THE LOST PRINCESS OF AEVILEN

D.C. PAYSON

Month9Books

THE LOST PRINCESS OF AEVILEN by D. C. Payson
All rights reserved. Published in the United States of America by Month9Books, LLC.
No part of this book may be used or reproduced in any manner whatsoever without written permission of the publisher, except in the case of brief quotations embodied in critical articles and reviews.

Paperback ISBN: 978-1-951710-27-9
ePub ISBN: 978-1-951710-28-6
Mobi ISBN: 978-1-951710-29-3

Published by Month9Books, Raleigh, NC 27609
Cover design by Danielle Doolittle

Month9Books

For Henry, John, and Helly

1

Julia held tightly to the armrest as her father yanked the steering wheel rightward and accelerated up the driveway. The car's wheels spat dirt and gravel behind them, Richard paying no attention at all to the familiar "*Children at Play*" and "*Caution: Animal Crossing*" signs. He pulled into the circular drive in front of their house and slammed the brakes. The car came to a screeching halt.

Richard turned around to face Julia and her younger brother. "Julia, help me pack up the art and get it into the van. Nico, find your mother, and help her with whatever she needs. The fire department is closing off this area at noon, which gives us less than an hour and a half. No time to waste!"

He threw open the car door and rushed toward the house,

yanking Nico along by the hand.

Julia followed behind in a daze. The Santa Ana winds had picked up, and the wildfire was spreading. Fast. "Uncontrollably," the radio newscaster had said. It just didn't seem possible that all of Malibu was at risk, not on such a beautiful morning.

Julia reached the threshold of the door and hesitated, looking for a moment up into the hills. She could see distant plumes of gray smoke.

Maybe the fire's course will change. Maybe we're overreacting.

"Julia, get in here," Richard barked. "Help me with this painting!"

Julia snapped to and headed into the house. Her mother, Pamela, frantically sorted through drawers for things to save while Nico filled boxes with the family photo albums. Julia took hold of one side of the painting and helped her father move it from the wall, through the front door, and down the path to the family minivan. No sooner had they slid the canvas into place than Richard started hustling back to the house.

"Wait! Dad, are you sure we have to do this?" Julia asked.

Her father stopped and turned, his eyes bearing down on her. "Julia, if we don't use the time we have now, lots of things we care about might be lost. We can hope that this is all for nothing, but let's act as if everything we don't save in the next hour is going to be gone forever, okay?"

Julia's pulse quickened. She nodded. "Okay, Dad."

They spent the next hour in a flurry of packing, grabbing, moving, and jostling. Her father and mother issued a continuous stream of orders as they tried to save their most beloved and valuable belongings. By the time the family finished, they had crammed artwork, heirlooms, and albums into every last inch of the minivan.

"Good job, everyone," Richard said, reaching up and pulling the rear hatch closed. "Last thing: I've left boxes in your rooms. Go fill them with what you want to save, and we'll load them into my car. The fire department will be here in ten minutes to evacuate the neighborhood, so keep that in mind. Remember, only what can fit in the box!"

Julia rushed back inside, across the living room strewn with detritus, and through the short, bare-walled hallway to her room. When she got there, she froze, staring blankly at the accumulated possessions of her seventeen years. She had lived with most of these things for so long they had faded from her day-to-day consciousness, little more than three-dimensional wallpaper. Yet now, faced with the impossible task of choosing once and forever between them, they all seemed precious, not wallpaper at all, but threads of emotion and memory that were part of the fabric of her life.

She glanced out her bedroom window. The smoke was nearer now. Thicker. Blacker. Julia took a few steps closer to the glass and squinted. She finally caught sight of the flickering flames of an actual fire at the top of the hill—a fire that was moving slowly and inexorably toward them.

"Five minutes, everyone!" Richard shouted.

Julia felt a sudden rush of adrenaline. She grabbed her camera and laptop and put them in the box. Next came her jewelry and favorite clothes, though she had only added a few sweaters and a pair of jeans by the time the box was out of room. She removed the sweaters and replaced them with her journals, then retrieved the first of three binders from the stamp collection she had inherited from her Aunt Sisa. It was a huge, thick volume representing decades of effort in careful acquisition, mounting, and annotation. There was no way that it was going to fit in the box. Julia tried to stuff it in, using her weight to press down harder.

A knot grew in her stomach, her father's words echoing in her mind: *Only what can fit!*

"Get in there!" she commanded, pressing harder and harder until she heard a muffled *crack*. She relented and slouched back onto the floor.

Her eyes welled up as she looked at her favorite indie-band posters, her blanket, all the clothes now strewn across the floor, the stamp collection, tennis racquet, childhood doll house, stereo, TV, pictures, books, trophies, and shoes. They would all have to be left behind. It felt like a betrayal.

"Julia, it's time to go!" her father called from the hallway. Julia turned to see him standing by her bedroom door. Though he offered a reassuring smile, Julia noticed the seriousness etched onto his face. He stepped forward and picked up her box.

"We'll be fine," he said, gently squeezing her shoulder. "No matter what happens, we have each other. But we have to go now."

Julia nodded. "Okay, Dad," she said, wiping away a tear with her finger. She looked around her room one last time. "Please, God?" she said. She looked up blankly at the ceiling before following her father out the door.

2

"The scene down here, Maria, is a devastating one. Firefighters are still struggling with the out-of-control blaze. Families downwind are scrambling to pack up their most precious belongings before the fire reaches them. As you can see from these images taken just moments ago, there are already many families whose lives will never be the same, their homes consumed by the most destructive wildfire in a generation."

Julia sat transfixed, watching the TV. She absorbed very little of the newsman's melodrama. It didn't matter; she already knew the truth. Her home in Malibu was gone. The things she left behind were also gone. Her old life had burned down with them.

Pamela sat down beside her on the sofa and kissed her on the head. "I think we should turn this off," she said quietly. "It's not doing anyone any good right now."

Julia reached for the remote and clicked off the television. She wasn't sure she liked the silence that now greeted her. At the very least, the noise and flashing images on the screen had anchored her to a still-turning world; now she was adrift in a sea of unhappy thoughts. She inhaled deeply and lay down against the threadbare pillows of her grandmother's sofa.

Growing up, dinner at Ina's house had always been reserved for special occasions. It meant dressing up, remembering your table manners, and talking about the sort of dull things that grandmothers like to talk about. Julia wasn't sure what Ina dinners were going to be like now that they were moving in, but she dreaded having to repeat the whole stilted affair night after night after night.

Much to Julia's surprise, her grandmother came down the stairs in a pair of blue jeans and a light, cotton blouse, an outfit far removed from the Christmas suits she recalled seeing her in as a kid. Even in jeans, Ina radiated formality. Her steps were evenly paced and deliberate, her posture impeccable, not a single strand of her snow-white hair out of place. As she came around the banister, she flashed a tight-lipped smile at her assembled family, something that might have seemed trite were not her blue eyes twinkling with kindness.

Moving to her spot at the head of the table, Ina gestured for the family to sit. The food smelled delicious. Though still feeling out of sorts, Julia appreciated the normalcy of a home-cooked meal.

Ina reached out her hands, and the family formed a chain around the table.

"We are blessed to be here together," she said, her German-sounding accent tingeing the words. "May he who gave us form give us the strength to endure our challenges, the wisdom to cherish the blessings we still have, and the courage to embrace the future."

"Thank you, Mom," said Richard. "That was a lovely grace."

Ina smiled. "I know how you're feeling. It will be hard at first, I remember. But everything does seem to work out, doesn't it? Look at you all. I have such a beautiful family."

Richard nodded. "Yes, family matters most. So long as we're together, safe, and in good health, I'm sure we'll be okay." He picked up his fork and fidgeted with it. "You know, maybe you should tell the kids about what you went through. It might help them see what they still have. Come to think of it, it could be good for all of us to hear your story."

"Oh, Richie," Ina replied. "That was a very long time ago."

Richard looked back at her insistently. "Please?"

Ina reached for her water, but she could not avoid the fact that all eyes in the room were on her. She put the glass down and sighed. "Okay, Richie, okay. As you know, I had to run away from a war. It was a very terrible time in my country. Some men had come to power promising a better life for everyone, but they succeeded only in turning countryman against countryman, even brother against brother. It all happened so quickly that we didn't realize that we had to run until it was too late. Really, it was a terrible time. I cannot tell you how frightening it is to face that sort of danger."

"So what happened, Ina?" Julia asked.

"In the end, I was the only one to get away. They killed my father and brother, and they would have gotten me, too, had not a woman named Balyssa saved me. She helped me come here. Of course, those first few nights in California were very hard. You must remember, I was completely alone with nothing but the clothes on my back. I actually had to sleep on the beach until a minister from a church in the Palisades saw me and offered to help."

"Did you speak any English before you came?" Julia asked.

"No," said Ina. She chuckled, her eyes drifting off. "I spoke a rare language unique to the small valley where I grew up. It is quite a lot different from English, but back then I was pretty good at picking up new languages."

Nico's face brightened. "Did you make new friends?"

"Oh yes. But it took a little while. I had to learn a bit about California, which was so different from my home culture."

"Don't you ever miss your old country?" Julia asked.

"Yes, of course. Every now and again, I think of it and miss it very much. But I don't know if it's really any better, even after all this time. I don't dare go back. I will always have my memories, just like you will always have your memories of Malibu."

"But Ina, wasn't the war over a long time ago?" Julia pressed. "Why didn't you go home after it ended?"

Ina was silent. She looked down at the table and repeated quietly, "No. I don't want to go back."

"Grandma, how could you not … "

"Stop it, Julia. Stop it!" Ina snapped. "Don't ask me again! My family is here now, and that's good enough for me!"

There was an awkward silence. Ina looked down at her plate and started cutting her meat with short, rapid strokes, a tight scowl on her face.

"Sorry, Grandma," Julia said sheepishly. She poked at the salad on her plate, unable to understand why Ina wouldn't want the one thing that she herself wanted more than anything else in the world: her old life back.

3

The smell. The very first thing that Julia sensed as she awoke the next day was the smell. It wasn't the salt of the ocean that used to waft in through her open bedroom window; rather, Julia smelled the particular and peculiar scent of *old,* the minor rot that comes with long stretches of time passed without wear. It was the smell of Ina's house, not of the bungalow in the Malibu hills.

She opened her eyes and rolled onto her back, staring at the ceiling as a quartz clock on her nightstand loudly ticked off the seconds of her new life. She shot a glance at the box at the base of the bed, the one that contained all her remaining belongings. Julia expected—almost wanted—to cry, to buckle under the great weight of all that she had lost. But she didn't; she was blank. Numb.

Slinking out of bed and into the shower, Julia cranked the water to hot and leaned against the wall. She didn't care for the greenish, sixties-era tile in front of her, so she closed her eyes and dreamed of the ocean view she used to have at home.

Back in her room, Julia put on her jeans and a clean t-shirt from the small stack of clothes that had survived the fire. Glancing at her reflection on the back of the door, she teased her shoulder length crop of sandy-blond hair. Julia tried to give it enough volume to hide the widow's peak she had inherited from her father and grandmother. She reached for her makeup bag but changed her mind after she saw the heaviness around her eyes in the mirror. It wasn't a day for makeup.

Julia turned her attention to the box, sifting through the things inside: journals, jewelry box, laptop. Camera. Her camera had always helped her through difficult times in the past. The act of shooting photos was calming for her, and the lens helped to her to *see*—not just capture images, but to engage with what was in front of her. She picked the camera up and pointed it toward the door, then she clicked the shutter. The camera beeped, and soon an under lit, grayish-brown scene appeared on the small previewing monitor on the back. Julia let out a grim chuckle. The image wasn't beautiful, but the darkness and unresolved shadows matched the way she felt.

It's a certain kind of therapy, I guess.

Camera in hand, Julia headed out of her room and down the stairs. She found her mother, brother, and grandmother sitting around the breakfast table.

"Good morning, Julia," Pamela called from the head of the table. "We have cereal, fruit, and a few pieces of bacon left. If you'd like, I'd be happy to make you some eggs."

Julia took a seat beside her brother and put the camera down on the table. She heard a loud slurp and looked over to see Nico grinning at her, spoon still halfway in his mouth.

"Lucky Charms!" he said, his eyes alight. "Grandma got them for me!"

"They're not good for you, you know," Julia said.

Nico smiled widely, showing the big gap between his front teeth. "They're great for me."

"No, all that sugar will rot those teeth of yours."

"I see you have your camera," Pamela interrupted. "You know, just up the road is a beautiful park full of old, live oaks. I think you'll enjoy shooting them. It could be a great way to get to know Brentwood."

Julia munched on a piece of bacon, lost in thought.

"Did you hear me, love?" Pamela asked.

" … Yeah, Mom," said Julia, looking up. "That sounds good, but I, uh … "

Pamela cocked her head, her eyebrows arched. "Yes?"

"I thought I might go back to the house in Malibu and take some pictures there."

Pamela sighed. "Julia, sweetheart, the house is gone. I don't even know if it's safe for you to be up there, and I'm sorry, but I can't give you the car today. We have way too much to do to get settled in here."

"But, Mom—"

"I can take her," Ina said. "I feel terrible for what happened last night. I had no right to speak to you like I did. Of all people, I should know better than to minimize the pain of someone who has lost a home. If your photographs will help give you closure, I would very much like to be a part of that."

"We're going to go see our burned down house?" said Nico. "Woah."

"No, Nicholas, not you this time," said Ina. "Just Julia."

"Aww," he said, dropping his spoon in his bowl. "That's not fair."

"I don't know how I feel about this idea," Pamela said. "It's probably dangerous up there." She saw the dejection on Julia's face. "But, if you promise it's just pictures … "

"Just pictures, Mom," Julia said.

"Just pictures," Pamela repeated. She shrugged. "Then I guess … just be safe, okay?"

Julia got up and hugged her Mom. "We will, Mom, thanks!" She turned toward Ina. "Thank you too, Grandma. This means a lot to me."

The old diesel engine of Ina's Mercedes purred, baroque music pouring forth from the radio. Julia had always found classical music boring, but today it helped to sooth her harried mind. She let her head loll to the side and watched the manicured hedges and gates streak by. The knot in her stomach grew when Ina turned down the ramp to the Pacific Coast Highway.

"Would you prefer to listen to something else?" Ina asked.

Julia sat up and looked ahead. "No, I'm fine."

"Julia? Are you alright?"

Julia breathed in deeply and exhaled. "I'm sorry, Grandma, I guess I'm a little stuck in my head." She took in the familiar homes along the highway and the chaparral hillsides. Everything looked normal. The plants were their standard greenish-brown, the $10 million "beach shacks" along the road their usual mini-fortress selves, the expensive, foreign cars lined up along the curb as on any other day. It felt like regular old LA.

"Are you sure you're ready for this?" Ina asked. "Maybe we should give it a few days?"

Julia shook her head. "No, Grandma. I want to go. I would rather deal with it now."

"Very well, my dear."

The traffic slowed as they drew near to the intersection with Topanga Canyon Road, backing up cars for the better part of a mile. Police had set up a checkpoint of overlapping cruisers and orange, safety barrels, and most traffic was being rerouted either back toward Santa Monica or up the road to Topanga.

"Do you think they'll let us through?" Julia asked.

"I can be quite convincing," said Ina. "Just let me talk to them."

When they got to the intersection, Ina ignored the swinging arm motions of the traffic officer trying to get her to U-turn. Instead, she drove up to him, her window rolled down.

"I live in Malibu," she said calmly. "My granddaughter and I evacuated yesterday, and we would like to check on our house."

"Have you called the fire department to see if your lot is in one of the safe areas?" the officer asked.

"I called this morning, yes."

"Alright. Do you have an ID?"

Ina looked up at the cop. "Officer, I have lived in Malibu for forty years, I need to check on my home. Now please let me pass."

Julia reached across her, her own driver's license in hand. "Here's an ID."

An ear-splitting *HONKKKK* rang out behind them.

"Please be patient, sir!" the cop barked at the angry driver. He turned back toward Ina and Julia and waved them through. "Be safe up ahead. There's still some debris on the road. Drive slowly, please."

"Thank you, officer," said Ina as she guided the car between the barrels, past the parked squad cars, and down the PCH.

Julia felt a jolt run through her as they rounded the hillside and caught sight of the first cluster of charred plants, and then seemingly an endless landscape of them—blackened fingers rising from the earth. She recognized the driveways they passed, but this wasn't the Malibu she knew. Stone or concrete skeletons were all that remained of many once-living homes. The streetside buildings still stood, but the ravages of the fire marked everything: the scorched trunks of old palm trees; the blanket of ash over driveways; the lines of parked emergency vehicles at otherwise empty beachside restaurants. Even the beaches, usually teeming with surfers, sat abandoned. It was like war had come to Malibu.

Ina stopped the car at the base of the steep driveway leading to Julia's former home. She moved a barrel out of the way then returned to the car and slowly accelerated up the winding path.

Julia could barely read the driveway signs anymore. Their paint was bubbled and peeling at the edges, and a thick layer of black char obscured most of what was left of the words. Little flecks of ash hung in the air. As they neared the top of the driveway, Julia caught sight of a once-beautiful Eucalyptus tree, the one she used to play on as a little girl, now black and lifeless. Her heart began to stir. Finally, she saw what was left of the house. There were no blue walls or tiled roof. No wisteria-covered pergola over the deck. Only the outdoor fireplace and concrete foundation remained. What hadn't been consumed by the fire sat in a mound of debris.

Julia's emotional dam broke, and tears streamed from her eyes. She let out a gurgled sob, but she didn't turn away.

Ina brought the car to a stop, parking well short of where the front door had been. They got out and approached the debris pile. It wasn't smoldering, but it had a strange smell—an acrid, ashy-metallic smell. Julia held her camera, but she couldn't bring herself to raise it. She just stood and took in the sight of her home, something she had always taken for granted, now reduced to nothing. She sat on the ground, put her camera down, and covered her face with her hands.

"My house, Grandma. The place I lived my whole life."

Ina came up beside Julia and placed an arm around her shoulder. "I know. It was a wonderful home."

A light breeze brought the salt smell of the ocean. Little wisps of ash rose from the ground then settled as the breeze subsided.

Julia sobbed again. "Why did this happen?"

Ina sighed. "I used to ask that question a lot. Sometimes I would blame the gods, and other times I would blame mankind. After being angry for a long time, I realized that I would never really know. Eventually, I learned that 'why' is less important than 'now.'"

"What does that even mean?" Julia asked, wiping her eyes on her shirt.

Ina pointed to her head. "'Why' is only up here. But in the 'now' are the breaths that we take, the love that we feel, the movement of our bodies going forward. Life continues, even amidst great change. Your destiny lies ahead, not behind."

"Destiny? That's cheesy." Julia chuckled between tears, but she secretly appreciated her grandmother's words.

"Malibu will always be in your heart, Julia. You grew up here, and it has shaped you. You are every bit as free-spirited and wild as these hills, and I see the beauty and vastness of the ocean in your eyes."

Julia smiled. "Thanks, Grandma." She turned her camera toward herself and clicked the shutter. She checked the preview. The photo captured her tear streaks and puffy redness, but also her smile and her grandmother's hand on her shoulder. She felt some of her energy coming back, her life returning. Breathing in deeply, Julia stood up and walked toward the debris pile.

"Maybe you shouldn't go over there," Ina said. "It may not be safe."

"Don't worry, I won't go much closer."

She spotted what looked like an out-of-place, gray block lying just outside the concrete footprint of the house. On closer inspection, she realized it was a book, the cover charred, but the layers of pages seemingly intact. Julia bent down, zoomed in on the book, and snapped a picture. She reached out and tried to take hold of it, but no sooner had she touched the cover than it disintegrated into ash.

"Crazy," Julia said under her breath.

"Incredible, the power of fire," said Ina from behind.

Julia looked back and nodded.

"We used to say back home that fire was the oldest of all powers, older even than the gods themselves. It was neither good nor evil, and indeed could be used for either purpose."

Julia clicked off another picture. "I'd like to hear more about your home, Ina. You never really talked about it when we were kids."

"Oh … Aevilen," Ina said wistfully. "It was very beautiful, a valley surrounded by mountains. No cars or planes. Just a beautiful, pristine valley. I lived in the capital, a grand fortress city built over a river. In our language, it was called *Erantioran*, Riverstride."

Julia put her camera down and looked over at her grandmother. "That sounds amazing. Please don't get mad at me for asking, but why wouldn't you want to go back to that?"

Ina shook her head. "I know I said that I fear it's still not safe. That's true. But I also feel great shame at having left."

"Ina, there's no shame in running away from a war. Your father and brother had already died. Anybody in your shoes would have done the same thing, just like we ran from the fire."

"It's different when you leave your people behind," Ina said solemnly.

"What do you mean?"

Ina shook her head again. "I never even told your grandfather."

"Ina?"

"The Vorravers were the ruling family of Aevilen. My father was the king."

Julia's eyes bulged. "Wait, you were royalty?"

"You would have been a wonderful princess, Julia," said Ina distantly. She looked back at Julia and smiled. "But it's of no matter anymore. That's a world away and a lifetime ago. Let us live our lives here, in the now."

Julia walked over and wrapped her arms around her grandmother, holding her in a firm embrace. "Thanks, Ina. Thanks for everything."

Ina hugged her back. "You're welcome, my dear."

Julia spent the better part of an hour wandering around the property snapping pictures, alternating between shots to capture the destruction and shots to help her remember her beloved Malibu home. She tried to be present, to use the opportunity for catharsis and closure. In many ways she succeeded, each new photo getting her closer to Ina's 'now.' But a thought kept distracting her: *Ina's a princess.*

Julia had to know more.

4

Julia closed the bedroom door behind her and rushed over to her box with barely-contained excitement. She put her camera down and retrieved her laptop, opening it up and tapping the spacebar to bring it back to life. When the screen came on, her heart jumped with excitement.

She went straight to Google.

A-I-V-A-L-I-N-enter.

Did you mean AVALON? appeared in link-blue, above a few hits for sweaters.

"No, I didn't," said Julia aloud.

A-I-V-A-L-I-N- -P-L-A-C-E, enter.

No results.

"C'mon … "

A-V-A-L-E-N- -P-L-A-C-E, enter.

No results.

A-V-A-L-I-N- -V-O-R-R-A-V-E-R, enter.

No results.

Julia frowned. "Really?"

V-O-R-

Just then, a knock came at the door.

"Come in," Julia called.

"Do you have a moment?" Ina asked, cracking open the door.

Julia closed the computer and looked up. "Sure, Grandma."

Ina walked over and sat at the base of Julia's bed. She held a box. "You know, it took me many years to adjust to my new life here in Los Angeles. I hid my past from everyone … Perhaps I mistook my weakness for strength. I am glad that we spent that time together today and that I don't have to bear my secret alone anymore."

"I enjoyed it too, Grandma. Don't worry, I won't tell anyone."

Ina flashed a mischievous grin. "I want to give you something."

Julia furrowed her brow. She didn't have the heart to tell her grandmother that she was starting to doubt her story, but she also wasn't sure she wanted to keep playing along.

Ina opened the box and took out a white, woolen garment. Holding it still-folded in her hands, she extended her arms toward Julia. "This is for you."

Julia received it gingerly. The wool was very soft and had been reinforced along the edges with a heavier cloth to give it structure. There was no label on the outside, but the wonderful fabric and pretty white color filled Julia with high hopes. She stood up and swung the garment open.

Julia gasped. It was a shawl covered in the finest embroidery she had ever laid eyes on. All throughout were incredible, interlocking patterns rendered in golden thread.

"I wore that the night I escaped," Ina said. "It is one of only a few items I have left from my old home. It sat in the attic for many years, but I think it's time for it to come out once again. I was a princess when I last put it on; I hope you feel like one when you wear it."

Julia swung the shawl over her back and looked in the mirror. She grappled with her lingering doubts as she took in the regal image before her. As an LA girl, she was well versed in fashion; she knew that even the couturiers at Chanel weren't making things like this.

"Do you like it?" Ina asked.

Julia nodded, barely able to take her eyes off the mirror. "It's amazing. Thank you."

"I'm so glad," said Ina. She got up from the bed. "I hope you find an occasion where you can wear it. But do keep its origin between us—I don't think anyone would believe you, anyway."

Julia smiled. "You're the best, Ina."

Ina laughed. "I am not sure about that, but thank you, my dear."

As Ina made her way out of the room, Julia removed the shawl and turned it over in her hands, admiring the intricate stitching. She no longer doubted that there was history here, though what it really was she still needed to discover. *The attic,* she thought. Julia didn't want her family to catch her rooting through her grandmother's belongings, so she'd have to wait—but not for long. She needed to know the truth.

5

Julia bided her time, half-heartedly flipping through a book as she kept an eye on the light from her parent's bedroom. Finally, it went out: *go time.*

She tiptoed out of her room and down the hallway to the attic door. Unhooking the old latch, she ducked inside and closed the door behind her. The beam of her flashlight illuminated the narrow, steep staircase leading to the attic.

The small hallway echoed with the creaking of old stairs as Julia ascended. At the top, she came to her deceased grandfather's writing niche, still arranged much as she remembered it: the mahogany desk against the window, a typewriter to the left, and a big, wooden swivel chair turned to face the stairs. What was different was the dust that blanketed everything in a thin coat of forgotten gray.

"Love you, Grandpa," Julia whispered, though she wasn't here for him. She flashed the light toward the crawlspace door. She had been in that space only once before, during a game of hide-and-go-seek years ago. It had scared her: a dark, cold space filled with sheet-covered furniture, like something out of a bad horror movie.

Julia braced as she turned the knob and opened the door. Stale, musty air wafted out. With her flashlight, Julia could pick out countless pieces of old furniture, boxes, and rolled-up carpets. No monsters or moving shadows. She reached her arm through the door and along the interior wall until she found the light switch.

She flicked it on and scanned the room.

Bureaus and trunks, she thought to herself. *Ina would have stored the shawl in a bureau or trunk … too important for a cardboard box.*

There were no bureaus, which made things easier, though there were four large trunks in the middle of the room. Julia made her way over and checked their tops. One had less dust on its lid than the others. Someone had opened it recently.

"Here we go," Julia said as she dropped to her haunches and took hold of the lid.

The trunk released a peculiar odor as she opened it, but Julia cared about the contents more than the smell. On the right side were stacks of clothes, cool vintage pieces that at any other time might have captured her attention. But not tonight. She focused on the left side, on the odd-looking leather trousers and the small, porcelain box. She took out the pants and unfolded them on the floor beside her. There was no label, and the hide had grown stiff from years of inattention. They were very high-waisted, and featured two rows of beautifully polished horn buttons running up the front.

Exotic, just like the shawl, Julia thought. She was on to something.

Julia returned the pants to the chest then took out the porcelain box. She opened it. Inside was a necklace, a thin chain with a silvery metal pendant at its center. The pendant was slightly larger than a quarter and shaped like an abstract shark's tooth with a hole cut in it toward the top. Julia took it out and held it up to the light. It seemed to give off a faint bluish reflection.

Julia felt a strange attraction to the necklace. It held her gaze the same way seeing a famous work of art or an A-list celebrity did. But this connection was deeper. Although she'd never seen the necklace before, it was somehow familiar to her. The longer she looked at it, the more she thought she could feel the metal warming in her hand.

This is a bad idea, she thought. *I should put it back*. But she couldn't put it down. Her eyes lingered.

Ina might not mind if I wore it for a day or two. She gave me the shawl—maybe I could have this, too, if I asked.

Julia slipped the chain over her head. The pendant sat high on her chest, the metal beautiful, almost entrancing, against her skin. She smiled as she placed a hand against it and allowed herself to imagine fanciful settings—restaurants, concerts, dates—where she might wear it.

"This is so cool," she whispered to herself. The necklace wasn't the proof of Ina's heritage she had been looking for, but it still seemed like a treasure. Like the shawl, the necklace made Julia feel special, even royal.

Julia looked back in the trunk and shuffled through the clothes on the right side, but the stack proved to be nothing more than old designer dresses, top to bottom.

She said she came with nothing more than the clothes on her back. Maybe this is it?

She opened up one of the other trunks close by. It was full of carefully stacked plates and serving dishes. Pretty, but ordinary. She looked at the other trunks and thought about going through those as well, but she was growing tired. Somehow, she knew that they were dead ends, anyway. Still, finding the necklace seemed like a stroke of good luck, and maybe it would be enough. She could research the pendant's symbol on the internet and hopefully learn something from Ina herself about the necklace tomorrow.

Julia closed the trunks, turned off the lights, and headed back to her room. She closed her bedroom door behind her and faced her mirror.

Hey, I'm Julia, she greeted an imaginary classmate, her confidence swelling. A gentle warmth radiated across her chest. She could already see herself wearing the necklace with a V-neck top and gray skirt the next time she went on a date.

She pulled her pajamas out of her bureau and was about to put them on when suddenly her ears picked up a strange sound outside her room. She froze. A moment later, it came again, a woman's voice:

"Elleina!"

Julia crept forward and poked her head into the hallway. The house was dark. "Nico?" she called in a loud whisper. "Dad? Mom?"

She kept still, waiting to see if the sound would repeat. Only silence.

"You're tired … just get some sleep," she said to herself, retreating to her room. She put on her pajamas, turned off the lights, and climbed into her bed.

As she lay down, she thought she heard the voice again. "*Elleina!*"

She ignored the noise, exhausted but glad to have stayed up late. Visions of wearing her grandmother's necklace and shawl brought a smile to her face. Strange as it would have seemed when the day began, she was almost looking forward to tomorrow.

Julia closed her eyes and felt a wave of calm come over her. She could feel her mind letting go of the day, her lingering anxieties, and then, finally, all remaining vestiges of conscious thought. She fell into a deep, restorative sleep of the sort she so desperately needed; so deep, in fact, that she didn't even stir when, minutes later, a brilliant light began to emanate from under her blanket.

"*Elleina! Vasansonnelaen!*"

6

Julia was awoken by a chill that gripped her. Los Angeles was usually warm in September, so the cold came as a surprise.

She reached down for her blanket and grasped only air. Groping farther, her hand met a cold, stone floor. Her eyes sprang open.

"Mom?" she called, jerking herself upright. "Dad?"

There was no reply, only the slight echo of her voice off the walls.

She looked around frantically. Blue-tinged moonlight streamed through a pair of arched, glassless windows, providing just enough light for her to see a column in the middle of the room and strange furniture along a nearby wall. She looked behind her and saw a large mirror.

"Okay, Julia, okay," she said, forcing herself to take a deep breath. She closed her eyes. "Breathe … you're just dreaming."

Julia would deal with this nightmare the way she had learned to confront nightmares as a child: she would ignore it. She lay down again and focused on her breath, disregarding the cold and discomfort. It was not long before she had fallen back to sleep.

Julia could feel the warmth of sunlight embracing her, a welcome change from the cold she had experienced several hours before. She stretched out her arms and yawned. When her elbow collided with stone, her eyes sprang open again.

In startled confusion, she took in the room around her. It was magnificently opulent, like something from a Venetian palace but born of a very different culture. An iron column rose from the middle of the floor and split into eight slender tendrils, each forming a ridge for the flower-like arched ceiling. The walls were carved in deep relief and painted a rich variety of colors, alternating between scenes of nature and panels of strange writing. On either side of the room were several cabinets with stone pedestal bases, and over by the window were two ornate metal chairs and an accompanying table. Julia cast a quick glance behind her, this time seeing the large, golden mirror in full.

Her heart beat rapidly. Her breathing accelerated. Julia struggled to understand what she was seeing. This felt much too real to be a dream.

"HELP!" she cried out.

There was only a brief echo, then silence.

She jumped to her feet and ran over to the window. She looked out onto a wide, mountain ravine filled with the ruins of an ancient complex. The buildings combined the colonnades of Ancient Greek temples and the thick, square, corner towers of Bhutanese dzongs. They were like nothing she had ever seen. Several buildings had dried-out, old trees growing from their center courtyards with carefully sculpted branch structures, like bonsais but on a much larger scale. A gust of wind whistled as it passed through the buildings' collapsed roofs, fallen walls, and scattered stones. This was a place long abandoned.

Withdrawing from the window, Julia fought to control her thoughts. She slumped to the floor, her palms and face sweating as she neared the point of intense, inescapable fight-or-flight anxiety. Suddenly, an alien warmth spread across her chest. Surprised, she placed her hand against it and looked down.

Her necklace, the one that she had taken from Ina's trunk, was glowing.

The warmth continued to spread until Julia felt as if her body were encased in a shell of protective energy. She wasn't sure how or why, but she found the necklace's warmth calming. Turning inward, she focused on her breath, bringing her mind back to the present. Soon her panic was gone.

What just happened? Julia wondered as the necklace's warmth and glow began to fade. She had never believed in the supernatural, but what she had seen and felt were undoubtedly real. Unsettled, she took the necklace off and looked at it. The centerpiece commanded her attention, her eyes locking on it in a way that felt almost irresistible. Mesmerizing.

Ina, what's going on? What is this thing?

Her conscious brain wanted to leave the necklace behind, to be free of its strange influence, but her subconscious resisted. Somehow, somewhere deep inside her, she knew that she needed it. That it was important. Conflicted, she tucked the necklace into the pocket of her pajamas.

I'll figure this out later, she thought. *First, I need to figure out where I am.*

Standing up again, Julia made her way to the closest cabinet. It had an elegant design, made from a dark red-brown wood bound together by silver metal joints at its corners. She tried to pull the doors open, but they only jiggled. After a minute of searching, she found a silver pin on the top side that held the doors closed. She pulled it out and tried the doors again; this time, they swung open freely.

Inside were two shelves. The top held a pair of large, stoppered jugs, the bottom several stacks of folded clothes. She picked up one of the jugs, feeling the liquid slosh inside. A strong, unpleasant odor like that of apple cider vinegar wafted up from the partially rotted stopper, making Julia think twice about removing it. She put the jug back and turned her focus to the clothes underneath.

Looking through the piles, which seemed to be mostly heavy robes, she found a white, woolen sweater. She pulled it out and held it against her body.

Better than pajamas, she thought, setting it aside.

She closed the cabinet doors and returned the silver pin at the top.

Going from cabinet to cabinet, Julia searched for other helpful items or clues to her whereabouts. She came across ceramic bowls and cups, other assorted clothes and blankets, and even a collection of covered-toe sandals. By the time she was done, she had found a pair of leather pants that she could wear and a pair of sandals that fit her. However, nothing had told her where she was.

Scanning the room one last time, she caught a glint of light reflecting off an object on the table. It was a silver oval set into the lid of a wooden box. She went over to look at it more closely, and her heart skipped a beat; the oval was engraved with a symbol matching the pendant of Ina's necklace!

Julia took out the necklace from her pocket and held it up against the oval. It really was a match! She tried to open the box, but it was locked. Turning it around, she couldn't find a latch or hole for a key.

Standing in puzzled silence staring at the box, Julia suddenly became aware of something else: the necklace was warming in her hand. She felt her eyes being drawn back to the engraving on the box. She ran her fingers over it, an intuition coming to her. *This is the key …*

Julia pushed against the metal oval. There was a popping sound as an internal mechanism released.

A mix of wonder and trepidation came over her as she stared disbelievingly at the unlocked box, then at her necklace. Her mind struggled to accept what she already knew to be true: Ina's necklace was feeding her thoughts, perhaps even guiding her. Was it benevolent? Was she still just dreaming? She had no way of knowing, but the longer she stared at the pendant, the more compelled she felt to put it back on. She slipped the chain over her head, relieved to feel the metal against her skin again.

Turning her focus back to the box, Julia carefully opened the lid, revealing a small, leather bag and two folded, yellow notes inside. She removed the bag, finding it surprisingly heavy. Uncinching the drawstring, Julia turned it upside down. A large, gold medallion slid out and clanged against the table. Julia's eyes widened. It was by far the largest gold object she had ever seen, six inches in diameter and a quarter inch wide. She picked it up with both hands, admiring the portrait of a young girl on its front. The girl's hair was braided, and she wore a simple, ivy crown. She looked very familiar somehow, but Julia struggled to identify the face. Turning the medallion over, Julia found the sharktooth-like symbol again, this time circumscribed by strange-looking writing. Her necklace warmed. Her eyes were drawn to the script in the same way they had been drawn to the box's metal oval earlier. Unconsciously, she began passing her thumb over the words.

Suddenly, she heard a man's voice: *"Go'eorra, Mosen Elle—"*

Julia gasped and looked up, the medallion almost slipping from her fingers.

"Who's there!" she yelped. She swung around, but the room was still empty.

She looked down at her necklace. *That came from you, didn't it?* She took a deep breath and ran her thumb over the words on the medallion again.

The voice returned: *"Aevilen Go'eorra, Mosen Elleina."*

As if in a trance, Julia ran her thumb over the writing repeatedly, the voice echoing with each pass. Slowly, it began to change, each additional tracing of the words bringing a new voice closer to the point of intelligibility. Finally, what had begun as an overlaid whisper became understandable: "Servant of Aevilen, Princess Elleina."

Elleina … Ina!

Julia knew why she recognized the girl on the medallion. It was Ina as a young girl!

Princess Elleina of Aevilen, Julia repeated in her head. She looked out the window past the nearby fortress in the ravine, seeing a broad mountain valley in the distance.

A valley in the mountains, just as Ina described. Is that where I am? Ina's home?

The intuitions, the voice, her necklace … what was happening? And had she really come to understand some new language just by touching it?

She looked up at the walls, scanning the carved scenes and the panels of writing. She walked over and ran her fingers across one of the inscriptions, her necklace casting a faint, blue glow against the stone. Soon she heard another voice whispering in the back of her mind. It was again male, but different from the first. And this time, she heard the translation immediately:

"The Shaper took Her into His arms, and they made their love complete on the sacred plateau He had crafted for Her. Of their godly passions were born the Ogarren, rock and vine and dirt and grass absorbing their energies and coming together as one ... "

In an adjacent scene, Julia spotted a beautiful woman embracing a bearded man with small figures rising from the ground around them. In that moment, it was confirmed: she could read a language she had never seen, understand a language she had never heard.

Her heart fluttering, Julia rushed back to the box and removed one of the notes. Unfolding it, she saw that it contained a similar script to the one found on the coin and walls. She began tracing the words. The voice that came was a young woman's:

Eovaz,

I write to say that I have always admired your loyalty and courage. You have given up much to serve as my Guardian. I do not know how or when, but I will see to it that your sacrifice is rewarded.

May the Shaper protect you always.

Elleina

A tear welled up in Julia's eye. The voice was Ina's, albeit a much younger Ina than Julia had ever known. She had written these notes. She had been in this room. Julia's mind wandered with thoughts of the grandmother she knew, the one back in California, and her mother, brother, and father. She so wanted to be back with them.

Glancing at the face of the medallion, she recalled her grandmother's words: *I know it's hard, but 'why' is less important than 'now.'*

Julia nodded. She wiped her eyes and focused.

Whatever brought me here can send me back, she thought. *Let's figure out what's going on and get out of here.*

Julia gathered herself and picked up the second note from the box.

To Elder Domin,

I am leaving but will call on you when I return. I know your kind has always tried to stay away from our politics, but I hope you will keep the long-standing relations the Vorravers have enjoyed with the Rokkin in mind when this period passes. My heavy heart knows there will be much to rebuild, and we will need your assistance. I am sending a royal marker with my message so that your smiths might begin work without delay when the time comes.

May the Shaper protect you always.

Princess Elleina Vorraver, Servant of Aevilen

Julia looked out the window, her gaze drifting across the valley. *Ina ... how did I get here?*

She placed her hand against her necklace, believing that it had played a part.

Send me home, she pleaded silently. *If you brought me here, send me home!*

She opened her eyes again. Nothing had changed. She sighed, disappointed but unfazed. The necklace frustrated her with its mystery, but it had also given her a deep-seated calm and resolve. She knew she didn't have many options: wait and hope that she might be sent back as inexplicably as she'd been summoned, or figure out how she had been brought to this place and how to get home herself.

She took in the view of the ravine and the desolation of the abandoned ruins.

I can't wait here for a rescue that might never come. I have to find Eovaz and Domin, whoever they are. They'll know how I can get home.

7

Julia changed into the clothes she had found, then she collected the gold coin and notes and packed them in the drawstring bag. After cinching the pouch to the waist of her pants, she walked over to the large, banded door by the window and lifted the latch that kept it closed. Prepared to pull with all her might, she was surprised by how easily it swung open. What she saw through the doorway, however, soon replaced her relief with concern.

There was a solid, wood surface in front of her. It didn't look like another door.

Rushing through the short hallway, Julia searched for a handle but found none. She pounded on the barrier with her fist. "Hello?" she called, the hollow report of her strikes echoing off the stone around her. "Hello!"

You're not trapped … you're not trapped, she repeated to herself, scanning the barrier frantically as her anxiety rose. In her frustration, she pounded on it again, and again a hollow *thud* resounded through the corridor.

Suddenly, Julia realized that she had heard that sound before. Back in Malibu, when her father had hung the TV in her room, he had showed her how to find wall studs by knocking. Hollow meant no stud; the wall would be thin there. But this wasn't a wall.

Julia went side to side knocking on the wood. The sound stayed the same. She tried going up and down, and, sure enough, every few feet the sound changed for an inch or two, becoming higher-pitched and tighter.

This isn't a wall … it's a piece of furniture!

Turning around, she leaned up against the right side of the barrier and held her breath.

1 … 2 … 3!

Julia pushed with all her might. The barrier crept forward, grinding against the stone floor and opening up a several-inch wide crack. Julia turned around and tried to peer through the crack, making out the outlines of a balustrade and also several books scattered across the floor on the other side. She reached her arm through and probed the back of the barrier, feeling empty cavities and regularly spaced shelves.

It was a bookcase!

She put her back against the wood again and heaved, the bookcase lurching forward another several inches. The crack was nearly wide enough for her to squeeze through.

Almost there.

"Okay," she said aloud, psyching herself up. "Let's get out of here."

She lowered her shoulder and pushed with all the strength she had left.

"Goooooo!" she cried out, spurred on by the sound of grinding wood. Julia fought for every last inch until, finally, out of breath, her legs aching, she slipped down to her knees. She looked up at the crack and let out a sigh of relief. She would fit.

After waiting a moment for her legs to recharge, Julia stood and shimmied through the opening. She stopped, stunned, as the room came into view.

It was a cavernous, multi-level library filled with colored light. Above her was the largest stained glass object she'd ever seen, a 100-foot diameter, domed ceiling formed from crystal panes arranged in floral and ivy-like patterns. Vibrant streams of green, red, and yellow illuminated row after row of ornamented bookcases below. It would have been a sight to behold in a prior era, but most of the cases were now empty, their contents spilled across the floor or missing entirely. Julia felt a deep unease welling inside her as she walked between the empty shelves and over the piles of books.

Something terrible happened here.

She made her way to the central staircase. As she rounded one of the massive, metal columns supporting the ceiling, Julia caught a faint whisper, barely distinct from the light breezes whisking through the library. She ignored it. But then a more defined murmur came from behind her, breathless but unquestionably a voice:

"Elleina!"

Julia looked over her shoulder. An ethereal robed figure stood beside a bookcase. It reached out a partially translucent hand toward her.

"Elle—"

Julia screamed. She ran down the stairs as fast as her legs could take her, bounding two or three steps at a time. She didn't slow down until she had burst across the threshold of the library, running into the sunlight. Glancing over her shoulder every few seconds, she charged down the narrow road ahead of her, past the porticos of the temple-like buildings flanking the library. She didn't stop until she reached the top of a short but grand outdoor staircase.

Julia ducked behind one of two huge statues at the top of the stairs and tried to catch her breath. Panting, she looked back at the library. The hooded figure had not followed her. She kept her eyes on the doorway for a minute longer, then she released her tension and slipped down the statue to the ground.

As she rested, Julia glanced over at the statue across from her. She was now able to appreciate its incredible size. Standing at least twenty feet tall, it was of a man with an impossibly large beard covering his torso, his hands clutching a giant hammer. Scooching forward, Julia turned around to see the equally large statue behind her. It was of a beautiful woman, nude except for a vine that wrapped around her leg and covered her groin, part of her torso, and breasts. She wore a wreath of flowers on her head, and her hand sat gently on the head of a maned, wolf-like creature. Julia recalled the figures carved into the wall of the library and the words that she'd heard in the back of her mind.

"The Shaper," she said as she looked at the statue across from her. "And you … " she continued, shifting her gaze to the woman, "you are the Goddess."

These gods had great significance for this place, yet something inside Julia also stirred to see them. The figures were at once unfamiliar and familiar. They reminded her that she was stranded in a foreign land, yet somehow she felt like she knew them well beyond just her ability to identify them.

Julia glanced back at the library doorway one last time, then she stood up and descended the stairs. There was a mosaic spanning the width of the road at the bottom of the steps that seemed to mark a boundary of some sort, separating the upper part of the ravine and library-temple complex from a wider area below. The road past the mosaic was no longer patterned, and even the buildings, though large in size, lacked the ornamentation of the library and temples behind her.

Julia stopped to examine the mosaic. Its central symbol was unmistakable: Ina's necklace pendant again. Except this time, it was surrounded by a ring of objects resembling peacock feathers, beneath which were two lines of writing rendered with blue stones. Julia sensed that there was something gravely serious about the mosaic and the library complex behind her. She looked up at the two huge statues one last time before she turned and hurried toward the front wall of the complex, paying no heed to the variously standing, dilapidated, and collapsed structures she passed. Whatever her interest in discovering the secret history of this place, it was superseded by her desire to get out and find help.

Arriving at an open archway in the fortress wall minutes later, Julia leaned against a pillar to catch her breath. She looked out over the landscape beyond. She felt at once exhilarated and daunted. A steep, winding road led away from the complex, with a vast plateau ringed by other mountains in the distance. Dense forest covered the plateau's near ground, though there was a more open plain beyond. Julia thought she could make out a city on the horizon. Her heart swelled with hope.

Roads connect people, she thought as she focused on the road, readying herself for the journey ahead. *Help is ahead, somewhere. This road will lead me home.*

8

Julia was not usually afraid of heights, but the butterflies in her stomach fluttered as she peered over the edge of the road. A sheer rock face plunged hundreds of feet down. All that separated her from the drop was a foot-high stone guardrail. She stepped back and traced the narrow road with her eyes as it cut back and forth across the mountain. The landscape was barren at this altitude, offering only a few small patches of scrub grass. Julia knew that there would be no refuge if the weather changed, and she would likely not find water or food for a while. She could only hope the road would be passable all the way to the base of the mountain.

Roads connect people, she repeated to herself. *I can't stay here.*

Her sandals clacked against the worn paving stones as she walked.

A strong sun beat down on her, and the altitude made breathing difficult. Occasional gusts of wind swept up the mountainside, forcing her to stop and brace herself. But despite the obstacles, Julia pressed on, step-by-careful-step.

Slowly, the landscape around her began to change. As the slope leveled off, golden mountain grasses and clutches of white and yellow wildflowers started to appear. Farther on, she saw a few small, twisted trees, and then a bush teeming with red berries. Her stomach growled.

Probably better hungry than poisoned, she reasoned, thinking back to some of her early camping lessons in Girl Scouts. Still, her head was beginning to throb, and she knew she'd have to find water and food soon.

The forest is close. I'll find something there.

As she neared the final stretch of her descent, Julia stopped for a moment to rub her legs, doing her best to ignore her thirst. The plant life grew larger and denser with every step, and the road seemed to disappear among the shadows of the primeval forest ahead.

She summoned her resolve; there was no turning back now.

Julia cautiously glanced from left to right and back again as she passed through a stand of hundred-foot trees at the boundary of the forest. The dense underbrush and subtle changes in topography across the forest floor limited her visibility. By the time she had walked only a few hundred yards in, she felt as though she'd been swallowed. Julia felt insignificant next to the ancient pines looming overhead. The rustling branches and ever-shifting patches of light played tricks on her eyes. The smell of decomposition and pine sap hung heavily in the air. The forest was at once a grand and claustrophobic space.

Julia's thirst had grown to the point where she felt almost desperate to find water, but she didn't dare leave the road to explore. She knew that the road was the only thing keeping her from being lost among the monotony of repeating trees, roots, and shrubs.

Roads connect people, she tried to reassure herself, though her confidence was beginning to wane. Her legs grew heavier with each step, and the deep, aching pain in her head was getting worse. Julia stopped to sit on a large tree root abutting the road. Looking up, she could only see a few small patches of daylight above—the forest hid even the time of day from her. She inhaled deeply and slowly exhaled in an effort to maintain her composure, but she could no longer control her emotions. She burst out sobbing.

"What's happening?" Julia cried out, her voice cracking from the dryness in her throat. "My house burns down, and now I'm lost in the middle of nowhere? What is going on? Why? Why!"

Julia was exhausted, and she knew that no one would be coming to help her. For a moment, she felt dizzy and thought she might pass out. But then an intuition made her reach for her necklace, and she felt it warm. It seemed to flip a switch inside her. She wiped her tears and ran her fingers through her hair.

I must keep moving, she thought. *It's not about 'why,' it's about 'now.' Help isn't far away. I just need to get out of the forest!*

She stood up and was about to continue down the path when she heard a faint sound in the treetops. She perked her ears and listened.

Birds!

The chirping sounds were the first familiar thing she'd come across all day. She scanned the trees but was disappointed to see only dense branches and rustling needles. The sound continued, a high-pitched rolling, warbling song that seemed to last longer than the birdcalls she knew from back home. Soon Julia heard other calls of the same type from elsewhere in the forest, their origin no less hidden than the first.

Suddenly, her necklace began to change, its warmth replaced by a faint chill.

Wait, why is my necklace … ? Julia looked down at the pendant for a moment then back up at the trees. *Something's wrong.*

Her search for the birds taking on a new urgency, Julia tried to zero in on their calls. The sound of a translating voice grew louder in the back of her mind as the song continued back and forth.

"Chosen of the Goddess?" called a distant voice, fading in and out of intelligibility.

"No, trespasser," the near one replied. *"Within thorn's flight."*

Julia finally spotted movement along a nearby branch. She stared at the area for a moment and shuddered as the creature came into view. It was not a bird at all, but rather something that looked like a cross between man and monkey. It had a humanlike face with sharp, angular features and long, slender limbs that clung tightly to the tree trunk. The rough texture of its skin provided near-perfect camouflage in the forest understory. Had she not seen it moving, it's unlikely Julia would ever have spotted the creature at all.

The creature uncurled its tail from an overhead branch and drew it back like a whip. Just then, Julia's necklace released a brilliant burst of light, simultaneously sending a wave of cold across her chest.

I have to get out of here!

She turned and ran, adrenaline breathing new life into her legs. She felt a sudden, biting pain in her right calf, but she didn't dare stop. For several hundred yards, she ran at top speed through the trees and over rocks and roots, spurred on by the calls of the creatures and the whirring sounds of small projectiles shooting past her. She kept going until her legs weighed her down like leaden logs. Eventually, she could not force even a small jump out of them, and her foot caught a low root. She crashed to the ground.

Julia remained still, gasping for breath, clutching her wounded leg. She was bleeding. The projectile had gashed the bottom of her pants but had only grazed her skin. She perked her ears for the creatures and heard nothing. Looking down, she saw that her necklace was dormant.

Are they gone? Am I safe?

Julia picked up a rustling sound in the distance. She froze, unable to run. But listening further, she realized it wasn't the sound of tree creatures or branches rustling in the wind; it was a different, more hopeful sound. Water!

Calling on her last reserves, Julia struggled to her feet and trudged off the road in the direction of the sound, pushing her way through a thicket. The canopy gradually opened up overhead, letting more light into the understory. She had to fight her way through the distinctly younger growth, sapling needles scratching at her exposed face and pulling at the fibers of her sweater. Squeezing her way through one final wall of brush, she found herself on an embankment overlooking a wide riverbed with a narrow but fast-moving stream in the middle.

Momentarily safe from the forest creatures and with a cure for her dehydration ahead, Julia felt the profound joy of survival overcome her. She lowered herself down from the embankment and rushed as fast as her exhausted legs could carry her across the riverbed toward the running waters. She sat down next to an eddy at the river's edge and dipped her hands into the near-freezing stream. No sooner had they filled than she rushed them to her mouth and drank deeply. The icy water burned against her dry throat. She suppressed a minor wave of nausea, reaching back in to drink several more times. Her fingers were numb by the time she had quenched her thirst.

Julia found a large boulder nearby and hid behind it. Removing her necklace, she used the pendant's point to help tear away the bottom part of her pants before cleaning up the blood on her leg with river water. There was an odd tingling sensation radiating from the wound, but she was relieved to see just how shallow the cut was. There wouldn't be much risk of infection.

What were those things? Julia wondered. She was well-traveled and well-studied, but even wracking her brain continent-by-continent, habitat-by-habitat, she couldn't come up with anything that even remotely matched the bizarre—and dangerous—creatures she'd seen. She knew she'd gotten lucky in her first encounter; only an inch to the left and she might have faced a very different outcome. It was only her necklace that had saved her.

She closed her eyes and tried to concentrate on a mental image of the pendant, squeezing the metal with her hand. She wanted to tap into its power, to control it for the first time.

Ina, where should I go? she called out in her mind. *What should I do? How do I get home?*

She waited for a response, but none came. Julia sighed. *I guess it doesn't work that way.*

Putting the necklace back on, she leaned against the boulder and watched the rhythmic chaos of the rapids. Her head felt woozy, as if she were spinning around in the river's frigid waters. Another wave of nausea came over her. The midday sun was warm, but a slight chill from her necklace nipped at her breast.

What the heck?

She wanted to get up and get moving again, but she felt an almost overwhelming sluggishness. She tried to will her leg to rise, but it lay dead against the rocks in front of her, attached to her body but no longer a part of it.

Wait, why …

Her head began to loll, her eyes slowly closing. With her last ounce of energy, she slid down the boulder to her side. A second later, she slipped into blackness.

9

Julia was startled back to consciousness by a loud sound in the forest. Her eyes shot open, and she bolted upright, checking her surroundings in all directions. It was already dark, faint rays of moonlight all she had to see by. She perked her ears, but all she heard was the babbling of the river. Her heart pounded.

Wha-what happened to me? she wondered, rubbing her temples with her hands. *What was that noise?* Her head hurt, and her stomach ached with hunger, but at least she could move her body again.

It was cold. She hugged her knees to her chest and pulled further into the nook of her boulder, sheltering herself from the wind. She inhaled deeply to slow her rapid pulse.

Then suddenly, from a short distance downstream came a loud, sustained scream: "AI-AAIYAAAAAAAAAAAAAAAAH!"

The sound shattered the peaceful stillness of the night. This was a bestial yell: deep, brutal, primal. Julia hugged her legs even tighter, praying that she would remain hidden.

Another scream rang out, though this one was different; rather than a wall of furious noise, it had variations in pitch and cadence. Quietly, in the back of her head, Julia could hear the whispers of a translation. Though the drawn-out words remained incomprehensible, she knew she was hearing language ... maybe even a human language. She was certain it was not coming from the creatures that had stalked her earlier; their birdsong was etched indelibly in her memory. It seemed likely to be human. Her fear gave way to curiosity.

Carefully inching out from under her rock, Julia crawled along the riverbed. She moved slowly and silently in the direction of the sound, hoping to see its source. As she came around a small bend in the river, she saw the flickering orange of firelight only a hundred yards ahead of her. Another yell pierced the night, making her jump behind a nearby log. But she could no longer suppress her desire to find out who or what it was.

Arriving at the riverbank a minute later, Julia climbed up and slipped through some low brush. She finally caught sight of the fire itself in the middle of a small clearing ahead of her, though there was no sign of whatever had been screaming. She crept forward. At the edge of the clearing, she pressed her body against a tree and poked her head out to get a full view.

There was a cooking spit set up over the campfire, a rabbit-sized animal roasting over the flame. The air was rich with the smell of meat, which made Julia's belly growl. A large leather satchel sat near the fire, close to which appeared to be a patch of bare ground where someone had made a place to sit or lie down.

Julia could hear the sounds of heavy footsteps across the way, in the woods on the far side of the clearing. Taking a step out from behind the tree toward the fire, she spotted a huge, hulking shadow. She pulled behind her tree again and kept watching, but the shadow disappeared from view, moving farther into the forest.

Shoot.

Suddenly, Julia's eyes detected movement to her side. Faster than she could react, a hand shot out and clutched her throat. The world around her blurred as she was swept to the ground and pinned against the earth. She squealed in terror but was powerless to resist.

"*VARNI FAN MA IORN!*" a voice demanded, drawing closer with each word.

The light of the fire revealed her captor's face. It was a man! Julia tried to scream, but he tightened his grip around her throat.

"*VARNI FAN MA IORN!*" he repeated, this time louder than before. Julia could hear the translating voice in the back of her head growing in volume, but it was still too faint to understand. She sobbed as she struggled against the man's immovable arm, her necklace growing colder and colder.

"*TAM,*" he said, staring deeply into her eyes as he reached down to his side with his free hand. " ... *IN SILENCE YOU DIE!*"

Julia saw the gleam of metal rising above her. She tried to scream again, but it was no use. She braced for the inevitable end.

Just as the man was about to strike, a tremendous flash of blinding, blue light shot from her necklace. He let go of her throat and staggered backward, covering his eyes.

Julia had her chance; wriggling and writhing, she broke free. She ran toward the river, driving forward through the brush. *"HELP!"* she shouted in English. *"HELP ME!"*

The man behind her yelled something, but she was too focused on getting away to understand. A hand grabbed her ankle like a vice. She lunged but went nowhere, falling to her knees.

"Let me go!" she shouted, kicking. *"LET ME GO!"*

The man pulled her backward then shot forward and pinned her arms to the ground. His hazel-green eyes locked onto hers. "Be still."

Julia futilely tried to wriggle free again.

"BE STILL," he repeated.

Julia relented, letting her body lie limp against the ground. Her mind raced with nightmarish images of the fate awaiting her. She could only hope that whatever was going to happen, it would be over quickly.

The man let go of her arms and sat up at her side. "You don't look like a Party spy," he said. "But you still should not have come here."

Julia was too overwhelmed to respond. She rolled into a ball on her side, facing away from her captor. Unexpectedly, she felt her necklace warming.

"I am sorry for attacking you. I was surprised to hear someone coming through the brush."

Julia continued ignoring him, though as her necklace warmed further she could feel herself re-centering.

"Are you hungry?" the man asked. He waited a few moments for a response then stood up and walked off.

It took Julia a minute to realize that he wasn't there. She sat up and looked over in the direction of the fire. The man was squatting next to it, turning the spit. She watched him, still wary but no longer deathly afraid. He was young, perhaps only a few years older than she was, with a powerful physique that showed even under his animal-hide getup. He had a long crop of reddish-brown hair pulled back into a ponytail and a thick but meticulously kept beard.

"It's warmer over here," he called without turning. "I would be happy to share some of my *tira* with you."

Sitting amid the riverbank bushes, Julia was both frozen and starved. The fire looked warm, and the food smelled delicious. She got up and tentatively made her way over, sitting down just out of arm's reach from the man.

He extended a meat-laden skewer in front of her. "You should eat." There was a great intensity in his stare, but also pensiveness and sincerity. "I do not know who you are, but we can talk after you've eaten." He could see Julia eyeing the meat but also hesitating to reach for it; he scooched closer and gently clutched her arm, guiding it to his offering.

Looking into his eyes again, Julia could see that the invitation was genuine. Hunger overpowered what was left of her fear. She grabbed the meat from the skewer and devoured it as quickly as chewing and swallowing would allow.

The man laughed at her ravenousness then reached to get her another piece.

Julia ate without interruption, the man patiently offering her piece after piece in silence until she'd had her fill. It was only after she leaned back on her hands to digest that he finally spoke.

"I am Thezdan, of the Guardian Clan. Why are you here?"

Julia looked up at him and shook her head. It was a question that she herself wished she could answer.

"You are young; do you even know of my clan?"

She shook her head again.

Thezdan furrowed his brow. "Then why are you here?"

"*I don't know*," she replied, without realizing it, in English.

Thezdan's eyes widened.

Julia shook her head and put up her hands, realizing her mistake. She could hear translated words but had never tried to speak them. She grabbed her necklace, hoping that it might allow her to speak as well. As it warmed in her hand, she focused, waiting for the words to come.

"I. I. I am ... am sorry," she began, struggling to channel the language. "I. I. Am Julia. This. Necklace, it ... "

Julia was frustrated at being so tongue-tied. Looking across at the confused man, she felt a new intuition come over her. She offered her free hand and gestured for him to take it.

"What is this?" he asked.

Julia tried to ignore the misgivings evident in his stare. She gestured again, and he reluctantly reached out and took her hand into his.

As their palms met, Julia closed her eyes and felt an electric wave of language, emotions, and even faint memories come through to her, as if she had plugged into his consciousness. First, she focused on the language, absorbing a lifetime of listening and speaking. Then she turned toward the memories. Rather than focus on any single one, she let the vast tapestry pass by, the images and emotions giving her an impression of the man. He was decent, loyal, and courageous. But he also harbored a deep frustration and a hidden but terrible anger.

Julia opened her eyes again to see Thezdan peering quizzically at her. If he had felt anything these past few moments, he showed little sign of it.

"My name is Julia," she began, the language now coming to her fluently. "Where are we? Why were you yelling?"

"How did you find me?" Thezdan asked, ignoring her questions.

"I heard your screams, then saw the light of the campfire. I didn't know you were going to try to kill me."

Thezdan's eyes narrowed. "But how did you end up in the forest? This is a very dangerous place for the *uninvited*."

"I woke up yesterday morning in an old, ruined fortress up in the mountains. I followed the path, and it led me here."

"What do you mean you woke up in a fortress? You mean the old monastery? What made you trek up there in the first place?"

"I didn't," said Julia. She was quiet for a moment, reflecting on how scared she had felt when she first woke up. "I just woke up there, okay? Look, I have no idea where I am or how I got here. I just want to go home."

"You really ... do not know where you are?" Thezdan repeated haltingly.

"Well, I think I'm in Aevilen," said Julia. "Where my grandmother was from."

"That's right," said Thezdan. "These are the Western Woods of Aevilen."

Julia sighed. "I know you probably don't believe me, but until a few days ago I'd never heard of Aevilen. I'm from California, in America. I just put on my grandmother's necklace and went to sleep in my bed. Then I woke up here. In a freakin' abandoned monastery."

"So that artifact belonged to your grandmother?" asked Thezdan, his voice tinged with anticipation. "And it brought you here? Who was your grandmother?"

Julia checked her necklace. It was still warm. She looked back at Thezdan. "Her name is Elleina."

Thezdan was stunned. His father had told him stories about the flight of Princess Elleina, heir to the Vorraver throne. He also told of her eventual return, that the same magic that had sent her away would one day bring her back. Thezdan had always believed these stories to be myths; yet now he found himself staring at a strange, young girl who bore a remarkable artifact cast in the shape of the royal symbol.

Thezdan asked, "Are you a Vorraver?"

"My grandmother's maiden name was Vorraver, yes," Julia said. She shrugged. "Maybe that makes me one?"

Thezdan studied the girl. She was wandering alone deep in Sylvan-watched woods. She claimed to be a Vorraver, a direct descendent of the Lost Princess, yet she seemed very much a foreigner, nothing like any plains-dweller he'd ever met. None of it made sense, yet something deep inside himself was telling him to believe her.

"Thezdan, why do you want to know?" Julia asked anxiously.

"Princess Elleina Vorraver was said to have escaped a long time ago via the monastery you mentioned," Thezdan said finally. "My grandfather died protecting her."

Julia leaned forward. "Was his name Eovaz?"

Thezdan nodded, smiling appreciatively. "The Princess told you of him?"

"Yeah, she did. But I also found something that mentioned him back at the monastery." She reached into the bag that hung at her side and withdrew the two notes. Scanning them quickly, she found the one she was looking for and held out for Thezdan to take. "I think my grandmother wrote this a long time ago."

Thezdan pored over the note, mouthing the words as he went. When he had finished, he refolded it and looked up, staring at Julia in silence.

Julia furrowed her brow. "W-What is it?"

"I'm not sure," he said. He stood up and beckoned for her to follow. "Much has happened since Princess Elleina left. But it's late, and you should get some sleep. Come. I will give you some skins so you can sleep by the fire."

"Wait," Julia said. "Sleep here? Have you forgotten that you attacked me? And aren't those awful forest creatures up there somewhere? Thanks for the food, but—"

"By the Goddess, I swear that no harm will come to you by me. The Sylvan will not bother you, either. By our heritage, members of our Clan and our guests may enter the forest. So as long as I am with you, they will leave you be."

It seemed a strange explanation to Julia, but Thezdan's confidence persuaded her. "Then I could have used you earlier," she said, turning over her leg to show off her cut. "I think one got me with one of their arrows."

Thezdan came around to look at the wound more closely. "This was caused by a Sylvan thorn?" he asked, concerned. "When?"

Julia pulled her leg back, not wanting to be fussed over. "Sometime earlier today? I'm fine. It's not that deep."

"How are you feeling?"

"I told you, I'm fine. What's this all about?"

"Sylvan thorns carry poisons," said Thezdan. "Even if one just grazed you, you may have been exposed."

Julia swallowed hard. "Maybe that's why I fell asleep by the riverbank. I've never felt so tired."

"Tired?" Thezdan repeated. He chuckled, suddenly much more at ease. "That's good. There's no need to worry then. I take that one when I'm sick!"

"Really? Phew. You had me worried for a second!"

Thezdan got up and headed over to his pack. "I apologize for alarming you. Do you think you'll still be able to sleep tonight even after sleeping all day?"

"Maybe. I'm not sure why, but I actually still feel tired. The real issue is these woods. I know you say that the tree creatures won't bother me, but they're not the only thing I'm worried about. Right before you attacked me, I saw a huge shadow moving around just outside the clearing, somewhere over there. It's probably still out there."

"Was it taller than me and this big around?" Thezdan asked, holding his arms out wide.

Julia cocked her head, eying him skeptically. "Yeah … "

Thezdan smiled. "That wasn't a monster. That was Scylld! Allow me to introduce you!"

Thezdan turned toward the forest and brought his cupped hands to his lips, blowing across the knuckles to produce a low-pitched whistle that filled the forest with sound. Almost instantly, a rumble reply came from within a stand of nearby trees, followed by the sound of heavy footsteps approaching.

Julia nervously awaited sight of the creature. The footsteps got closer and closer, louder and louder, until finally it came into view at the edge of the clearing: a huge, hulking creature, built like a man but easily several feet taller and thicker than any man she had ever seen, with a cracked hide that from across the camp appeared to be made of stone. It had a smooth, mouthless, and noseless face with two black stones set where a man's eyes would be. Julia watched it make its way toward Thezdan, transfixed by its size. She reflexively reached behind and put a hand on the ground, ready to turn and run.

"Julia, meet Scylld," said Thezdan. "He is one of the Ogarren."

The creature came to rest in front of them, raising one of its long, thick arms up and across its body in something resembling a salute.

"O … g-garren?" Julia stuttered.

"Yes, you know, the ones mentioned in all the children's stories. Have you not heard of them?"

In fact, she had; she remembered hearing that name when she had traced the words on the panel in the library. "Born of godly passions … " she whispered.

Thezdan turned toward the creature. "That's right. Scylld is one of the few remaining. The Ogarren are living earth, beings created by the energy released by the Goddess and Shaper as they communed on the plateau here in Aevilen."

"Is he actually made of rock?"

"Yes. And soil, and leaves, and vines. Whatever the Goddess and Shaper touched as they were together took on their energies, and those things coalesced into the Ogarren."

The creature knelt, letting its arms rest palm-up against its legs. Julia sensed that the Ogar was offering itself for her to examine.

"May I touch him?" she asked.

"Sure," said Thezdan. "I don't think he'll mind."

She got up and moved to within arm's reach of the Ogar. She could see that Thezdan had not been lying about its body. The rocks that formed its skin fit very tightly together, though in some places she could see vines and twigs poking through. Looking up at the creature's head, she saw the two rounded, black stones, their polished surfaces reflecting the lapping flames of the campfire.

"Are these his eyes?"

"Yes, they are. His other senses are not like ours, though. He feels sounds with his whole being. He does not taste since he does not eat. Nor does he smell. And touch … " Thezdan chuckled, gesturing toward the creature's four thick, triangular digits set like an eagle's talons in his giant hands. "Just don't ask him to fasten your sandals."

Julia was so focused on the eyes that she barely registered Thezdan's joke. "Beautiful," she muttered under her breath.

The creature came to life again, returning to its feet and rising to full height. It took all of Julia's bravery to remain in front of it, so puny did it make her feel. It loomed easily three or four feet overhead, and she imagined her arms might only make it halfway around its tremendous girth. As their eyes fixed on one another, the Ogar brought its claw-like hand forward and opened it at Julia's side. She glanced at the open hand then back at the creature. Her necklace warmed. Somehow, she knew that it was inviting her to connect with it in the same way she had with Thezdan.

How do you know about that?

Julia placed her hand into the creature's palm. No sooner had she closed her eyes than an overwhelming torrent of life-energy poured into her. It was much too much for her to absorb: thousands of lifetimes' worth of visions and sounds and experiences. Like a dam faced with restraining the ocean, Julia tried to relax her mind enough so as not to break amid the flow.

Suddenly a deep, booming voice came to her:

You have courage, young Vorraver, and greater strength than you yet know. You will need both. This land is threatened by a darkness that would see it changed forever. You must defend it! Assemble the divided key, and fulfill the promises made by your ancestors!

She reopened her eyes. Thezdan was standing next to her, clutching her shoulders.

"Julia!" he called in a loud voice. "Julia!"

Julia shook her head to clear the lingering cobwebs and slowly removed her hand from the Ogar's. She didn't know what to make of the experience. Where did that voice come from? What did it all mean? Her whole body tingled, feeling as though she'd been touched by the divine. Looking up at Scylld, she felt an even fuller appreciation of the ancient power that flowed from his very core.

"Are you okay?" Thezdan asked. "You seemed to be passing out."

"I'm fine, thanks," Julia replied. She thought about sharing her experience with Thezdan, but decided to keep it to herself for now. It felt important, but it didn't make sense yet. She needed time to process.

The Ogar raised an open hand and bowed its head. Julia smiled and bowed deeply in return.

Thezdan raised an eyebrow, not knowing what to make of the spectacle. "Um, why don't I go get you those skins I promised you?"

Julia walked over and settled in close to the fire, letting the warmth envelop her. "Can I ask you something?" she called to Thezdan.

"What is it?" he asked, his voice muffled by his pack.

"Why did I find you alone in the forest? Why you were yelling?"

When after a few moments he didn't reply, Julia turned around. She was surprised to find him standing just behind her.

"I am here to train," Thezdan said, his body tense. He dropped a small stack of skins at her side. "To find the Rage that made the Guardians the greatest warriors in history. And when I do, I will use it to reclaim what was taken from us."

10

It was barely after dawn when a heavy hand woke Julia from her sleep.

"We have to go," Thezdan said quietly.

Julia sat up and tried to shake off her grog. "Am I going with you?" she asked through a yawn. "Where are we going?"

"I have an appointment in Breslin to trade some skins and foraged greyroot for supplies. Afterward, I will take you to meet an old friend of my father's. There aren't many left who would know anything about royal artifacts, but he would be one. Hopefully, he can help you."

Julia hesitated. She wanted to trust him, but he was still a stranger … a stranger she'd found screaming in the woods. "I'm just going to slow you down," she replied, shaking her head. "Why don't you just drop me off at the closest village? Anywhere with a phone should be fine. I'll just call my parents and they'll help me get out of here."

"A *phone?*"

Julia mimed a telephone with her hands. "Yeah, you know … "

"Like animal horns?" Thezdan asked, confused.

"No. The thing you use to talk to people far away. Don't you have them?"

"Is that another royal artifact? I have never seen it."

Julia shook her head, flustered. "Why don't you just drop me off at the nearest town, anyway. I'll figure it out."

Thezdan laughed dismissively. "You would be in danger the moment I left. It is a miracle you were not killed by the Sylvan yesterday. And out on the plains, there are horrors greater than anything you might find here among the trees."

"What do you mean?"

"It is dangerous in town, in the countryside, and in the little villages and hamlets we'll pass. All of Aevilen is dangerous, for me and especially for you. The eyes will never stop watching. Even the kindest-looking old farmer would report you to a Party guard. The extra rations he'd receive would go a long way toward clearing his conscience. And were anyone to discover you are a Vorraver … "

"Then?" Julia pressed.

"Then I don't know. But the last time the Party chased a Vorraver, they sent an army, and your grandmother barely escaped."

Julia fell silent, frightened by the images running through her head.

"I'm telling you the truth," said Thezdan, offering a hand to help her up.

She took it. "So, you're going to keep me safe, then?"

Thezdan's eyes locked on hers, and he suddenly seemed at a loss for words. A moment later, he offered a shallow nod and turned away.

Julia was impressed by the litheness with which Thezdan moved through the forest. Despite the large, well-stuffed pack on his back, he never seemed even slightly encumbered as he climbed over obstacles or uneven stretches of ground. Scylld followed behind, a chorus of cracking and snapping sounds suggesting that the Ogar had a more direct approach to dealing with obstacles. Though stressed by their pace, Julia was happy to be traveling with them. Yesterday, the forest had seemed a dangerous labyrinth; today, with two companions to guide her, it was a place of ancient and pristine beauty. She had been on many hikes in her life. Still, there had always been signs of humanity: trash left on a trail, signs pointing the way, and other cars or tourists nearby. This was different. Old trees soared overhead in all directions, their trunks covered by thick, green climbing vines and patches of green-blue moss. They passed a few trees in particular that stood out, remarkable not just for their height or circumference but also for their thick, rough bark. By the light streaming through the canopy, Julia traced the canyons that crisscrossed the surfaces of these trees. She imagined them as wrinkles on the faces of wizened elders who kept silent watch over life in the forest.

Thezdan noticed her fascination. "You keep looking around like it's your first time amid trees. Are there no forests where you're from?"

"I went to see the redwoods once," Julia replied. "So, I've seen big trees, but we spent most of the time in the car. I never really felt like I was in nature. This is what I imagine the redwood forests were like a thousand years ago, before anyone discovered them."

"This forest shall remain as it is until the end times," said Thezdan. "The Sylvan will see to that."

"They protect the forest?"

"Yes. They attack any human who is not a Guardian or accompanied by one. For centuries, the Guardians ensured that those who entered the forest made respectful passage through, only traveling along the paths the Sylvan themselves had cleared."

"Your Clan lives here, in the forest?"

Thezdan's pace slowed. He took a deep breath. "In the past, only a small number of Guardians lived in the forest. It was how we paid tribute to the Goddess. The rest lived in the Trebain, just east of Riverstride."

"My grandmother mentioned Riverstride. I think she lived there."

"Yes, that was the royal seat. The Trebain was close by because, in the old days, the other duty of the Guardian Clan was to protect the royal family."

"That's why your grandfather died protecting my grandmother," Julia said somberly.

"Yes, along with many other Guardians. The Revolution was a disaster for all Aevilen, and the rule of the People's Party even worse."

"I didn't believe my grandmother when she said it wasn't safe for her to go home. It's been fifty years! How can this still be going on? How can it still be so dangerous? Why haven't they been toppled yet?"

Thezdan grit his teeth. "Because no one has been able to unite a population scared into submission." He stopped walking and looked over at Julia. "Can I ask you something?"

Julia leaned against a tree to catch her breath. She was grateful for the break. "Sure. What's up?"

"Why did Princess Elleina send you? Why didn't she come herself?"

Julia looked down. "It's not really like that. I don't think she meant for me to come."

Thezdan cocked his head. "No?"

"No. I found her necklace in a trunk and put it on. I didn't know what it was."

"That it was a powerful artifact held by the royal family of Aevilen? How could she not have told you about it? Why would she have put it in a trunk to be forgotten?"

"I don't know," said Julia. "She didn't really talk about Aevilen much when I was young."

Thezdan crossed his arms in front of him, a forlorn look in his eyes. "My father always believed she would return, and that when she did things would change. I'm glad that he never found out that she had forgotten us."

Julia shook her head. "Don't say that. That's not what happened.

Ina's not like that."

Thezdan turned and started walking again. "It doesn't matter now. Let's keep going. We're not far from the road."

True to his claim, only a few minutes later they came upon a road snaking its way through the forest. Julia expected things to be easier from then on, but the opposite was true: the even surface allowed Thezdan to pick up his pace. She had to jog to keep up, and it wasn't long before she had to stop, cramping and out of breath.

"Hold up! You're going too fast!"

Thezdan stopped and walked back to her. "We have a lot of ground to cover today. If you're too tired to continue, perhaps Scylld can help."

As if on command, the Ogar presented its back to her and knelt down.

Julia looked back at Thezdan disbelievingly. "You want me to ride him?"

"If you're too tired to keep a good pace, yes."

"Uh, how would I even get on?"

"Just climb up and put your legs on either side of his neck. You can hold on to his head."

As unsettling as the idea of riding the Ogar seemed at first, it grew on Julia as she thought about trying to keep up with Thezdan on the road. Rising from her stump, she went over to Scylld and began awkwardly clambering up his back, surprised that the Ogar could tolerate her groping and kicking. Soon, she was seated with her legs around his neck, gripping his head like a giant pommel.

"Now what?" she asked.

"Now?" said Thezdan, smirking impishly. "Now you hold on."

Julia looked down, panic-stricken, as the creature began rising to its feet. She hugged its head for dear life, one of her arms partially covering its eyes.

"Careful!" laughed Thezdan. "He won't know where he's going!"

The vines that were part of Scylld's body suddenly started growing, forming loops in the areas around Julia's feet. Though unnerved by the sight, Julia knew that these vines were meant to help; she tucked her feet in the loops and instantly felt more stable.

"There! That's better!" said Thezdan.

Julia shot back a cold stare.

Thezdan laughed again as he turned to head up the road. "Enjoy the ride!"

Julia managed to keep her composure as the Ogar started moving. His plod made for a bumpy journey, but after the first few steps, she relaxed a bit. It was indeed better than walking.

11

"*Wait, Julia! Don't go too far ahead!*"

"*Chill, Mom! It's not my first time on a horse!*"

"*There's no rush. Take a deep breath and enjoy the—*"

"*Giddyap, Bluebird!*"

"*Julia! JULIA! WAIT!*"

"Julia? Is everything alright?"

Thezdan's voice snapped Julia out of her daydream. "Hmm?"

"You were kicking Scylld," he said, looking up at her with a mix of amusement and confusion. "Is something the matter?"

"Oh," said Julia. "Sorry about that, Scylld!" She reached forward and rubbed the Ogar's stone hide where her heel may have struck. "I guess I got a little carried away. Riding Scylld reminded me of going horseback riding with my Mom in Montana. I would kick my horse when I wanted him to go faster."

"You want him to go faster?"

"Oh, no! No, this speed is just fine."

Thezdan chuckled. "Good. I don't think you'd enjoy the ride very much if Scylld were running!"

The forest was brighter here, and the sunlight brought rich plant life to the understory. Flowering vines grew along the trunks and lower branches of the trees nearby. Much of the area surrounding the road was blanketed with low-lying shrubs. There was also a slight dampness to the air, matched by the churning hum of a nearby river.

"Why is the river so much louder in this part of the forest?" Julia asked.

Thezdan slowed his pace slightly, answering in a hushed voice, "The earlier stream was just a small tributary. By the time it gets here, it has combined with a hundred other streams from the western mountains. The river you hear stretches all the way to the Giant Steps at the end of the plateau. It is an effective boundary between the forest and the Aevilen plain.

"Why are you whispering?" Julia whispered back. "Do we have to be careful?"

"We will be alright, it's just better to be quiet."

Something was amiss. Looking around them, Julia thought she could see some mist from the river, and maybe even a trace of the plain Thezdan had mentioned. Then ahead of them, she noticed that the road they were on intersected with a wide, well-traveled footpath.

"Thezdan, where does that lead?" she asked, pointing toward the path.

Thezdan glared at her and shook his head. He covered his mouth with his hand.

Julia fell silent, chastened. She peeked up the path as they passed, seeing little more than the same trees, shrubs, vines, and roots that she had seen for hours now. But then she caught a glimpse of something in the distance, well-camouflaged against the surrounding trees: a wall made from whole logs! It looked like something from the old frontier forts she had seen pictures of in her history books. Her mind raced. Was it a human settlement? The city of the forest people? A gate? The only thing she knew for sure was that Thezdan wanted to avoid it. She wondered why it made him so uncomfortable.

Only a short distance past the footpath, the road turned toward the sound of the water. The forest opened up in front of them, a flood of brilliant daylight filling Julia's eyes. Ahead of them was a stone bridge over a wide river, a vast stretch of open grassland beyond. The bridge was very old and so narrow that a man could not have lain down across its width. There were no handrails, ropes, or walls, and the guardrail stones, like those of the mountainside road, came up only just high enough to keep a wagon wheel from slipping over the side. Beneath the bridge ran the angriest river Julia had ever seen. The roaring, yellow waters in the canyon raised the hairs on the back of her neck.

Thezdan stopped a few yards shy of the crossing and spun around.

"You'll have to cross under your own power."

Julia swallowed hard. "Wait, what about Scylld?"

"He is not coming with us. He will remain in the forest."

The Ogar kneeled, and Julia climbed down from her perch on its shoulders. She stared nervously at the bridge. "That doesn't look safe at all."

"Safe?" said Thezdan. "The bridge has stood for a thousand years. Surely that makes it among the safest in Aevilen."

Julia glowered at him. "That's not what I mean."

Thezdan looked back askance for a moment, then he turned and waved her forward. "It's only walking. Let's go."

Julia followed, but her will gave out once her feet met the first stones. She watched Thezdan move farther and farther away; he seemed to pay no mind to the lack of handrails and the rushing waters below. Queasy from the sight of the raging river, Julia decided there was only one way across. She dropped to her hands and knees and began to crawl. It was slow, and the old stone hurt her knees, but it was getting her where she needed to go. Then she heard howling laughter.

Thezdan.

She clenched her jaw and continued, inch by inch, to make her way across the span. Arriving at the far side a few minutes later, she stood and stomped over to him, her face twisted into an angry scowl.

"What's the matter with you?" she snarled. "Why are you such a jerk?"

"I'm sorry," said Thezdan, trying to appear sincere. "But ... "

He started to laugh again under his breath. " … in Aevilen, we *walk* across bridges!"

Julia deepened her scowl. "Call me crazy, but I don't like narrow, little bridges over killer rivers. And at least I'm not a lunatic who screams at trees!"

"No. But you did choose one as your guide!"

Julia's cold façade started to crack. She looked up at his twinkling eyes and started to laugh, giving him a playful eye-roll.

"A bridge-crawler and a lunatic—what a fine pair of traveling companions!" said Thezdan as he turned up the road. "Come, Julia. Even if we stick to walking, we've got quite a ways to go."

12

The dirt road leading east from the bridge stretched out into the distance and disappeared over a hill more than a mile away. The landscape reminded Julia of the Carmel Valley back home, with its gentle undulations and fields teeming with golden grasses, wildflowers, and scrub. There were also occasional patches of bare, dry earth and signs of past settlements peeking out from the growth, including a low, partially collapsed wall that ran along the road.

"Is it safe for us to be out in the open like this?" Julia asked. "Couldn't somebody see us?"

"There is virtually no patrol activity west of Breslin during the day. Anyway, I know most of the hunters out here. I give them *braeden* bark to tan their skins. They won't give us up."

"How far are we from Breslin?"

"About seven rests," said Thezdan. "At a good pace, we should be able to make it before midday. Are your legs feeling any better?"

Julia shrugged. "Not great, but I'll make it."

"If you get tired, we can take a break up the road. We're going to change our clothes in an old storage house not far from here. We'll need to wear Party garb as we get closer to town."

"Disguises? Just who exactly are we pretending to be?"

"Peasants. I keep a number of field tunics with all the proper insignias. One of them should fit you, don't worry."

They came to an intersection with a rough road that cut its way into the fields. Thezdan turned onto it, leading them into the seemingly empty countryside. As they came up over a small hill, Julia caught sight of a dilapidated stone structure, alone among the meadow grasses.

"That's the storehouse up ahead," said Thezdan. "It was a crop house once. All that you can see around here were some of Aevilen richest farmlands. My father once told me that when he was a boy, this whole area was an endless sea of beuwit stalks so tall that a man could have hid among them."

"What happened to all the farms?" Julia asked. She looked over, recognizing the pain in Thezdan's eyes.

"The Revolution happened," he said. "The All Aevilen People's Party happened. And while your grandmother escaped, there was a Purge, and then a Second Purge, and then a Third. Party soldiers destroyed all of these farms and killed most of the farmers." He pointed at a nearby patch of dried earth. "That was once a home. Burned, like the rest of them."

Julia tried to imagine the farmhouse on a cultivated plain. She could see small clusters of brick peeking out from the ground, which reminded her of her burned house in Malibu. She had to fight back tears. "Why? Why would they do that?" she asked distantly.

"Control. They wanted to move the farms closer to the city so that they could watch the farmers. Though these lands are more fertile, the Party believed that the farmers here were spoiled by their plenty. Too hard to control."

"Why hasn't anyone done anything?" Julia said. "Why doesn't the world know about this? This should be in the *LA Times*, CNN!"

"We have no contact with the lower continent, if that's what you mean. The Giant Steps are only passable several times a century, and not even once in my lifetime."

"All this? Just for control?"

"Yes. The People's Party used the difficulties of a few bad harvests to prey on everyone's baser instincts. They told the suffering tradesmen in the towns that the farmers were hoarding food; they told the farmers that the monks had angered the gods and brought about a drought; and they told everyone that the Vorravers were the greatest evil of all. The Party started a Revolution. By the time the fires had stopped burning, the most influential farmers were dead; the temples and monasteries were destroyed; and the entire royal family—your family—was slain."

Thezdan's face twitched. "The Party's cruelty knows no limits.

We have suffered three great Purges. Countless deaths. They boast of the 'paradise' they have created, but all around, there is only misery. The people of Aevilen now do just about anything to survive. Most would send their relatives to the headsman if they thought it to their advantage. We live in a trying time, Julia. Before long, none will be left who remember the Aevilen that once was, and the old ways will be lost forever."

Julia had read about man's capacity for evil in history books, but it had always seemed distant. Seeing the burned landscape around her and the deep pain in Thezdan's eyes, knowing that he'd lived through it, shook her to the core. "How have you survived?" she asked, her voice quivering.

"The Party sent its armies against us during the Third Purge. I fled with the children and women to the forest while my father, Eobax, and the warriors stayed behind. I've heard that each of their swords had the blood of forty men on them by the time they were overwhelmed."

Julia didn't know what to say. She placed a hand on his arm, but Thezdan didn't respond to the gesture.

"Let's go," he said, turning away.

Julia followed Thezdan in silence. These were blood-soaked grounds. Unlike Malibu, most of the families in these houses had not escaped their fires. She imagined what it might have been like for her grandmother to be trapped like that with her family. She could no longer suppress her emotions in the face of the violence and tragedy surrounding her. Tears welled in her eyes.

When they arrived at the dilapidated crop house a few minutes later, Thezdan saw the streaks on her cheeks. Julia, almost ashamed in the face of his stoicism, looked away.

"You do not need to hide your sadness from me," Thezdan said. "You express what we all feel. But harden your heart, Julia. In town, your emotions would give us away."

She nodded, wiping her face with her sweater. "I understand. I'll be fine."

Thezdan walked through an old doorway, now just an empty space between the walls, and returned carrying a stack of folded garments.

"Put this on," he said, passing one to Julia.

Julia unfolded a hooded shawl made from coarse, brown wool. On the back was a symbol of three overlapping rings. "All peasants wear this?"

"That's right. Peasants and hunters both. The one thing in our favor is that it's easier to blend in when so many wear the same thing."

Julia opened the shawl and put it on. It hung from her slender frame like a set of drapes. She held out her arms, showing off the excess fabric. "Is this a problem?"

"I don't think so. Not many people wear shawls that fit well. Young people usually wear ones they've inherited from dead family members, and the older generations wear ones they were given before the famines. So long as you play your part, we should be fine."

After sliding on his own shawl, Thezdan walked around to the back of the house and emerged pulling a four-wheeled wooden wagon. It looked like an oversized version of a kid's toy, with a long bar extending out front that connected to either side of the front axle. The wheels had deep dings and cracks from years of hard duty.

"Climb in," he said.

Julia climbed over the side of the wagon and took a position up front. Thezdan placed his pack next to her then went back inside the crop house. He came back with two large stacks of tanned animal hides.

"What are those?" Julia asked.

"They're feral borum hides, mostly," said Thezdan, dropping them in the wagon bed. "They roam the western fields, and the Party allows designated hunters to take them. The guy I'm going to see in Breslin usually gives me better terms for these than for the smaller *tira* hides from the forest."

"If you see a borum, will you point it out to me? I don't think we have them back home."

Thezdan moved into position inside the u-shaped bar. "Look! Here's one now!"

Julia swiveled her head around but saw only empty meadow. She looked back at Thezdan. He smirked and pointed at himself.

Julia laughed. "So, you're our beast of burden?"

"That I am!" he said, pushing hard against the bar to set the wagon in motion.

Julia leaned up against the stack of skins. She was torn between excitement and apprehension as she watched the landscape roll by. Thezdan guided the wagon back toward the main road and then east, away from the river. Listening to the soothing monotony of footsteps and clacking wheels, her eyes began to grow heavy.

"Thezdan? Is it safe for me to take a quick nap?"

"So long as you put your hood up, it's fine. I'll wake you when we get closer."

Julia pulled the oversized hood up and over her head and adjusted her position against the skins. She closed her eyes and emptied her mind, repeating her mantra from before.

This road will lead me home.

13

The landscape had changed by the time Julia awoke. The open, swaying meadow was gone; instead, she saw rough farmland broken into alternating fields of long, stalky crops and low-lying vegetables. The plant rows were dotted with farmers hard at work, each wearing a brown tunic with the Party's insignia embroidered in large format across the back. At the far edge of the fields were several long houses with mud-brick walls and thatched-grass roofs.

Julia peeked out from under her hood, trying to avoid focusing on anyone or anything for too long. The farmers seemed to ignore the wagon, though Julia caught one woman looking up from her work and, for a brief moment, their eyes met. In those eyes, framed by a drawn, gaunt face hollowed out by malnutrition, Julia saw desperation of a sort she'd never seen before. Startled, the woman immediately turned her gaze back to the ground and began furiously raking at her crop.

"Where are we?" Julia whispered to Thezdan.

Thezdan turned his head slightly, just enough to hide his face from the farmers. "These are the outskirts of Breslin. Try to ignore the farmers, for everyone's sake."

Julia watched an older man near the side of the road use a bony, kinked finger to scratch at the roots of a stalk. He seemed very frail.

"These ones are relatively well off," said Thezdan. "Life is tough for farmers. All of this harvest will be seized come the fall, and most will go to soldiers. Disease and starvation kill hundreds of farmers every year."

Julia felt her chest tighten. She looked away, frustrated by her own powerlessness. She wanted to jump off the cart and rush over to help these people, but she knew that to do so was to invite catastrophe for everyone—including her.

"You can see Breslin ahead," said Thezdan. "In my grandfather's time, it was a trading hub for the western farmers and Rokkin. As we get into town, be careful not to stare at anyone or anything. You must play the role of the visiting hunter. Even the smallest thing may lead a suspicious villager to call the guards on us."

"Okay," said Julia. She slid down and let her gaze fall loosely but continuously on the wall of the wagon bed, doing her best to ignore the world around her. It was the only way she knew how to keep up the charade.

The telltale sound of wagon wheels against cobblestones announced their arrival in town. Unable to suppress her curiosity, Julia let her eyes wander again, taking in the buildings around them.

The town had a medieval European feel to it, the road bound on either side by two-story stone structures with tiled roofs. By the beautiful white and gray-blue stones that made up the buildings' facades, it was clear that Breslin had been wealthy, once. Its trading past lingered in old merchant stalls that dotted the road and in the shop signs carved above doors. Decay had long since overtaken that splendor. The merchant stalls were rotting, and most of the buildings had open holes in their facades, boarded up windows, or leather tarps on their roofs.

A man emerged from one of the homes and swept the street behind them, the rasping of his broom the only sound Julia heard other than the cart wheels in this seemingly-abandoned town.

Thezdan steered the wagon into an open square. Julia could imagine this square as the bustling center of civic life in a prior era. Today, however, there was only a single person: a woman in a brown dress made from the same course fabric as the peasant tunics gathering water from a fountain in the middle. Like the farmers, she rarely looked up, and her quick movements and shuffle-steps showed a deep underlying skittishness.

A large, well-maintained barracks adorned with Party banners loomed over one side of the square, standing out like a sore thumb among the decrepit townhouses around it. On the opposite side was a single-story smithy that belched puffs of gray-black smoke from two chimneys on its roof.

Thezdan brought the wagon to rest in front of the smithy, then he jumped down and made his way to the back to collect his cargo.

"I have to go inside to drop off these skins," he said quietly, without looking at Julia. "Remember to ignore everything and everyone in this town. Pretend they don't exist. If you end up in trouble, knock on the door three times. Now, kick the side of the wagon if you understand."

Julia tried to appear as though she were just shifting her weight as she tapped her foot against the wooden wall of the wagon bed. Thezdan knocked on the other side to acknowledge her gesture. Then he reached in, grabbed the skins, and headed toward the door. He knocked twice and stepped back.

A minute later, the door opened. The man in the doorway was perhaps thirty years old, a lean figure bursting with muscle. He had a ghastly collection of scars that ran up his arms and a cracked, soot-stained face. Julia couldn't hear what Thezdan was saying, but she saw the man checking the square for signs of activity before nodding almost imperceptibly toward the interior of his house. Thezdan entered, and the door closed swiftly behind him.

Julia lowered her hood over her brow and tried to stare at nothing. *If I can't see them, they can't see me.*

Soon, she slipped into a daze. She might have fallen asleep again but for a gentle rapping against the wagon. She hadn't heard any approaching footsteps, so it came as an unwelcome surprise.

"Hail to the Party, and fair day to you, hunter," came an artificially feeble voice. "Might you have any rations to spare for your fellow citizen, a veteran?"

Julia turned her head to see a man standing beside the wagon. He was hunched over a cane, and he wore a patch over his right eye that partially covered a scar that ran all the way down to his mouth. As Julia's gaze met his, he smiled a mostly-toothless grin.

"I don't have any rations, I'm sorry," she replied.

The man's smile disappeared. "I know you have rations!" he growled, banging his cane against the cart. "I watched you and your fellow hunter come in here with those stacks of skins. You think I don't know what those are worth? You don't think you should have to share with your brother citizen?"

"I-I'm sorry!" Julia said. "Honestly, I don't have anything!"

The man clenched his jaw, his brow contorted with anger. Suddenly, he raised his cane to strike. Julia shrieked and lurched away, her tunic slipping lower on her frame. Peeking back at the man, Julia could see that his expression had shifted from anger to frightened bewilderment. She followed his eyes down, and soon knew what had him so transfixed. Her necklace had been revealed, and it radiated a brilliant, blue light.

Julia covered her necklace with her hand, but it was too late. The man dropped his cane and began running. Julia's mind raced. Should she go get Thezdan, or just hope that the man would disappear down an alley?

She watched the beggar run over to the barracks. He banged on the door, turning every now and again to make sure she was still there. When the door finally opened, the beggar gestured furiously in her direction then stepped aside to make way for a trio of armed guards. They carried long staves with curved blades at the end, and their metal armor glimmered in the sunlight. The leader of the pack had a polished helmet that hid his face, but his quick, purposeful strides laid bare his fervor.

The moment she saw the guards, Julia knew she had waited too long. She jumped down from the wagon and banged on the door three times. Looking over her shoulder, she saw that they were closing in quickly. She banged again.

"Where are you, Thezdan!" she whisper-shouted. "Open up!"

"Halt, hunter!" shouted the guard captain.

Julia ignored him and started banging frantically against the door. Just as the guards were coming around the side of the wagon, the door to the smithy swung open. Thezdan loomed large in the doorway, the other man standing only a few feet behind him.

"Hail, Revolutionaries," Thezdan called. "We are here to deliver skins to Citizen Vonn."

"Hold for inspection," the guard captain commanded, his tone brimming with bad intent. "We have reports that your companion has something around her neck that we should investigate. She will come with us."

Julia looked up at Thezdan and shook her head with a rapid but contained motion.

"I'm afraid we have to leave," Thezdan replied. "On Party orders we are to deliver plough blades to some farms in the Western Territories, and, as you are well aware, we will need to finish the trip before dark."

The guard captain ignored Thezdan. He reached out toward Julia and made a 'come' motion with his hand. "To me, hunter."

Suddenly the man behind Thezdan lurched forward and grabbed Thezdan's arms. "These hunters are enemies of the Revolution!"

"Arrest them!" cried the captain as the other guards readied their weapons.

"You fool," Thezdan growled. He turned his wrists and thrust his body backward, pushing the man holding him to the ground. Pulling his tunic up as he spun, he drew his sword and in a single motion sent it flying toward the guard captain. It whizzed by Julia's ear and passed clear through the captain's throat, blood spurting from the entry wound.

Stunned, the other guards watched the captain crumple to the ground.

Thezdan lunged toward the nearer of the two. The guard tried to push him away with the shaft of his polearm, but Thezdan ripped the weapon from his hands and delivered a forceful kick that sent him sprawling to the ground. Thezdan then spun around and slashed at the neck of the other guard, catching it flush. Julia turned away in naked horror as his severed head fell and then rolled several feet away.

Thezdan turned toward the guard on the ground, who spotted him coming as he struggled to get up.

"Please! Ple—" the guard whimpered.

Thezdan drove the polearm's blade into the guard's midsection. The guard briefly screamed in agony, then his eyes stilled.

Thezdan walked back to the house and found the smith scrambling to his feet. He grabbed him by the throat. "You betrayed me."

The smith sobbed meekly, his face showing the terror of a man facing his own death.

Thezdan let go. "I will show you mercy, but not because you deserve it. A worse fate awaits you in the manacles of the Party. So run, and understand how my Clan has lived; or stay and suffer."

The man slumped to the ground. Thezdan came out of the house and grabbed Julia's shoulder. "We have to go. Now."

Julia stood in despondent silence, frozen. She had never in her life witnessed killing; here, she had just seen three men die. Viciously. She watched Thezdan run over to the corpse of the guard captain and yank the sword from his throat, fresh blood dripping from the blade. A wave of nausea washed over her.

"Now!" Thezdan repeated.

Julia stared at him blankly, frozen in fear.

"WE HAVE TO GO!"

She could hear the distant cries of panicked villagers, and from the corner of her eye, she caught sight of one of the guard's dangerous pole weapons lying on the ground. It had been meant for her. The nipping cold from her necklace made her snap to. She ran to Thezdan's side.

Thezdan reached into the wagon bed and grabbed his pack. He quickly removed his Party tunic and jammed it into a side pocket. He stuck out a hand toward Julia. "Your tunic will slow you down. Take it off! Quickly!"

Julia pulled her shawl over her head and passed it to Thezdan. He hurriedly stuffed it into the other side pocket then slung the pack over his shoulder. "Can you run?" he asked.

Julia nodded tensely.

"Follow me! Run as fast as you can!"

They sprinted through the square together, the clip-clop of their sandals reverberating off the walls of the stone buildings. Julia looked over at the barracks from which the guards had emerged earlier, finding no signs of activity. Then suddenly, from atop the building, a horn blared a dreadful, deep roar. She turned to locate the source of the sound, but Thezdan grabbed her by the sweater and yanked her forward. "DO YOU WANT TO DIE HERE?"

Julia was startled, but the yank refocused her. Getting away was the only thing that mattered. With Thezdan leading, the two ran back through the town, retracing their earlier route. Just as they turned the final corner, the dirt road leading back toward the forest coming into view, Julia heard an ominous rumbling sound.

Thezdan grabbed her arm. Extending her stride, Julia allowed him to pull her faster than she herself was capable of running. Even at that pace, however, the rumbling gained on them. Thezdan kept checking over his shoulder, growing more desperate with each stride. Then it appeared: an iron chariot pulled by two hairy, yak-like creatures covered in leather armor, each with a set of massive horns extending forward like a pair of knight's lances. The driver wore the armor of a guard captain, and at his side he swung a ball and chain with rhythmic menace.

"Run!" Thezdan cried, letting go of Julia.

As Julia sprinted toward the dirt road, Thezdan turned and grabbed hold of one of the old rotted merchant stalls. Unbowed by the charging chariot, he engaged all his strength and pulled the stall from its anchors, heaving it to the ground.

Julia ignored the crashing sounds and kept running. At the end of the paved road, she stole a glance behind and saw Thezdan running toward her. The chariot had stopped and was now backing away from the barrier. Thezdan shook his head and waved her on.

"Go!" he yelled. "We're not safe!"

Catching up with her, he grabbed her hand again and pulled her forward along the dirt road. The air shook with another loud crashing sound as the chariot smashed through the barricade.

Julia shrieked but didn't break stride. "What are those things?"

"Black borum! Quickly! This way!"

Thezdan pulled Julia off the road and down one of the many crop rows. The stringy plants were not tall enough or dense enough to make hiding among them an option. Thezdan didn't stop, and it took only a moment for Julia to realize that they were heading toward the long houses at the edge of the field.

Thezdan checked over his shoulder again, his eyes widening. The chariot was cutting a swath through the plants straight toward them.

"Hurry!" he yelled.

Julia fought to get more out of her legs. Her chest burned, but she would not give up now; she focused on the house in front of her and ran. The chariot was so close she could feel the vibration of the earth as the two borum beat their way forward.

No sooner had they cleared the edge of the house than Thezdan took hold of Julia's arm and hurled her to the side. She flew through the air and rolled as she hit the ground, stunned but unharmed. She looked back in time to see Thezdan diving away from the borum and charioteer, the ball of the charioteer's weapon barely missing him as it crashed through the mud walls and into a wooden column of the longhouse.

Sheer terror and adrenaline coursing through her body, Julia jumped up and started banging on one of the shuttered windows along the side of the house. "HELP!" she cried. "OPEN UP! PLEASE!"

There was no response.

"Keep going!" Thezdan shouted, running toward her as the charioteer readied for another charge. He reached out in stride and grabbed a farmer's hoe from against the wall.

Julia pushed off and began running again, watching over her shoulder as the sinister combination of beast and machine churned toward them, the guard swinging his ball and chain maniacally overhead.

Thezdan stopped, turning to face the chariot. He pounded the butt of the hoe into the ground. "Goddess, receive me!" he shouted defiantly.

As the chariot closed, Thezdan began running toward it, screaming aloud the primal yell Julia had heard back in the forest. Then, just as a borum horn was about to impale him, he stepped to the side and spun around, swinging the hoe like an axe at the charioteer. At the same time, the charioteer swung his ball and chain and the two weapons collided, the ball and chain winding around the shaft of the farm tool. Thezdan dug in his feet and pulled, sending the charioteer over the chariot's side and onto the ground.

The unguided borum charged mindlessly forward. Julia ducked behind the far side of the house to avoid them. She heard a thundering cacophony as the animals and chariot went by and watched as they slowly came to a stop.

As she came out from behind the house, she saw Thezdan, his arms covered in blood. She leaned up against one of the long house's corner columns and slid down to the ground, spent.

"We don't have time now," said Thezdan, fighting to regain his breath. "We have to keep moving."

Julia held her head in her hands, trying to contain her emotions. "What the hell is happening?"

"I will explain everything," said Thezdan, dropping down on his haunches beside her, "but you have to trust me just a little longer. We can't wait here, but we'll be safe soon!"

Julia looked up into his eyes. She felt her necklace come to life, which combined with his steadiness calmed her just enough for her to regain her wits. She wiped her face and nodded.

"We have to take the chariot," said Thezdan, helping Julia to her feet. "The Party will kill these farmers for not assisting the guard if they find the chariot here."

He walked over to the grazing borum and grabbed the reins; the giant beasts barely seemed to notice as they continued nibbling on withered stalks. He stepped up into the chariot and reached back for Julia. "Come, hop on."

"Do you know how to drive one of these?"

"Black borum? Honestly, no. But as a boy, before the Party restricted borum ownership, I used to drive the wagon we used earlier with field borum. My father had a big one that we called Yemeth, and Yemeth could run at least as fast as these two louts."

Julia wasn't reassured by Thezdan's story. "Just be safe, okay?" She climbed up next to him and grabbed the rail with a death-grip, prepared for the worst.

Thezdan saw her bracing and shook his head. "You can relax," he said. "I'll drive carefully."

After a quick flip of the reins, the borum came to life, lifting their heads from the turf and beginning the journey forward. After a minute of gentle maneuvering, the chariot was back on the dirt road and heading away from the town.

Julia checked over her shoulder; the road behind them was empty.

"What now?" she asked. "I don't think we can go back there."

"No, we can't; the original plan is dead. I'm going to take you back to the forest. We'll be safe there, and I think I know someone who might be able to help you."

"Are you sure the Party won't follow us?"

"No. During the first Purge, their army chased your grandmother all the way to the Order of the Key Monastery, the one you saw up in the mountains. During the march there and back, the Sylvan killed almost a third of their troops. Since then, the Party has avoided the forests."

"Wow," said Julia, struggling to imagine the scale of such a culling. "I'm glad they're on your side."

"It's not so simple, but I agree with you," chuckled Thezdan.

It took Julia a while to shed the lingering fear she felt from the day's events, but once they were out of the planted farmland and into the open countryside, she actually began to relax slightly. She looked out and wondered what the vast stretches of meadow might have looked like in prior years when they, too, were tilled and planted. Several times, she spotted grazing borum in the distance, presumably the field variety Thezdan had mentioned earlier. They were less hairy, and their horns weren't quite so long or as pointy as those of the borum pulling the chariot. There were also quite a few patches of dried earth, signals of tragedy along the road.

She looked over toward Thezdan, who either hadn't noticed her shift in focus or chose to ignore it. A part of her remained frightened by him, his strength, his hidden anger, and his capacity for violence. But he had looked out for her so far and had proved himself an able protector. She was grateful to have found him.

"Thezdan?"

"Yes?"

"Why are you helping me? Why didn't you give me up in town?"

" … Why would I do that?"

"I'm pretty sure I just cost you a trading partner. Maybe even your ability to return to Breslin at all."

Thezdan tugged on the reins and brought the chariot to a halt. He turned around. "I told you that I would keep you safe."

"You did. Thank you for that."

Thezdan nodded. "I am a Guardian, which makes me a man of my word."

Julia smiled. "Well, I'm a Californian, so I can make promises, too. If you help me get home, I will do everything I can to make people aware of what's going on here. Those farmers shouldn't have to suffer like that, and you shouldn't have to live in exile in your own country. When the world knows, change will come."

Thezdan's hazel-green eyes twinkled. He turned around again and whipped the borum back into motion. "Perhaps we will be saved by the return of a Vorraver after all."

14

Thezdan and Julia arrived at the narrow bridge leading to the forest in the early evening, about an hour before sunset. Thezdan pulled the chariot off the road and brought it to a halt.

"We'll have to go by foot from here," he said, dismounting.

Julia hopped down from the chariot and sat on the ground nearby. She was pretty stiff from standing in place for a few hours, and she needed a moment to rest her legs.

Thezdan drew his sword and hacked at the straps connecting the borum to the chariot harnesses. Once the animals were free, he cut their armor loose and delivered a few quick whacks to their rears, sending them running off into the countryside.

The once-menacing chariot now sat in a heap like a piece of

roadside junk. Thezdan grabbed hold of it and walked it over to the edge of the riverbank, then he sent it into the roaring waters with a strong shove. Julia sprang to her feet just in time to watch the rapids swallow the chariot whole. A single detached wheel made a brief appearance downstream, discomfiting evidence of the river's power.

"They'll be able to track us to the river, but no farther," said Thezdan, turning to walk toward the bridge. "Let's go. I want to arrive before dusk."

"You know," said Julia, "you still haven't told me where we're going. Not really, anyway."

"As I said before, I know someone who may be able to help you."

"A friend of yours?"

Thezdan sighed and kept walking.

Julia didn't quite know how to respond. She followed in silence as they neared the bridge, wondering what he was hiding. Those thoughts soon gave way to other concerns, however, as they came up to the first set of the bridge's stones. The pit in her stomach returned.

"Stop here," said Thezdan. "I need to teach you something."

Julia's body tensed. She hoped that his 'teaching' would have little to do with the extremely narrow bridge in front of her or the river below.

"There may come a time when you have to cross this span, or another one like it, and you will not have time to crawl. From a very young age, you've been able to walk a distance the length of this bridge without deviating but a few fingers either way from your path, and yet you do not trust yourself to do it here."

Julia nervously shook her head.

Thezdan continued, "What are you afraid of?"

"W-what is this about?"

Thezdan took a step toward her. "By blood I am a Guardian. By fate I may now be *your* Guardian. But that does not mean I alone can protect you. You must find the strength inside you so that it will be there when you need it. So, I ask again, what are you afraid of?"

"Well," Julia said, looking past him, "I'm guess I'm afraid of the river, of ending up like the chariot."

"And you should be. But I am not asking you to swim."

Julia flashed an insincere grin.

Thezdan faced the bridge. A moment later, his legs burst to life. Julia watched in amazement as he sprinted across the span, seemingly oblivious to the danger below. At the far end, he turned around and drew his sword.

"Trust yourself!" he yelled.

He began running back across. Suddenly, he let out one of his brutal screams and slashed his sword in front of him, the first strike in an elaborate sword dance. Leaping, whirling, and tumbling, he moved across the bridge, striking in all directions with his sword. It was a beautiful display of precision and strength, made all the more incredible by the stage on which it was performed. Closing within yards of Julia, he launched himself into a giant forward roll, driving his sword toward her in a dramatic final thrust. Its point came to rest only an inch from her breast. Julia looked down with a mixture of awe and fear, at a loss for both breath and words.

Thezdan looked into Julia's eyes with a strong, purposeful stare. "I have done that sequence over a thousand times since my father taught it to me as a young boy. It is almost as natural as walking. I have learned to trust myself and my training, and that trust has made me stronger. Now: walk across this bridge. Trust yourself."

Julia tried to imagine herself doing as he said. She looked past Thezdan to the bridge in front of her.

"When you cross, look at me," said Thezdan. "Let your general awareness and peripheral vision guide your steps."

Julia nodded. "Okay. I'll try."

Thezdan turned and crossed the bridge again. At the far side, he waved for her.

Julia took a deep breath. She forced herself to take a step, then a few more. With each one, her mind fixated more and more on the danger beneath her, until, suddenly, she stopped.

"I don't know if I can do it," she said, her voice too soft for Thezdan to hear.

Thezdan waved her on again. "Trust yourself! You are stronger than you know!"

Julia dropped to one knee and closed her eyes. Her necklace sprang to life, radiating warmth greater than any she had felt it emit before. She gathered her breath, building courage. Then she rose to her feet, opened her eyes, and began walking. The first few steps were not easy, but they showed the truth of Thezdan's words.

I can trust myself.

She walked half way across the bridge, then stopped.

"Come, Julia!" Thezdan called. "You can do it!"

Julia ignored him. She clenched her jaw and focused on her endpoint. Her mind was still.

I can trust myself!

She pushed off hard against the stone. Faster and faster she went, running at top speed over the narrow span. The sounds of the wind and river below filled her ears but her concentration never wavered. Finally, she burst across the last few stones and onto the dirt road at the end. She had made it.

Thezdan clutched her arms. "You surprised me," he said, smiling broadly.

Julia smiled back. "Maybe I surprised myself."

"Never forget what you felt here. There is great strength inside you, strength that you may need to call on again one day."

Julia nodded, feeling the natural high of someone who had just accomplished something beyond what they thought possible.

"Unfortunately, we can't stay and revel in your victory," said Thezdan, turning to walk up the road. "We're not far, but it's getting late. We should go."

Julia took another moment to catch her breath then scrambled to catch up. "Wait. Where's Scylld?"

"He is probably nearby in the forest. We will meet up with him tomorrow."

Thezdan and Julia walked down the road side-by-side, coming to the intersection with the footpath a minute later. Thezdan's pace slowed.

"Are we going this way?" Julia whispered, surprised.

"Yes."

"What's up there?"

Thezdan turned up the path. "People who can help you. I hope."

Halfway up, as they came around a small bend in the trees, the wall of wood Julia had seen earlier came fully into view. It wasn't a frontier fort log wall at all; it was a line of thick-trunked trees that had grown together so tightly that many of the trunks had fused. A large opening had been cut into the base of the central tree on the front wall, though a wooden gate sealed it closed on the far side. There was also a boxy guardhouse, almost like an enclosed kids' treehouse, built on a thick branch above.

Julia couldn't quite believe what she was seeing. This *was* a fort, but a living one, with actual trees for walls, branches for ramparts, and a broad canopy ceiling. Through the branches, she could make out a sheer rock face looming in the background, the first sight of the mountains she'd seen since entering the forest the day prior. This was a very narrow part of the forest, only several hundred yards separating the fort from the river.

"Who lives here?" Julia asked, amazed. "How did they get the trees to grow together like this?"

"We believe the Goddess herself commanded the trees to grow together. It was here when we arrived, and we have been here for centuries now, ever since we became aware that she wished us to serve her as Guardians."

Julia stood still for a moment. "Wait. We? Guardians?"

Thezdan bowed his head and kept walking.

"Thezdan, come on. Where are we going? Is this where you're from?"

"No. I'm from the Trebain," he said coolly. "As is most of my clan. But yes, now the surviving Guardians live here."

"Are you alright?"

"It's fine. You need not worry for your safety."

As they approached the gate, a voice rang out from the guardhouse. "Halt. Announce yourself!"

Julia looked up at the source of the sound. There was a teenage boy standing in one of the open windows, his hands clutching a bow and arrow trained on them.

"Notin, I had thought you braver than to shoot those pointed twigs at me!" Thezdan shouted. "Come! Let's fight like true Guardian warriors!"

The boy lowered his weapon and leaned over the rail of the window. "Is that you, Eodan?"

"Indeed, it is! I have come to see Alana and have brought an honored guest!"

Julia could hear a delighted laugh from the tower as the boy withdrew from the window. She heard him yell something into the interior part of the fort, though she couldn't quite make out his words.

"Eodan? I thought your name was Thezdan?"

Thezdan shook his head. "He calls me by a title I no longer accept."

Before she could ask any further questions, the large gate doors began to open.

"Let's go," Thezdan said, staring ahead blankly.

Julia wasn't sure whether he was addressing her or speaking to himself.

The interior of the fort was brimming with people, most of whom had stopped what they were doing and were facing the gates expectantly. A small horde of young boys rushed forward to greet Thezdan.

"Eodan! You're back!" shouted one at the head of the pack. He was older than the others, though barely a teenager himself.

Thezdan smiled at him and held out his arms. "Nobrun! How goes your training?"

The young boy ran forward into the open embrace but was surprised when Thezdan pivoted at the last moment and threw him gently to the ground.

"Not very well, it seems!" Thezdan said, jumping on top of the squirming boy and grinning broadly.

"Ease up on the young, No," called a gruff voice from behind the crowd.

Julia looked up to see an older man limping toward them. He had a long but well-maintained beard, and his nearly shoulder-length hair hung freely like a proud, gray mane. He had a truly incredible physique for a man his age, the ample armholes of his leather tunic revealing muscles larger and perhaps even better-defined than Thezdan's. As he hobbled forward, Julia could see that his right leg was turned in slightly, and that a metal brace had been wrapped around his leg near the knee.

Thezdan looked up, his grin fading. He let go of the boy and rose to his feet. "Hello, Lothic."

"I have missed you, Eodan," said Lothic, smiling genuinely as he came forward and clutched Thezdan's forearms. "These boys have missed you, too. They could use your guidance in training."

Thezdan shook him off. "Lothic, I am here because something strange has happened."

"Oh?" said Lothic, his expression shifting. "Are you alright?"

"Yes, I am fine," said Thezdan. "But I need to speak with Alana right away."

Lothic nodded. "Then go to her. I will not keep you."

"There is no need," said a woman as the crowd parted in front of her. She looked to be about Lothic's age, with pale blue eyes and a crop of long, gray hair tied behind her back. She wore a white robe held together by a large brooch made from twigs woven around a central flower. Her movements and posture radiated the quiet seriousness of authority.

Thezdan brought his hand up to his chest in a formal salute and waited for her to come. "Hello, Mother."

"Hello, Eodan," said the woman, who took his hands tenderly into her own. "It is *I* who have missed you most of all."

Thezdan smiled uncomfortably.

"So, tell me," the woman continued. "What is the trouble?"

"I have brought someone who needs your help," said Thezdan, beckoning toward Julia. "This is Julia."

The woman extended her two hands with their palms up and bowed her head. "Hello, Julia. I am Alana."

Julia tried to mimic the gesture, bowing her head and extending her hands in return. "It's a pleasure to meet you, Alana."

"We have so few dealings with the world outside the forest now that I would be surprised if there were anything I could do," Alana said. "But I will listen, of course. Perhaps we should discuss it in the Council chamber?"

"I think that would be best," Thezdan agreed.

Alana turned to the crowd. "Tell all the young No that they may take tomorrow off from their training. Tonight, let them enjoy the returning Eo's company, and stay up late hearing stories of his travels and travails!"

The young boys erupted in fits of glee and hollering and dispersed to share the good news. Thezdan's face brightened to see their excitement.

"Lothic, would you join us?" Alana asked.

"No," said Thezdan. "I don't believe his counsel is needed."

Alana looked at Thezdan with a surprised and disapproving look, but Lothic quickly interceded.

"It is alright, Alana. Don't let it trouble you. The Eo is probably right."

"I doubt he is," Alana replied. "I will call if I need you."

Lothic bowed his head. "I will await your call, then."

As Alana led them toward the back of the fort, Julia took in the sights around her. The fort's courtyard was a large oval around 150 yards in length and 100 yards wide at its center. There were several areas where large, lower branches came down from the trees like staircases to offer access to the higher reaches, and against the tree walls were many simple, two-story cabins, each with a narrow, man-made exterior staircase leading from the ground level to the second floor. The fort's cabins were arranged in such a way that a gray, stone chimney was shared by each pair. Most of the second story structures were made of newer wood and the chimneys of newer stone. At the back of the fort were several larger structures, including an open-air forge toward which Lothic was hobbling.

Surveying the people around town, Julia saw quite a number of women, girls, and young men. She estimated that there were at least two hundred, perhaps two hundred and fifty, people living here, a number that seemed to stretch the fort's capacity. Looking around further, she realized there were barely any men older than twenty and no children younger than five or six. She thought back to Thezdan's story about his father's death. It brought home to her the stark reality of the Guardian Clan's recent past. The men had been killed. Their absence left a gaping hole in the fabric of this town. It filled Julia with sadness to see so many children who were growing up without their fathers, uncles, and grandfathers.

Alana stopped in front of a building set against the fort's back wall. It had a second story balcony with a panel carved with an image of the Goddess at its center. Alana raised her hands and bowed before the icon, then she opened a large door and led Julia and Thezdan inside. A single oil lamp burned on a table by the door, providing just enough light to make out the basic features of the room.

Alana lit a small piece of kindling on the lamp and set to work lighting candles throughout the space. "I am surprised by the way you treated Lothic, Eodan," she said. "He has taught you so much. Why would you show him such disrespect, especially when he has so much more wisdom to share?"

Thezdan remained silent.

Alana looked up from behind a flickering, just-lit flame. "What has he done to deserve this from you?"

"I'm sure my father felt similarly when Lothic retired on the eve of battle," Thezdan replied.

"Oh?" said Alana, annoyed. "Why do you presume to know what Eobax thought about Lothic? They were like brothers."

Thezdan shook his head angrily. "Lothic was our Prime. I have thought about his actions a great deal during my time as a Searcher. I would not have permitted him to retire, not like he did! No Prime has ever retired and accepted the title of Lo with the enemy practically in sight. His injury is no excuse. He should have fought and died alongside my father and the rest of the warriors! And if he were half as good as father used to say, then he might have taken quite a few of them with him!"

Alana paused. "Your time alone in the forest has fostered an unfortunate and misdirected resentment. Had Lothic perished, a thousand years of training and teachings would have been lost, dead along with him. Instead, he was able to share with you and the other Guardians the knowledge he carried, and our Clan lives on."

Thezdan turned away. "Perhaps my father should have been the one to save the teachings."

Alana sighed. "One day, you will understand Eobax's decision. I miss him too, Eodan. But know this: you should trust Lothic. Respect him. He is a greater man than you know."

Alana finished lighting the last few candles then walked over to the circular table that dominated the center of the small but not cramped space. Pulling out a high-backed and beautifully carved chair at the head, distinct from the plainer ones around it, she beckoned for Julia to join her.

"It has been several years since we have welcomed a guest to our meeting table," Alana said. "You would honor us by sitting here."

"Thank you," Julia said, walking over.

"That is more appropriate than you realize, Mother," said Thezdan. "She is a Vorraver."

Alana shot back a disbelieving stare. "What do you mean, Eodan?"

"Look at her necklace!"

Alana looked at Julia and at the necklace that hung around her neck. "It is the royal symbol, yes. Anybody could wear such a thing ... though it would be dangerous to do so these days. Tell me, where did you get this?"

"It was my grandmother's," Julia replied.

"And your grandmother, what was her name?"

"Her name is Elleina."

Alana's eyes widened. "The Lost Princess Elleina? Truly? Please, have a seat, my dear. I would very much like to hear your story."

Julia sat down in the high-backed chair. Thezdan took a seat next to her.

"Elleina Vorraver left many years ago," said Alana, sitting down across from them. "What has brought you here? And why now?"

Julia shook her head. "I don't know. As I told Thezdan, I put on the necklace and was transported here as I slept. I woke up in the monastery up in the mountains."

Alana pressed her fingers together, her eyes deep in thought. "The Order of the Key monastery? Tell me, did Elleina give you the necklace? Did she say it was time for the Vorravers to return to Aevilen?"

"No, not really," Julia said, shaking her head. "I found it in a trunk in her home."

Suddenly the door sprang open. In walked a man nearly as tall as Thezdan but younger and of slighter stature. His eyes fell on Thezdan almost immediately.

"Mother, I need to speak with you," said the man, his tone urgent but controlled.

"Hello, Nonox," said Thezdan.

"Much has changed since you left, Thezdan. You would do well to address me as Sinox."

Thezdan let out a dismissive laugh. "Sinox? Who has made you Prime?"

"I have," interrupted Alana. "And I did so with Lothic's blessing.

Your brother is a fine warrior. He may be unorthodox for a Guardian, but with you gone, he is surely our strongest."

"It is the end of our tradition if our Prime fights by stealth and bow," Thezdan muttered.

"Mother, it is very important that I speak with you," Sinox repeated through clenched teeth.

"Then speak. Eodan can hear whatever you have to say."

Sinox paused. He looked over at Thezdan then back at Alana. "And what of the girl? I believe she may be the source of my news."

"She is with me," said Thezdan.

"Yes, I know," said Sinox.

"What do you mean, Sinox?" Alana asked. "How did you know?"

"The Sylvan saw her coming from the monastery road yesterday. They tried to catch her, but failed. They say they saw a magical artifact glowing around her neck."

"She is a Vorraver," said Thezdan, "which makes it our duty to help her, brother."

"What?" replied Sinox, shocked to hear the name. "The Vorravers have been dead for over a generation, and with them quite a few members of our Clan who tried to save them. Do not speak nonsense, brother. We have enough trouble already without you bringing us more."

"I promise I'm not trying to cause any trouble," Julia interjected. "I am just looking for a way to get home. Hopefully I'll be out of your hair soon."

"I apologize, Julia, for my son's harsh words," Alana said. "These are difficult times in Aevilen, which makes everyone cautious." She turned toward Sinox again. "You met with the Sylvan today?"

"I did. I went to see Nain to share reconnaissance on Party movements, and he told me what I've now told you: Sylvan scouts spotted this girl—sorry, Julia—alone in the forest and wearing a magic necklace."

"And what does Nain think of this?"

"I'm not sure. He did not share his thoughts with me."

"Well," said Alana, turning toward Julia. "If Nain were worried, he would have told us. I believe her. As strange as it seems, the magical artifact she wears and her arrival at the mountain monastery seem like much more than coincidence. Why a Vorraver would reappear after all this time is as perplexing to me as it is to you. But for now, we have a duty to help her."

Sinox nodded and shifted to a rigid, formal posture. He brought his closed fist to his chest in salute. "As you wish."

"Eodan," continued Alana, "I would like Lothic's counsel. You were right to come and to bring Julia with you. But in strange and surely significant circumstances such as these, it would be foolish for us to proceed without him."

Thezdan offered a reluctant nod. "Alright, Mother."

"Sinox, please ask Lothic to join us. I imagine you'll find him waiting."

"Right away," said Sinox, saluting again before departing.

Alana looked at Julia. "Tell me: how are you feeling? Do you need something to eat? To drink?"

"I am a little hungry," Julia replied. "It's been quite a day."

Alana smiled. "Please, let me get you something, then." She stood up and went to a cabinet nearby, returning shortly with a basket of nuts.

The nuts had sort of a strange, greenish-purple color. Not wanting to offend her host, Julia picked one up and popped it into her mouth. It had a very earthy flavor but a pleasant, sweet aftertaste.

Better than they look, Julia decided. She reached for a few more.

"Tell me, what has become of Princess Elleina? We were always told that she was sent away, but most of us doubted that story. I had always assumed that she perished in the attack on the monastery."

Julia smiled as she thought about her grandmother. "No, she's fine. She's back home in California, probably wondering where I am."

"California? Is that a territory on the lower continent?"

"It's in the United States. I don't really know where we are now, but California is very different. I mean, it has lots of paved roads, and *cars*, and technology everywhere. Here, everything seems to be old fashioned … almost medieval."

Alana laughed. "I'm not sure I understand, but I can tell you are sincere in saying it. Tell me, why did you put on your grandmother's necklace? Did you know it would take you back to Aevilen?"

Julia shook her head. "No. I put it on because I liked the way it looked. I found it while exploring my grandmother's old trunk, and after wearing it to bed, I woke up here."

"Will it not allow you to go back?"

"I tried going back to sleep, but I just woke up in the same spot.

I still haven't figured out how it works, but … "

"Yes?" Alana coaxed.

"Well, it almost seems to have a mind of its own. It helps me when I need it, warning me of danger or shining a bright light to scare off things attacking me." She raised her eyebrows playfully at Thezdan. "It has also guided me at times, as if it were feeding my thoughts. I never used to believe in magic, but this necklace—I mean, there's definitely something special about it."

The door opened. Sinox came through with Lothic following behind him.

Alana rose to her feet. "Lothic, thank you for coming. Something extraordinary has happened, and I am very much in need of your help."

"Whatever is required of me, Alana, you shall have," said Lothic, hobbling over to the table.

Once Lothic and Sinox were seated, Alana leaned forward. "Lothic, the girl before you is a Vorraver, the granddaughter of Princess Elleina."

Lothic was incredulous. He looked over at Julia, then back at Alana. "I see a resemblance, but Princess Elleina perished in the Order of the Key Monastery, and the Vorraver line died with her."

"No, Lothic," said Alana. "It seems the stories of her escape are true."

"I have never believed those stories," Lothic said, shaking his head. "What has made you suddenly so certain?"

"Look at the necklace she wears," said Alana. "It matches the Vorraver seal!"

"Nain believes that necklace to be a powerful artifact," Sinox added.

"An artifact?" asked Lothic. "What do the Sylvan have to do with this?"

"The Sylvan have nothing to do with this," said Sinox. "But they saw the necklace glowing around her neck."

"I was telling Alana about it before you came in," said Julia. "It does more than just glow."

"I have seen it myself, Lothic," said Thezdan. "You know more about strange metals that the rest of us; perhaps you should examine it." He looked over at Julia and extended his hand in front of her. "Please, let Lothic give it a look. In this matter, he can be trusted."

Julia placed a hand on her necklace. She knew its importance. It had helped her to brave Aevilen's challenges, understand its people, and avoid its dangers. She was loath to give it up.

Thezdan could see her hesitation. He gently clutched her free hand. "It's okay. I promise the necklace will be returned to you."

Julia closed her eyes for a moment, tapping into the intuitions fed by her necklace. It warmed to her touch, a sign she took to mean that the Guardians before her could indeed be trusted. Reopening her eyes, she slipped the chain over her head and passed the necklace to Thezdan. Her heartbeat accelerated as she watched Thezdan turn and pass it on to Lothic.

Lothic put the necklace on the table in front of him. The others watched as he carefully examined the metal. He ran his fingers over its contours, his eyes and movements betraying a growing interest.

He reached for a candle, then he picked up the necklace and watched the light dance off its surface. He gripped the centerpiece between his thumbs and forefingers and twisted, gently at first and then forcefully, the strain on his face suggesting that he was applying every ounce of his strength.

"Stop!" Julia cried out, reaching across Thezdan for the dangling chain.

Lothic relented. He put the necklace back down on the table and slid it back to her. "You needn't worry," he said, smiling. "Even if Eodan and I were to combine our strength, we wouldn't be able to bend it."

Julia barely heard him as she grabbed the necklace from the table and put it on again. She was relieved to feel it back in place around her neck.

"What do you mean, Lothic?" asked Alana.

"It's magestone, Alana," Lothic marveled. "I have only seen magestone once before, in my training with the Rokkin, but it is something I could never forget. See the faint glow it casts in the light? It is unmistakable. The metal is so strong that only the oldest of the Rokkin can shape it, and the required exertion is so great that they risk death in doing so."

"So, the necklace is Rokkin," said Alana. "But what of its magic?"

"It was probably made by the Rokkin, yes. I don't know about its magic, but I have heard about magestone relics having special powers." Lothic looked down at the table and chuckled to himself. "You know, I always assumed that those stories were legends also.

And now there is a girl here, presumed granddaughter of the Lost Princess, with a magestone necklace in the shape of the royal seal. It seems there are many stories I will have to reconsider."

"It is frustrating that so much knowledge has been lost," said Alana. She sighed. "May Pestilence curse the Party for that … Still, I fear something is happening. There is a reason this girl has been brought back to us now. Somehow, we need to learn more about the necklace and its powers. Who do we know who could help?"

"Do you still have contact with the Rokkin, Lothic?" asked Thezdan.

"No," said Lothic, waving him off. "I cannot go directly to the Rokkin, and I have not seen Domin, my former master, since before we left the plains."

"Do we have any idea where Domin might be?" Alana asked the table. "Sinox, I know you have contacts in the capital. Do you happen to know?"

Sinox shook his head. "No. But I have never asked."

"Alana, I don't think Domin is the answer," said Lothic anxiously.

"What other options do we have?" she replied. "Domin was an Elder and head of the Rokkin smithing caste, no? Surely he will know something about a magestone artifact."

"Wait," Julia said. "I think I have a note for an Elder Domin written by my grandmother." She reached inside her pouch and found the note, then she passed it across the table to Alana. "So maybe he does know something. Maybe he really could help!"

"It is not about whether he knows anything," said Lothic. "It's about whether he would share his knowledge with us if he did. The last time, it cost him greatly."

"I do not claim to understand the affairs of the Rokkin, Lothic," said Alana, scanning the old note. "Nonetheless, this note definitely gives us cause to see him, and I do not think that he would turn you away. Julia, do you know what became of the royal marker referenced here?"

Julia took out the gold medallion and placed it on the table. "I think this is it."

Thezdan and Sinox stared at it in disbelief.

"Perfect!" Alana said. "Between that medallion and your necklace, Domin will surely not ignore us."

"Mother, wait," interrupted Sinox. "Is this really wise? I agree that there is likely great significance to Julia's arrival; her necklace and this medallion prove as much. But we are not as strong as we once were. Going out into Party territory and exposing ourselves could be dangerous. The forest protects us only so long as the Party remains unwilling to risk a significant number of soldiers in order to hunt us down. I do not want to change their minds."

"I appreciate your caution, Sinox," replied Alana. "And I believe you are right to see danger ahead. That is why we must learn more about Julia's arrival and her necklace: so that we can protect ourselves from whatever is coming. Lothic should be able to find Domin and get answers to our questions without bringing much attention to us."

Sinox bowed his head. "Just be prepared, Mother. The plains have gotten no safer in recent years, and the Party no saner."

"We will be careful, Sinox," said Alana. "And prepared."

Lothic resigned himself to her judgment. "I am to find Domin, then?"

Alana nodded. "Yes. I think he can be of great help to us."

"Very well," said Lothic. "I believe I know where he can be found. I will leave in the morning."

Alana smiled. "Thank you, Lothic." She turned toward Thezdan. "Eodan, I would like you to accompany him. Based on the supplies you leave us from time to time, I gather that you have some experience safely moving about on the plains."

"Wait, what about Julia?" Thezdan said, surprised. "Should I not stay with her?"

"She will stay here, safe in the forest with me. Besides, she could probably use some time to rest and recover. Is that alright with you, Julia?"

"I guess so?" Julia replied nervously. "Would you be back soon, Thezdan?"

"We shouldn't be gone long … not more than a day. But are you sure?"

Julia looked over at Alana. She sensed sincerity and kindness in her eyes. "It's okay. I'm sure I'll be alright."

Thezdan sighed. "If it is your wish, Mother, I will go with Lothic."

"Thank you, Eodan. You will leave in the morning. I do hope that you will take some time to be with the No tonight. They would so love to hear your stories."

"Of course," said Thezdan.

Alana pushed back from the table and stood up. "Eodan and Lothic, I wish you luck and success on your journey. Sinox, please check in with your sources on the plains—see if there is anything strange going on with the Party. The sooner we find out, the sooner we can begin to prepare. Also, let us keep Julia's heritage a secret for now, even from our clansmen. There is much for us to learn, and we must be sure that she is safe in the meantime."

"Yes, Mother," said Sinox.

Alana began making her way to the front door.

"One last thing," she said, turning around to face the group again, a big smile on her face. "Tonight we shall celebrate the return of an Eo. Enjoy yourselves, all of you!"

15

"Hail to the Party, Revolutionary Grimmel!"

Grimmel frowned as he alighted from the carriage, pausing to adjust the engraved, golden breastplate he wore over his tunic. His eyes scanned the decrepit, old village and the disheveled citizens standing in rows in the middle of the square.

"Remind me why I was summoned here?" he growled. "Did we not train and arm you to handle fellow citizens who step out of line?"

"Yes, Revolutionary Grimmel. Something unusual happened. We felt it was important enough to deserve your personal attention."

Grimmel laughed contemptuously. "So then, what happened, Commander?"

The commander came around to Grimmel's side and gestured

toward the smithy at the far end of the square. "Over there. Three of our soldiers were killed as they tried to question some interlopers."

"Interlopers? How bold. Southsiders?"

The commander shook his head. "No. They were disguised as hunters, and they were trading illegally with the citizen blacksmith. We've interrogated the blacksmith. He revealed that one of them was a member of the Guardian Clan. Eobax's son, no less."

"Really?" said Grimmel, genuinely surprised. "What about the second?"

"We don't know. The charioteer we sent to capture them was also killed. But Revolutionary ... um ... "

"Yes?"

"There are reports that she had a magical necklace of some kind."

"A magic necklace? What do you mean?"

"A citizen over there," said the commander, pointing to the man. "He approached the hunters. He startled the girl, and when she flinched, her magic necklace was revealed. He says it glowed like the sun!"

Grimmel's eyes narrowed. "You brought me here to tell me that a piece of metal reflected the sunlight?"

The commander reached up and awkwardly scratched behind his ear. "Well, I don't think, Revolutionary, well, the word came to me from below that it was, was, brighter—"

"Stop," said Grimmel, dismissing the commander with a wave of his hand. "I will speak to the citizen who saw the hunters, address the crowd, and be gone. I do not wish to waste any more of my time.

And Commander … I don't expect you to give me occasion to return here. Do you understand?"

The commander nodded meekly.

Grimmel turned and began walking toward the rows of people in the square, his ambling gait accentuating his girth. In his presence, an obvious tension gripped the crowd, hundreds of eyes tracking his every movement.

He approached the man that the commander had pointed out to him earlier. "Hello, citizen."

Staring straight ahead, the man called the expected reply: "Hail Great Revolutionary Grimmel!"

"You may address me now," said Grimmel.

The man looked tentatively to his right, checking to see if it was, in fact, safe to look at the Supreme Leader of the People's Party. "D-do you wish to hear of the girl, Rev-Revolutionary?" he squawked.

"I do," Grimmel replied leadenly.

"Well, uh, I came up to her, and, and, we spoke for a moment, and I guess I fr-frightened her, because she fell backward. And then I saw it!"

"And what was that, citizen?"

"It, uh, was, uh, a necklace of some sort … a magic necklace! It glowed bright blue!"

Grimmel's expression changed. "Bright blue? Are you sure it wasn't a reflection, citizen?"

"Yes, Revolutionary. I, uh, I'm sure. It was a bright, blue light, and it was coming from the necklace itself!"

"I see," muttered Grimmel, rasping the sharpened spines of his gauntlet against his armor. "Tell me, citizen, what kind of necklace was it?"

"Well, um, I-I don't know?"

Grimmel lunged forward and grabbed hold of the man's tunic, the gauntlet spines digging into the man's flesh. Pulling the beggar closer, he stared into his eyes. The beggar caught a brief glimpse of the red-tinted flame behind Grimmel's pupils. He suppressed a scream but his mouth was agape, contorted by physical and psychological agony.

"Citizen, you'd best search further into your memory!" said Grimmel.

"Oh please!" sobbed the beggar. "Please Revolutionary! Have mercy!"

Grimmel released his grip and the man fell to his knees in a quaking heap. Grimmel knelt down beside him and spoke directly into his ear. "The necklace. Was it all metal? Was it thick? Thin? Was there writing on it? Or a symbol?"

The beggar looked up. "Yes! Yes! It was in the shape of a symbol, Revolutionary!"

"Tell me what it looked like!"

"I think it was one of the forbidden ones! The one like an arrowhead with a hole in it!"

Grimmel was stunned. *The royal symbol? It's not possible, not now!*

Grimmel stood, paying no further attention to the beggar. He walked over to the podium. Their final victory was so close at hand, so very close. Yet, for the first time in ages, he found himself questioning its inevitability.

"Citizens," he began, his booming voice filling the square, "now is a time for vigilance! We must be ever watchful, lest the progress of our glorious Revolution be lost at the hands of criminals!" He looked out across the square, soaking in the rapt attention of the crowd. "Citizens, will you stand with me and fight for the Revolution?" he called out.

"We will! We will!" the crowd shouted loudly in unison.

An arrogant grin crept up Grimmel's face. Victory was still assured. By the Master's hand, these lives would guarantee it.

16

Julia sat at Alana's side at the end of a long table lively with feasting and conversation. Theirs was the women's table, a large bonfire in the middle of the fort separating them from Thezdan and the men of the Clan. Candle-filled lanterns hung overhead, their soft glow catching the branches and canopy above in a way that made the fort's courtyard feel like an enchanted hollow.

The table in front of her offered a great variety of foods gathered from the forest: grilled meats, fish, edible flowers, roots, vegetables, mushrooms, and more. At Alana's insistence, Julia tried a little bit of everything, and was astonished by the richness and complexity of the flavors. The night was turning out to be everything she had imagined an old-fashioned feast might be.

"Out of curiosity," Julia asked between bites, "why do you put the men and women at separate tables?"

"It is our tradition," said Alana. "Now we are apart from the men of the clan, as if they were away in a distant field. After they hear our laments, they will cross the courtyard, past the bonfire, and reunite with us. Then we will sing and dance to celebrate the reunion."

Julia smiled, appreciating the symbolism. She turned toward the men's table, but it was obscured by the flames of the bonfire. "Can I ask you something else?" she asked quietly.

"Of course."

"What happened to Thezdan? Why did he change his name? And why does he seem to spend most of his time outside the fort?"

Alana nodded to acknowledge the question, but the sadness in her eyes made Julia regret asking it.

"My son changed his name because he wished to leave," said Alana. "A Thez is a 'Searcher,' one who lives separate from the Clan. It is not a common path for a Guardian."

"But *why* did he leave?"

"Only he could tell you, but ... " Alana peered through the bonfire as if trying to catch a glimpse of her son.

"Please, Alana? I want to know him better, to trust him."

"Of course. You ask a fair question, though it is not an easy one for me. In truth, I believe that Eodan has always felt guilty that he did not die alongside his father. A month before the Revolutionary Army came, he completed his sixteenth year and became a warrior, earning the En title. We knew that there was a new Purge underway, but we didn't realize until much too late that we were one of its targets. When word came that five thousand army regulars were gathering in Riverstride with orders to march on the Trebain, Eobax knew that any who remained in the town would die. He ordered our son to lead the women and children to the forest while he and the Guardian En bought time by making their stand in the Trebain.

"Eodan resisted, of course. He tried to persuade his father that the job of leading the flight to the forest should be given to the Prime: Sithic, the man you know as Lothic. As fate would have it, Lothic was hurt later that day when he fell helping to prepare the ramparts for the defense. His leg was broken. Though he offered to stay, Eobax demanded that he accept retirement and be carted off to the forest with the rest of the Clan. It humiliated Lothic, but he accepted the judgment of the Eo. My son, too, ultimately accepted his father's judgment, though never wholeheartedly. Eodan was brilliant during the escape. He disguised our movements well, effectively deployed scouts, and faced obstacles with a clear head. He was a natural leader, even in his youth. But shortly after we arrived here, he began to change.

"As Administrator, I elevated him to Eo, effectively making him a leader of the Clan. Wearing the same title as his father only worsened his guilt. He did a fine job helping to adapt the fort to a much larger population, but he lost interest in day-to-day affairs. He only wished to grow stronger so that he might exact his revenge on the Party. He trained with Lothic until he believed that Lothic had no more to teach; then, one day, about two years ago, he left. He occasionally comes by to leave us iron, skins, or food at the gate, but he has been living outside the Clan. Until today, I had not seen him for a long time."

Julia sat in silence, thinking about what Alana had just shared. She remembered the anger she sensed when she clutched Thezdan's hand, and it made her heart swell with sympathy for the burden he carried, hidden, inside.

"I have faith that it will end well, though," said Alana, forcing a smile. "I still believe that, one day, he will return to us and embrace his role as a Guardian Eo. But come: this is a night for celebration. Can I offer you another roasted *cambrea* root?"

Julia partially covered her mouth as if to protect it from even one tiny bite more. "No thanks, I am totally full. Everything has been delicious. Thank you, again."

"I am happy to hear it. I know it must be hard for you to be here, away from your family in a land you do not know. At the very least, I hope we can make you comfortable and keep you safe."

Alana's smile brightened. She reminded Julia of her own mother, not because of similarities in their eyes or lips, but because of the earnestness and kindness that both women carried at their core. Julia smiled back, a tear welling up in her eye. "I appreciate that, thank you."

Alana placed her hand over Julia's, squeezing it gently. "Are you alright?"

"I miss my family," said Julia. "Being with you makes me think about my mom. She and I haven't really had many close moments like this recently. I miss her."

"I know how difficult it can be to be apart. We have a tradition based on what you're feeling right now."

Julia wiped her eyes. "Oh, yeah? What's that?"

Alana rose from her seat and held out her hand. "Please, stand with me."

A hush came over their table as Julia stood up beside her. The men, though out of sight, noticed their silence and quickly fell silent as well.

"Let us watch the fire together," Alana said.

Julia felt a bit awkward, anticipating that, like a new student in a dance class, she would soon be lost in the ritual's choreography. But Alana offered no further instructions; instead, she began to sing in a soft, melancholy tone. Julia watched the fire, allowing her mind to let go as she listened to the song. The language was one she hadn't heard before, and no translation ever came. Other women added their voices. Each one knew her part and contributed to the beautiful, haunting harmony. The lapping flames and sorrowful melody filled Julia, bringing her back to her house in Malibu. She thought about her family—her mother, father, brother, grandmother—and how deeply she missed them, even after so little time apart. It wasn't until Alana let go of her hand that she realized that the song had ended.

"That was beautiful," Julia said, wiping her eyes again.

Alana held out her palms and bowed. "Thank you for honoring us, Vorraver Julia. That song is our lament, sung in the old language of our ancestors. We no longer know the meaning of each word, but the lament is still well understood: it is a song of sadness at being apart from the ones we love and a plea to the Goddess to bring us together again."

Julia was about to respond when she heard Thezdan's voice boom from across the courtyard. "Women of the Guardian Clan, your Warriors have returned!"

With that declaration, the boys and young men erupted into a chorus of hoots and shouts, then they rose from their benches and ran across the courtyard toward the women's table. The women greeted the approaching men with their own cries, their voices mixing into a great roar of frolic and excitement. Julia soon heard the sound of instruments filling the air, a group of musicians having used the chaos as a cue to start playing.

The musicians stood between the tables away from the bonfire. Five played what looked like smaller, rounder guitars, strumming out a fast-paced and lively tune; two others played wooden flutes; and the last one played an assortment of drums, including one very large one that let out a wonderful rumble when struck.

All the Guardians, young and old, were on their feet dancing to the music. Julia turned around at the table and watched, but she wasn't quite in the mood for dancing. She kept thinking of her family in California. She wished she could be so easily reunited with them.

"Do you mind if I sit here?" came a deep voice next to her.

Julia turned to see Thezdan standing there, his arms crossed in front of him. "Sure, go ahead."

"Are you feeling alright? Has my mother been good company?"

Julia chuckled. "Of course. She's been great."

"Why so glum, then?"

"Well … I never told you this, but just before I came here, my home burned down in a fire. I know that that's not anywhere near as bad as what you've been through, but being here, listening to the women's song, watching the bonfire here in the fort—it made me think about it. It made me think about my family even more. I miss them a lot."

Thezdan nodded. "Our circumstances are more similar than I realized. Both displaced, both searching—"

"Both trying to find our way back home?"

Thezdan laughed. "Yes, maybe." He stood up again. "I will disappoint the Administrator if I don't dance." He smiled and gave a casual salute, bowing his head slightly. "Have a good evening, Julia."

Julia enjoyed watching the Guardian party: the dancing, the drinking, the music, the laughter. The earlier pall she'd seen hanging over the fort had all but disappeared, and she was glad that these women, girls, and young men could have a chance to celebrate and enjoy life, if only for a brief while.

Suddenly, without warning, a high-pitched horn rang out from the eastern ramparts. The sound ran through the Guardian festival like a terrible wail. The musicians fell silent. The crowd hushed to a whisper.

Thezdan pushed his way through the crowd then sprinted toward the front gate, his mother and brother following closely behind.

"What is it?" he called in the direction of the guardhouse.

"A strange light approaching! Coming up the path!"

"Can you identify it?"

"No! Should I shoot, Eo?"

"Not yet! Call a warning!"

Julia chased after them, anxious to know what was happening. She heard the guard shout something into the forest, then she saw him reemerge on the interior ramparts a moment later.

"Eodan, it's still approaching!"

Thezdan waved for Sinox to follow. "Hurry, brother, come with me!"

Together, Thezdan and Sinox bounded up a branch leading to the upper walkways and ducked into the guardhouse on the other side. Thezdan soon caught sight of the small circle of yellow-white light moving toward them up the path.

He cupped his hands around his mouth and shouted, "Be still, or we will shoot!"

Despite his threats, the light kept coming. It was not more than fifty yards away.

"What do you think it is, brother?" Thezdan asked tensely.

Sinox's eyes tracked the approaching object, carefully studying its movements.

"Should I shoot?" the guard asked again.

"No, not yet," said Sinox.

"Sinox, tell me what you see!" Thezdan pressed.

"I'm not sure … It moves like a man, but that is not the light of a torch." Sinox turned and faced the guard. "Give me your bow."

The guard nodded, handing over his bow and quiver. Sinox took out two arrows. He placed one in his teeth and notched the other in the bowstring. Thezdan watched intently. Sinox had always been an expert scout, and he was an even better sniper.

Sinox drew the arrow back. He held it for only a moment—his target still approaching, now only thirty yards away—before letting it fly. It whizzed through the air and struck the dirt only a foot ahead of the moving figure. The small dust cloud from the impact glittered for a moment in the nearby light but did little to slow the figure's advance.

"You missed?" said Thezdan, surprised.

Sinox took the second arrow from his mouth and readied it in the bow. "No, I didn't. Call out a final warning."

Thezdan cupped his hands around his mouth again. "Stop now or die!"

The light continued toward them.

"So be it," muttered Sinox under his breath. He released the arrow and it flew true through the night air. But just before the fatal moment, it seemingly froze in midair then dropped harmlessly to the side.

"Goddess ... " Sinox whispered, his tone betraying a rising panic. "Brother, be ready!"

The figure came to a stop just short of the gate. It began to speak, its voice womanlike, yet otherworldly and ethereal. "Greetings, Guardians. I have come to speak with Princess Elleina."

Thezdan leaned out of the window and held out his hands to

indicate that he was unarmed. "Announce yourself!"

"You may tell the Princess that it is Balyssa. I will not leave until I speak with her."

Thezdan looked back at Sinox. "Balyssa? Is this a name you know?"

Sinox shook his head.

Thezdan knew that they didn't have many options. Their guest could not be ignored. "I'm going to go down, brother. You keep watch from here."

Sinox grabbed his shoulder. "Should you call Scylld?"

"No. I do not want our visitor to think I am committed to hostility. I will take care of this myself."

"Just be careful, Thezdan … My arrows will not protect you."

Thezdan nodded. Without further word, he ducked through the hole leading back to the interior ramparts of the fort.

"What is going on, Eodan?" Alana called from below.

"We don't know," Thezdan replied as he descended the branch-stairs. "There is someone outside who announced herself as Balyssa. She has asked to speak with Princess Elleina."

Julia's ears perked on hearing her grandmother's name—and the name Balyssa. "I think I have heard of Balyssa," she said.

"What?" said Alana. "You know this visitor?"

"No, I don't know her, but I believe my grandmother did. She told me once that Balyssa helped her flee, but I'm not sure how."

Alana looked worried. "Someone from Princess Elleina's age has come here in the middle of the night to see her? Something is not right. You should not go out there. Tell her to return in the morning."

Thezdan grabbed a torch from the front wall. "No. I don't know who it is, but this is not the sort of visitor who can be turned away. Let me go. Sinox will keep me safe from above."

Alana shook her head. "I don't like this, Eodan. You should not have to face this alone."

"Hold on," said Julia. "I'm going, too. Balyssa asked to see my grandmother, but Ina's not here. I am. Let me go with you."

"No," said Thezdan. "It may not be safe."

Julia took a step forward. "If she sent my grandmother away, she may have been the one that brought me here. I want to speak with her."

Thezdan looked into her eyes and saw her determination. He also knew that it was not his place to deny the wishes of a Vorraver. "Very well. Stay by my side, and if I say run, run."

Julia nodded. "I will."

Thezdan lifted the barricade lock and pushed open one of the doors just enough to slip through the gate. He headed toward the waiting figure, Julia following behind.

It was a woman, the youthful, delicate features of her face visible under her hooded robe. There was something strange about her, though: her pale skin exuded a ghostly, iridescent glow.

"Oh my gosh," Julia whispered. "It's the ghost from the monastery!" She reached for her necklace, seeking its guidance. This time, however, it offered no report, neither warming nor cooling in her hand.

The woman held out her arms and bowed. Thezdan reflexively pulled Julia behind him, shielding her with his body.

"Do not worry, Guardian," said the woman. "I am a friend."

"Who are you, Spirit?" Thezdan asked, his body tense.

"I am Balyssa, Eodan."

"How do you know who I am?"

"I have watched the Guardian Clan for a long time now. Your grandfather and I helped Princess Elleina escape many years ago."

Thezdan shook his head. "You could not have known him. You would be an old woman if you had!"

"I knew him well, Eodan. He was strong. But not as strong as you might become."

Thezdan took a step forward and squinted, trying to get a better view of their visitor. "Who are you that you do not age?"

Balyssa raised her head slightly, revealing her eyes for the first time. They were a stunning purple color. "I am not a mortal woman," she said. "I am a servant of the high and most beautiful Dancer. I straddle the world of the living and the world of spirits."

"Were you the person I saw in the library?" Julia called.

"Yes, young Vorraver. For years, I have stayed there trying to summon Princess Elleina. Those efforts have left me drained, which is why you see me as I am now. I am struggling to maintain my tether to this living form, and so I slip farther and farther into the spirit realm."

Thezdan gripped his sword, unnerved. "What brings you here?"

Balyssa extended her hand toward Julia. Thezdan stepped

backward, pushing Julia back with him.

"I must speak with the girl behind you," said Balyssa. "This world needs her."

"You can see that she is not the one you seek," said Thezdan. "Will you leave us now?"

"She is not Princess Elleina, no. But I know that she is a Vorraver, and I can sense the presence of the Vorraver key around her neck. So there is still hope."

"Wait," said Julia. "What do you know about my necklace?"

Balyssa's gaze shifted past them. Julia glanced over her shoulder and saw Alana and Sinox coming through the gate.

Alana came up beside Thezdan and bowed her head, extending her palms forward in the formal greeting gesture. "I am Alana, Council Member and Administrator of the Guardian Clan."

"Hello Alana," Balyssa said. "I apologize for the circumstances and hour of my arrival, but I need to speak with the young Vorraver."

"As with generations of Vorravers before her, she is under our protection," said Alana firmly.

"I am glad. She will need that protection, but not at the moment. I am not a danger to her or to you."

Alana's eyes narrowed. "Go on."

"I am here because this world is in terrible danger. I have been trying for a very long time to summon Princess Elleina so that we might have a chance to save it."

"Summon?" Alana repeated skeptically. "Save? I'm afraid I don't understand."

"There is a great deal for me to share. Invite me inside, and I will tell you what I know."

Alana paused, her eyes sizing up their visitor. "Do we have a choice?" she said with obvious reluctance. "Very well. Come, but please cover yourself. Your glow would frighten the younger No."

"That should not be necessary," Balyssa responded. "Give me the torch. My spirit form will fade against the light."

Alana gave an assenting nod, and Thezdan passed the torch to Balyssa.

As Balyssa pulled the torch in close to her body, her spirit-glow disappeared. In its place, the torchlight revealed a beautiful, pale-ivory complexion. Combined with the deep-purple of her irises and the few visible strands of her raven-black hair, Balyssa's beauty was surreal—at once discomfiting and captivating.

"As you can see," Balyssa continued, "my form is now well concealed."

Alana swallowed hard. "Thank you. Please follow me." She forced herself to turn around, dabbing sweat from her brow as she led Balyssa and the rest of the group back into the fort.

There were no signs of ongoing festivities in the courtyard. The bonfire still burned, but most of the Clan members were waiting in silence to see what had caused the earlier commotion.

"Is everything alright?" Lothic asked as they came through the gates.

"Yes," Alana replied weakly.

Lothic reached for the blade in his belt, his focus locked on the strange figure. "Is our guest welcome here?"

Alana placed her hand on top of his. "It's alright, Lothic. Please join us in the Council Hall."

Lothic continued to observe Balyssa, but he removed his hand from the knife. He fell in step behind Alana and walked with the group as they proceeded through the crowd of assembled townspeople to the Council Hall. Arriving just outside, Alana stopped and turned around.

"I need to address the Clan," she said. "Please head in and wait for me. I won't be long."

The rest of the group entered the Council Hall and sat down around the meeting table. Balyssa extinguished the torch she had been carrying, her ethereal glow returning in the dim, candlelit room.

"What are you that you glow like the twin moons?" asked Lothic.

"She is neither woman nor spirit," said Thezdan. "She claims to be a servant of the Dancer."

"In this age? Visiting us now, in the middle of the night?"

"I will explain, Guardian, soon enough," said Balyssa.

The room fell silent. They could hear the muffled sounds of Alana speaking to the Clan outside. Then, a few moments after her speech ended, the door opened.

"I regret the worry that we have caused the others," Alana said, closing the door behind her. She walked over to the table and sat down, her eyes trained on Balyssa. "We have done as you've asked; now, it is your turn. Tell me, why did you come to us at this late hour and demand an audience?"

"Thank you, Alana of the Guardian Clan," said Balyssa. "The hour is indeed late, much later than you even know. The members of your Clan are right to worry."

"Why is that?" said Alana. "Have I misjudged you?"

Balyssa shook her head. "No, I am a friend. But even my most beautiful and beloved Dancer fears what is coming. The fatal harvest of seeds planted many years ago. I—"

"We have no use for cryptic speech," Thezdan scoffed. "Be direct."

Balyssa turned toward Thezdan, letting an uncomfortable silence linger. "Very well, Eodan. I will speak plainly. I believe that the Party is a mirage, a manipulation designed to turn men against each other and to weaken the influence of the Goddess and the Shaper on Aevilen."

"What do you mean 'weaken the influence of the gods?'" Alana asked. "Yes, the Party destroyed all the temples and punish any who dare mention the gods. So what? What can the gods do for us now? They do not care about Aevilen. The only time we encounter them anymore is in our stories."

"Oh?" Balyssa replied disapprovingly. "Has my beloved Dancer ceased to feed the cycles of life with his Spirit Winds? Were you not given this home amid the trees by the Goddess herself? The gods still influence our world. They have many agents that they have empowered and through which they act. I am one, and you all are, too."

"I do not think that our faith alone makes us agents of the Goddess," said Alana, "though we are grateful for the protection of the forest."

Balyssa closed her eyes. The candles flickered as a strange breeze circulated around the room. "I can still sense the Goddess's blessing in you."

"We have no powers, I can assure you," Alana said. "I wish we did … some things might have turned out rather differently."

Thezdan leaned over the table, staring off into nothing, lost in thought.

"Eodan, is something bothering you?" Alana asked.

Thezdan looked up at his mother. "She refers to the Rage."

Alana frowned. "That's young boy nonsense."

"No!" said Thezdan. "I have felt it! I have been training, and perhaps soon—"

"Enough," Alana interrupted sharply. "Balyssa, so what is happening then? Why do you believe that the Party has religious aims? Have they really fooled us all?"

Balyssa nodded. "You must understand, the Aevilen valley is special. The Shaper has shared Aevilen with the Goddess since the First Age, when they lay here together. It has been shaped by both of them: His mountains make it nearly impregnable; and Her forests and fields make it rich in materials and life. Aevilen is a great prize."

Alana glanced over at Lothic then back at Balyssa. "A great prize? Now I ask you to speak plainly. For whom is Aevilen a great prize?"

Balyssa's expression took on a sudden, disconcerting seriousness. "Aevilen is valued by all of the gods, but most of all by the one that even among gods is feared … he who despises all that the Shaper, Goddess, Tempest, and my beautiful Dancer have brought into being. The gods of creation never call him by name, but I have heard men call him many things. The Unmaker. Oblivion. The Void Terror. In Aevilen, I believe you call him the Still Lord."

"The Still Lord?" said Alana, recoiling. "As a girl, I learned about how Still Lord cultists led the Eastern Uprising. But that was well over a century ago! Weren't they destroyed?"

"The uprising was put down, yes, but the cult was not destroyed," said Balyssa. "As they neared defeat, its senior members—they called themselves the Prelate—disappeared. I suspect they used their god-given powers to extend their lives, biding their time. They knew that they could never again reveal themselves as servants of the Still Lord, but they have continued their work. You must understand, Aevilen is something that the Still Lord greatly covets."

"It doesn't make sense," Lothic grumbled. "Aevilen is a small territory compared to the lower continent."

"It is small," said Balyssa, nodding. "But its protection and resources make it the ideal place to build an army. Given your isolation, you probably know little of the history of the lower continent, but the Prelate did not begin in Aevilen; they arrived here after fleeing up the Giant Steps to the east.

They had been defeated in a terrible battle on the lower continent at the hands of the great Warrior-Queen Maruana. She killed their Champion, but at a cost in life that would change her kingdom forever. The surviving Prelate fled north to the mountains. They had been close to victory, but now they would have to resummon their Champion and rebuild their army. By chance, the Giant Steps were passable that year, and they arrived in Aevilen. It was a revelation. They knew immediately that it would be the perfect staging ground for a new army. Here it could grow, hidden and safe from the risks of preemptive attack. And when they were ready, they could dam the rivers, open the Giant Steps, and march down to the lower continent to conquer the world."

"Hold on," said Sinox. "So where do you imagine this 'Prelate' is now? And where is this great army they're building?"

"I believe that the Prelate controls the People's Party, and that they are working to summon one of the Still Lord's Champions here. If they succeed, it will threaten all life in Aevilen and eventually all life throughout the world."

"The People's Party, threaten the world?" Sinox sneered. "Theirs is the army you fear? Ha! Aside from the small elite corps that everyone calls the 'Night Reapers,' the People's Army is an ill-fed, ill-equipped, ragtag outfit. You are right to say that they have done a great deal of harm here in Aevilen, but a great campaign on the lower continent? Impossible!"

"You are wrong, young Sinox," said Balyssa. "Their Army grows by the day. Have you ever seen the killing fields northeast of Riverstride? The great Pit where they have amassed the bodies of prisoners and victims of the Purges?"

"Of course," Sinox replied. "A vile monument to the depredations of the Party."

"That is where the Army grows. The Still Lord does not fight with mortal men. His agents raise armies from the dead."

Sinox grit his teeth. "Absurd."

Balyssa lurched forward, her eyes crackling with electric energy. "You know nothing. I have seen it! I watched his Champion raise the dead to fight against Queen Maruana's soldiers!"

A heavy silence gripped the room. Julia and the Guardians traded glances.

Balyssa sat back in her chair, her eyes still pulsing. "After the battle, I followed the Prelate as they fled. Here in Aevilen, I managed to report their presence to the Vorraver Queen Fel. She, like you, was skeptical. Still, she took precautions. When the Eastern Uprising came, her army was ready, and they easily prevailed. I lost track of the Prelate at the end of the Uprising, but I tried to remain watchful because I knew that they would return.

"I beg forgiveness from my beautiful Dancer for my failure, because the Prelate did not go far! Indeed, they have been hiding in plain sight, using politics as a disguise. The Prelate became the People's Party, I am certain of it now! What they called a "Revolution" and "Purges" were just great reapings, opportunities to build their army. Where people resisted the Party's control, the Revolution's false ideology provided a useful pretense for murder. As I said before, we are nearing the end stage of their plan. Their body harvest is nearly complete."

"Nearly complete?" Lothic repeated. "Then what comes next?"

"The return of their Champion, the Demon-Lich Kaal, and the raising of a great army of the dead."

"You speak with great conviction," said Alana, shifting uneasily in her chair. "But this seems beyond imagination."

Julia took a deep breath and spoke up. "I believe her."

All the heads at the table turned, five sets of eyes fixing firmly on her.

"Why?" asked Alana.

Julia placed a hand against her necklace. "I heard a warning when I connected with Scylld."

"What do you mean?" Alana asked.

"My necklace gives me certain powers. It activates when I really need it. That's how I became aware of the Sylvan watching me in the forest. That's also how I came to learn your language even though I'd never heard it before. When I connected with Scylld, this amazing voice came through him, and it told me that a darkness was threatening Aevilen. I didn't know what to think at the time, but it didn't feel like a dream. And now, hearing Balyssa, I realized that she was probably talking about the same evil."

"Scylld is the Ogar who travels with Eodan?" Balyssa asked.

Julia nodded.

"Interesting," said Balyssa. "So that voice you heard … " She fell silent, offering Julia a knowing smile.

"Your necklace is more powerful than I realized," said Alana. "May we see it again?"

Julia removed her hand, revealing the pendant. A twinkling, blue light filled the room.

"Remarkable," said Lothic.

"That necklace is why you were summoned," said Balyssa. "It is part of a key that we need to assemble."

"The divided key," Julia said under her breath, again recalling the mysterious voice.

"Yes!" cried Balyssa. "The key that will allow us to summon the Shaper's Champion and destroy the cult forever!"

"Wait," said Julia, refocusing. "If all you need is my necklace so you can make the divided key, what if I just gave it to you? Couldn't you send me home?"

"No," said Balyssa. "That would not work, unfortunately. I believe that only a Vorraver king or queen can recombine the pieces of the key. Until we know for certain, you will have to stay in Aevilen."

Julia shook her head. "Okay, but what if we did something else? Why don't you send me home, and I tell the world about what I've seen? My uncle works for—"

Balyssa laughed ominously. "I am surprised you haven't realized it yet, but this world and the world you came from are not the same. There is no way for you to summon help. There is no army you can bring, no weapons you can transport, to help in the fight ahead. You, young Vorraver, are the only one who can save Aevilen now."

Julia felt light-headed. Not the same world? All of her options had disappeared in an instant. She was at Balyssa's mercy. Trapped. "B-but I am not a Vorraver queen. I said I believe you, and I do! But the things you mentioned? I don't know anything about that! I'm not from here, even if my grandmother was! Let me give you the necklace, and maybe you can figure out a way to use it. You brought me here, why can't you send me home?"

"She's right," said Thezdan. "This is not her land, and this should not be her fight."

Balyssa locked onto Julia with a penetrating, supernatural stare, arcs of electricity flashing in her eyes. "I am too weak to send you home, but do you feel nothing for these people? Would you allow them to die without having tried to save them? Would you abandon the ancient heritage of your family and deny the gods they served?"

"I-I can't do anything!" Julia said, recoiling.

"I refuse to hear this any longer!" Sinox exclaimed. "Our visitor is clearly no ordinary woman, and perhaps she is as old as her story implies. But the dead rising? Hidden cults? Enough! We all know Grimmel leads the Party. He is a vile man, a rotten and malicious schemer, but he has meager talents. He is not in league with a god! Even if the Party were, in fact, a cult, what would you have us do? We are hollowed out. Two generations worth of our warriors lost their lives not even a decade ago. One day, we may be able to influence events on the plains, but that time is not now. There is only one thing we can do: nothing. With the Sylvan protecting us, the Party leaves us alone in the forest. Let us stay in the forest. We will protect the girl until you are strong enough to send her home, and we will leave the outside world to its fate. We have enough to eat, and we are safe. We can continue to monitor the rest of Aevilen. Perhaps when I am an old man and our Clan has been rebuilt, we can discuss involving ourselves in matters like this. For now, to even consider it would be foolish beyond words!"

"You cannot hide from what's coming," Balyssa scorned. "If their

Champion is reborn with an army behind him, these forests won't protect you. Your inaction will seal your fate!"

"What would have us do?" asked Lothic, gesturing for Sinox to hold his tongue.

"We must gather the other piece of the key, the one held by the Rokkin," said Balyssa. "They will not be as skeptical as you have been. Some Rokkin are only a generation removed from the last time Aevilen's Champion was summoned."

Lothic sat back in his seat, crossing his arms in front of him. "You came to see us; why don't you go see them yourself?"

"That is not possible. The Rokkin would not welcome me as a stranger. They are hostile to magic. In my present condition, I would not last long in Rokkin lands. It is one thing to turn away an arrow; it is entirely another to turn away a Rokkin's hammer."

"Then what?" Lothic pressed. "You expect us to dispatch some of our people to knock on the gates of Ymreddan? Our men would be strangers to the Rokkin, too, and we would be no more welcome than you."

"But you are not a stranger to them," said Balyssa.

"That's true," said Lothic, his anger rising. "I am worse than a stranger; I am a criminal!"

Sinox slammed his hands down and abruptly stood up. "We will not dispatch Lothic—or anyone else, for that matter—on these fool's errands! Even my contacts have no idea what happens inside the Rokkin keeps. What you propose is pointlessly risky. Alana, I hope you offer our guest a warm bed for the night and a full belly to travel on in the morning. There is no further purpose to her visit here!" Sinox's face hardened. He bowed in the direction of their visitor, then he repeated the gesture to his mother.

Alana reached out and placed a hand on his arm. "Stay, Sinox. I do not think we are finished."

"I have said what I needed to say," Sinox said, gently brushing Alana's hand aside. "I have no more to contribute."

The table watched as Sinox strode over to the door and exited into the night.

"I am sorry for my son's outburst," said Alana after the door had swung closed. "As Prime, he feels responsible for protecting our Clan. I fear that he may be too cautious at times, too risk-averse."

Balyssa smiled. "You are wise, Alana, a deserving Guardian Administrator. You see that *not* to act could be the gravest risk of all. Who will you send to meet the Rokkin to retrieve their piece of the key?"

"I think you misunderstand me," Alana replied. "I am not yet convinced of your plan, either. Rushing in headlong without knowing the threat that we face would be worse than hiding in the forests. No, we will do what we had planned to do even before you arrived: we will gather information. Eodan, Lothic, you will still go find Domin. You will have much to talk about with him following tonight's conversation. Perhaps he will know why the Rokkin have withdrawn farther into their mountains, and he might be old enough to know something about our guest's story."

"Yes, Alana," Lothic replied. "Eodan?" Alana asked.

Thezdan looked over at Julia briefly and nodded.

"Very good," said Alana. "As before, you may leave in the morning."

"So, I am still going to stay with you?" Julia asked.

"For now, yes," said Alana. "I will ensure that you are safe and well taken care of until Eodan returns."

"If you will permit me," Balyssa interjected, "I would like to work with the young Vorraver."

Julia shuddered. Out of the corner of her eye, she saw Thezdan trying to gauge her response, but she remained still and tried to suppress her emotions.

"Work with her?" asked Alana. "I'm not sure I understand. What do you need her to do?"

"As you know, she is not the Vorraver I thought I would find here, though I accept her as an heir to the bloodline. I don't know how much Princess Elleina shared with her about her heritage or Aevilen itself, but I suspect that there is a great deal for her to learn. I can teach her. Perhaps once she understands her history, she will embrace her duty."

"What makes you believe that you know more about Aevilen than we do?" asked Alana. "Or about the Vorravers, for that matter?"

"This conversation has shown me that much about Aevilen's past has faded into legend," said Balyssa. "Fifty years of Party rule has wiped out so much of your history, and we have frighteningly little time to rediscover it all. I wish to take Julia back to the monastery. I believe that the Champion's Gate may reside there, though I have not been able to find it myself. It may be hidden in an area meant to be accessed by the Vorravers alone."

"If you need someone to accompany you to the monastary, I will go in Julia's stead when I return," said Thezdan.

"No," said Balyssa, her tone cool and unwavering. "It must be a Vorraver, and it must be now. I fear it is already too late for us to stop the Still Lord from claiming Aevilen as his own, but we must try."

Thezdan leaned forward, placing a clenched fist on the table. "It is not your choice."

"It's alright, Thezdan," said Julia, covering his fist with her hand. "Maybe this is my ticket home. The voice I heard when I connected to Scylld also said something about fulfilling the promises of my ancestors. If we went with a Guardian guide, we should be able to get through the forest to the monastery and back in a day, maybe two, right? You said yourself that the forest is safe, so I don't see why I shouldn't go. If I help Balyssa find the gate, maybe the Champion really can help free you all, and I can be sent home."

"Are you sure?" Thezdan asked. He turned to Alana. "Who would you send as her guide and protector, Mother?"

"Endi and Entaurion. Of all our young warriors, these are our finest eyes. They will watch her and keep her safe."

"Not a single strong arm among them," Thezdan grumbled.

"I will give Engar over to the protection team," said Lothic. "His arm is plenty strong."

Thezdan's relief was clear. "I'm sure he'll appreciate the time away from the forge. Thank you, Lothic."

Balyssa smiled. "We will not need warriors, but I accept your supervision."

Alana turned toward Julia. "Are you sure that you're up for this?"

"Yes," Julia said.

"Thank you for your trust," said Balyssa. "Do not worry; I too wish to see you safe and well-protected."

"It seems we've set our course," said Alana, standing up from her chair. "Eodan and Lothic will search for the Rokkin Domin. Julia will travel to the monastery with Balyssa under our protection. Do any of you have anything further to say?"

The room was quiet.

"It is a shame that our celebrations were so short. Try to sleep well. If Balyssa is right, there may not be many restful nights for us in the days ahead."

17

Grimmel fixed his eyes on the heavy wooden door in front of him.

I cannot wait. I must tell him …

He pulled a kerchief from his pocket and wiped his face clean, then he bowed his head and pushed the door open. The candle flames inside the darkened chamber danced as the air from the hallway rushed in.

"Master, I have news."

"Come in, Grimmel," a voice calmly called from the room. "I know you would not disturb me if it were not important."

Grimmel looked up. Amid the darkness, he could see the outline of the Master's robe.

"So," said the voice. "What news do you bring?"

"There was an incident in Breslin," said Grimmel. "The crossroads village to the West."

"I know the one. Go on."

"Someone came to the village wearing an unusual artifact around her neck. I believe that it may be the one you had me look for early in the Revolution, the Vorraver one."

"What makes you believe this?" asked the voice in a controlled monotone. "It is not possible, Grimmel."

"It glowed a blue light, and the beggar who saw it described a shape that matched the royal symbol. There's more, Master; she was accompanied by a Guardian, the son of Eobax."

"I see ... this is becoming more interesting. Go on."

"The local smith was trading materials with the young Guardian."

"And the girl with the necklace? Who is she?"

"We do not know yet," said Grimmel.

"Why did the local forces fail to capture them?"

"The one chariot that was at the ready was destroyed, its rider killed. We believe that they escaped to the forest."

Grimmel looked downward and awaited a terrible response, but there was only silence. He looked up again just in time to see one of the candles tip over into a channel of flammable liquid. The flame spread quickly along the channel and into a great, stone basin at the middle of the room, erupting into a ball of red fire. The room came into full view, its vaulted ceiling and rough walls taking on the sinister red-black hue of the firelight. The robed figure now loomed large behind the fire, his nearly skeletal face and pale, deeply wrinkled skin projecting the infirmity of very old age. But as he moved toward Grimmel, his measured, powerful strides belied the seeming fragility of his body.

"Master, please!" Grimmel whimpered.

"I am not upset, Grimmel," the Master replied. He stopped and stood beside the basin. "I do not need to remind you how important these next few weeks might be, do I?"

"No, no! Whatever you would have me do, it will be done!"

The Master unhooked a pair of long scissor tongs hanging on the side of the basin, then he reached into the fire and withdrew a glowing, red stone. Once the stone was clear of the flames, he grabbed it with his free hand.

"Good, Grimmel. Good. I need you to send word to Redyar that he will have to step up his pace. Use this lifestone to convince him."

A long, emaciated hand offered up the red crystal, which Grimmel carefully received.

"Then, I need you to find that girl. She is likely harmless to us, but there is always the chance … "

"The chance of what, Master?"

The Master stared into the fire. A moment later, he reached for the tongs and withdrew another crystal. "It is nothing, Grimmel. But, just to be certain, I need you to bring me the great wolf you keep."

Grimmel bowed deeply, his words echoing off the floor as he spoke. "I will do as you command."

"And Grimmel, please share any further news on this matter as it arises, even if you think it trivial. I wish to give this my personal attention."

18

Dawn was just breaking, the earliest traces of morning light slowly appearing through the treetops.

Thezdan turned toward his mother with downcast eyes, his arms folded in front of him. "She is going to wake up in a strange place with her only known acquaintance gone."

"Eodan, do not worry," said Alana, smiling. "Julia will be safe here, and I will make sure that she feels comfortable. Besides, she needs to rest."

She was right; Thezdan knew that Julia needed sleep more than she needed goodbyes. He saluted his mother, returning her smile. "Then she is yours. You will take good care of her, I know."

"Of course," said Alana.

Lothic spun around to face them from his perch on the driver's bench. "Eodan, we have to go. If we are to see Domin and get back in a day, we cannot linger here."

Alana reached out and clutched her son's hands. "Be safe, Eodan."

"I will, Mother," said Thezdan. He turned and clambered up the side of the waiting cart, the sideboards creaking loudly as he did. He settled on the seat next to Lothic.

"I am glad we are leaving early," said Lothic, examining Thezdan's peasant tunic and its large party emblem embroidered on the chest. He glanced at his own and clenched his fist. "That way, only a few of our kin will see me suffer this indignity."

"One day, I will see to it that no one has to wear these tunics anymore," said Thezdan. "Perhaps that's a battle you'll actually join."

Lothic brushed off the intended slight. "May that day be soon," he replied. Facing forward, he called out to the borum attached to the wagon: "We go! O-na!" He snapped the leather reins down on the borum's hide, stirring it to life.

Unlike its long-horned cousins from a day ago, this borum was a rather pathetic creature: desperately thin with the stubbly, cropped horns of a farm animal. Sinox had captured it only several months prior, and it still looked like most of the other domesticated borum that moved goods throughout Party territory. That unremarkable quality made it an ideal companion for the day's journey.

Thezdan and Lothic gestured goodbye to the guards as the cart passed through the open gates. They headed down the path toward the main road. As they neared the intersection, Thezdan held up his hand.

"One moment, Lothic."

Lothic stopped the cart. "Is something wrong?"

Thezdan brought his cupped hands to his face and blew across his knuckles, making the resonant whistle that he used to call out to Scylld. A few moments later, he heard a distant rumble called in response, and knew his signal had been heard.

"Everything's fine," said Thezdan. "I want to bring Scylld with us."

"Is that necessary?" Lothic asked.

"After yesterday's events, the two of us shouldn't go alone," said Thezdan. "The towns will be on alert. The patrols will be larger and more frequent. If we are discovered, we will need Scylld's help to fight our way free."

"Very well, Eodan," said Lothic with a subtle shake of his head. "I hope he doesn't weigh down the cart too much, though. We can't afford to move slowly."

"I suppose we'll see," said Thezdan, leaning back against the cart bed. He closed his eyes for a moment, absorbing the early-morning sounds of the forest. "Lothic, I need you to tell me something."

"Of course. What is it?"

"I need to know more about the Rokkin we seek. Domin. He trained you, no?"

"Yes," Lothic said somberly. He paused for a moment. "What do you know of the Rokkin, Eodan?"

"Not much," Thezdan replied. "I saw a few as a No before we left the Trebain. They were usually headed toward Riverstride with ore to trade. Short, thick creatures with odd complexions."

"They are not all short, Eodan. You have only seen relatively young ones. The Rokkin grow larger and stronger throughout their lives as their bodies accumulate minerals from their food and drink. The older ones can be taller than you, and much, much stronger. Eventually, a day comes when, at the very peak of their size and strength, they outgrow the ability of their lifestone to bind them together and they break up into dust."

Thezdan tried to imagine the Rokkin as Lothic had described them. Larger. Stronger. Despite his efforts, his mind kept returning to what he had seen along the paths years ago.

"Do not underestimate Domin's strength," said Lothic. "You and I, strong as we are, would only be a match for a middle-aged Rokkin. Domin is old, and thus much stronger."

Thezdan was taken aback by Lothic's seriousness. He sat up again and looked over at the older Guardian. "Are you expecting him to attack us?"

Lothic shook his head. "I don't think so. Let's both hope that he does not."

"Why are you uncertain?" asked Thezdan sharply. "I thought that the only risk we faced was from Party patrols. What could make your old master want to attack us?"

"Because I am the reason he was exiled from Ymreddan."

Thezdan's eyes bulged. "What?"

"Yes, Eo. Domin was among the highest-born of the Rokkin, a member of the Elder Council, and head of the Smith's Caste. He was also given responsibility for improving relations between the Rokkin and the humans on the plains. These relations were quite good under the Vorraver, but worsened after the Revolution and the early period of Party rule. Domin had an idea that he figured could get Human-Rokkin relations back to where they had been before. He wanted to teach a few select men the techniques of Rokkin smithing." Lothic stopped for a second and chuckled. "He hoped that human creativity and Rokkin craftsmanship could prove a powerful combination, and that it could spark a new era of industry and trade throughout Aevilen."

"And did it not?"

"Well," continued Lothic, "you have to understand, Domin had trained for centuries as a smith. It would have been impossible for one of us to learn how to smith to Rokkin standards. But Domin was determined to try, and so he recruited a single apprentice."

"You."

"Yes, me," said Lothic. "I was a young man, only a few years older than you are now, when their emissaries came. With your father's approval, I accepted their offer. It seemed like an adventure into a hidden world. Domin … well, Domin proved a firm and demanding master, but not unkind. I worked with him for five years, learning about ores, metalworking, and fabrication. I knew that the other Rokkin didn't approve of my presence, but they showed me courtesy out of respect for Domin." Lothic chuckled again. "Who knows? Maybe with another hundred years, I might have gotten somewhere."

"So, what happened?" asked Thezdan.

"I still don't know. Not entirely. There was an Elder named Redyar. He came from the Miner's Caste. In their language, his name meant 'Weeper' because of two silver lines that ran down the sides of his face. He was old, even for a Rokkin—probably toward the end of his life. He hated Domin. Eodan, you have never seen such hatred. It was the kind that takes centuries simmering in tireless jealousy and malice to develop. I think he started spreading rumors that I had stolen a lifestone, an unforgivable crime in Rokkin society. The rumors were, of course, untrue. But one day, Redyar and a contingent of warriors burst into my quarters late at night. Redyar reached under my bed and pulled out a high-quality lifestone. I hadn't put it there, but the damage was immediate and irreversible. I was chained and brought before the other members of the Elder Council. Redyar demanded that I be killed for my supposed crimes. Domin defended me, suggesting that what I had been accused of was impossible. When Redyar produced the lifestone, I saw Domin's face grow hard. He walked toward his fellow Elders and pled for mercy, citing the damage that would come to relations between humans and the Rokkin were I to be executed. Redyar only pressed harder for blood. After the Elder's conferred in private, I was taken to the gates of Ymreddan and released. They told me that I would be killed if I returned. And then, moments later, a Rokkin was pushed out of the gates beside me. It was my master, Domin. They had sheared his magnificent gold beard and stripped him of his highborn finery. He was naked except for a pair of dirty trousers. He had been made an outcast."

Lothic looked away, pausing. "Even now, it causes me great pain to think about what happened to him," he said, deep sadness in his voice. "Outside those gates, I begged Domin to believe me that I had not taken the lifestone. He was silent. I told him to join me in the Trebain, but he declined. He ended up settling in a town south of Riverstride so that he wouldn't have much contact with his fellow Rokkin traveling along the northern and western roads. I made a point of checking in on him several times a year, bringing him grains for his stills. Our reunions were never particularly happy affairs; by the end, he would appear only long enough to receive the goods I had brought him before wishing me well and disappearing back inside his house. Then the last Purge came, and we Guardians fled to these woods. I haven't seen him since."

"I see," Thezdan muttered. "The pain of exile does grow with time ... I understand why you're anxious about the way he'll receive us. Still, it seems terribly cruel that he would have to endure such punishment over a jewel."

"You must understand, Eodan: Lifestones are the most important thing in all creation to the Rokkin. They see them as gifts from the Shaper himself, and perhaps they are. The Rokkin mine them; that's why you see their fortresses buried into mountainsides, with endless tunnels extending deep into the earth. How the stones work is one of the world's great mysteries. At the heart of every Rokkin is a lifestone. Most of the lifestones the Rokkin find are low-quality; these are never activated, and are typically ground up into powder and eaten during great celebrations. But every now and again, they come across fine examples, and each of these is destined to be a seed that will eventually become a new Rokkin. The quality of the stone determines what the new Rokkin will become in his lifetime."

"And the one Redyar planted on you was top-quality?"

Lothic nodded. "Yes. I'm sure you can see the problem." He winced as he adjusted his leg brace. "But that's enough history, I think. Why don't you call the Ogar again? He must be getting close now."

Thezdan raised his hands and blew across the knuckles, the forest echoing once more with the sound of his whistle.

Scylld's rumble response came almost immediately, much closer now than before.

"Listen," said Thezdan, pointing off into the woods. He hopped down from the cart. There was a nearby sound of a branch cracking, then another and another. Soon a shadow appeared between the trees, and then, finally, the hulking, gray Ogar emerged, walking toward them with giant strides.

"Scylld!" Thezdan called.

The Ogar came to his side and stopped. It crossed an arm over its body to salute the two men.

"We need your help," said Thezdan. "We are heading into the plains. After yesterday, the Party is sure to have stepped up their patrols. If we find ourselves in a fight, it could be against more soldiers than we can handle. Will you ride with us, just in case?"

Scylld tilted his head forward and offered a rumbling assent.

"Thank you, my friend," said Thezdan, saluting. "We don't want you to be spotted by passing soldiers, so you'll have to hide in the back of the cart. It should be able to support you."

"I hope you're right," Lothic muttered from the driver's bench. He had reinforced the bed years ago to support heavy logs, but an Ogar was another matter entirely.

Scylld followed Thezdan to the back and slowly climbed into the cart bed. The cart bowed in the middle, its metal axle strained by the great weight of the Ogar. When Scylld sat down, the whole cart shook; but in the end, it held.

Lothic sighed. "This cart must be blessed by the Shaper himself."

Thezdan set about carefully arranging grain around Scylld until he was well camouflaged, then completed the illusion by adding a few freight-stabilizing weights on top. He closed the back gate of the bed and made his way back to the driver's bench.

"Ready to go!" he announced cheerily, teasing a clearly unsettled Lothic.

"I hope our cart and borum can hold out," said Lothic. "It's going to be a long day for both of them."

Lothic whipped the borum with the reins. The creature pushed hard against its harness, and slowly—very slowly—the cart moved forward. With a little more coaxing, the borum got them up to a reasonable speed. Thezdan could tell that Lothic was relieved.

"See, Lothic, have a little faith," Thezdan teased again.

"A long day, indeed," muttered Lothic as he pulled the cart onto the main road in the direction of the bridge.

Thezdan laughed, paying no mind to the whining wheels behind them.

19

Julia awoke to the sun shining brightly through the window and filling her room with morning light. It had been the first full night of sleep she had had in days, and she was grateful to finally wake up in a place of relative safety.

She pulled back the heavy, woolen blanket that covered her and slipped on her clothes and sandals, then she walked over to the window and took in the courtyard below. Watching all the people bustling around reminded her of her old neighborhood in Malibu, when she'd wake up to see neighbors gardening and kids playing in their backyards. The sight of a teenage girl carrying a basket of foraged foodstuffs made her think of Maya, who used to come by and collect oranges from a tree in their backyard.

I'm sure everyone's worried about me …

Her mind wandered with thoughts of her mom, dad, brother, and grandmother again. She wished that she could be with them, and she even imagined for a moment that she could rush down to the courtyard and be greeted by them there.

Alana spotted her from below and waved, shaking her from her daydream. Julia waved back. She stepped away from the window and made her way downstairs.

"The Goddess's bounty to you, Julia!" said Alana as Julia came out of the house. "Did you sleep well?"

"Yes, thank you."

"I'm delighted. I know you needed it." Alana stepped back and turned toward two young men sitting nearby. "May I introduce you to the Guardians who will look after you in Eodan's absence?"

On cue, the two rose to their feet. They were both roughly Julia's age, but their similarities ended there. The first was lean, dressed in a long-sleeved, hooded tunic that partly obscured his face. He had a quiver at his side and a bow slung over his back, and he moved with long, delicate strides. The other was massive, his naked arms bulging with muscle. He wore a thick, leather doublet cinched by a heavy belt from which two large hammers hung on either side. Despite his size, he was boyishly handsome, his youthful features humorously incongruous with his hulking frame.

Alana welcomed the two young Guardians with a nod of her head, and they offered her the formal palms-up bow in turn.

"Julia, if you believe them to be worthy, these two En will accompany and protect you," said Alana. "They are honored to perform this role; it is a sacred one for us." She extended her free hand toward the hooded one, and he took a step forward. "First, I present you with Entaurion, one of our scouts. He has trained with Sinox, and has a very keen eye."

Entaurion turned toward Julia and repeated the formal bow.

"And here," said Alana, as she beckoned to the other, "is Engar. He is Lothic's apprentice at the forge and the strongest of all Guardians. Lothic has also trained him to be a fine warrior."

Engar flashed a mischievous grin, but a disapproving stare from Alana made him drop into a very deep formal bow. Julia laughed at the sight of the giant laid low.

Alana quickly turned around. "Do you not approve of them?"

Julia rushed to cover her mouth, nodding her head. "They will be great, I'm sure. I feel safer already."

Engar peeked his head up and smiled at Julia, who had to turn away to keep from laughing again.

"Very good," said Alana. "These two will protect you until we can find a way to get you home. I have also asked Sinox to keep an eye on you, so don't be surprised to hear Sylvan chirping overhead if you go into the forest. He often works with them to track what is going on around here."

"Alright ... " said Julia tentatively, recalling her original encounter with the tree creatures.

"You will be well looked after, don't worry," said Alana. "Come. Let me get you something to eat."

Alana led Julia and the two Guardians back to her home in the fort, which was largely indistinguishable from the other dwellings that ringed the interior walls. While the two Guardians waited outside, Alana prepared a simple meal of forest-scavenged nuts mixed with a sweet borum-milk yogurt.

"This is really good," said Julia as she savored a bite.

"I wish I could remember enjoying it like that," said Alana. "Having the same breakfast every day for years has a way of erasing such memories."

Julia was just finishing when a knock rapped against the door.

"Come in," Alana called.

"The robed stranger has returned, Alana," said Entaurion from the doorway. "She just passed through the front gate."

Julia closed her eyes and breathed in deeply, trying to settle her nerves.

Alana noticed her unease. "Do you no longer wish to go with Balyssa? Have you reconsidered?"

Julia wanted to say that she had, that she much preferred the idea of staying in the fort than wandering the forests with Balyssa. Then, she thought back to her intuition that helping Balyssa was her surest route home.

"I guess it's hard for me to feel comfortable with the idea of going anywhere with someone so strange," Julia said. "But I'm probably worried for nothing. I know that the Guardians will keep me safe, and I'll be back in no time."

Alana smiled. "I trust Engar and Entaurion to do just that. You're in good hands."

Julia followed Alana into the courtyard. It didn't take long for her to spot Balyssa, her long, hooded cloak showing barely any motion as she approached. There was an unusual steadiness to the way she walked. It almost seemed as if she were floating.

"Who is she?" asked Engar.

"Her name is Balyssa," said Alana. "She was the cause of last night's commotion. As I told you, it was mostly a misunderstanding. She is here to help the young Vorraver."

"Something seems … odd about her," said Entaurion.

"You are to be cordial and to treat her as a friend," instructed Alana. "Of course, you must also be sure that she never places Julia in danger."

"Then she will be with us?" asked Entaurion.

"No; you will be with her. She intends to take Julia to the mountain monastery."

"It pleases me to see you again, Julia!" Balyssa called. Her glow was not visible in the daylight, though her skin looked even whiter and her eyes more richly purple than they had the night before. "My most beautiful Dancer has cleared the skies above and offers us a gentle breeze for our travels."

Alana stepped forward into Balyssa's path and offered a shallow bow. "Goddess's bounty to you today, Balyssa."

Balyssa acknowledged Alana with a quick nod of her head, then she refocused her attention on Julia. "Shall we go?"

"I am ready," said Julia. "These two Guardians are coming with us to keep us safe."

"I am Engar," Engar declared, marching to the front of the group. "Guardian Warrior and Blacksmith's Apprentice. I am stronger than a borum and swifter than a kwia, and I am honored to be protecting the Vorraver Julia!"

"Very well," said Balyssa. "If you are the one chosen—"

"I am Entaurion, and I will also be joining you," said Entaurion. He looked over at Engar and shook his head disapprovingly.

"So, it is the four of us, then?" Balyssa said, examining the two Guardians. "Alana, I trust that, when asked, these Guardians will give me room to speak with Julia privately?"

"They are going with you to protect her," Alana replied coolly. "At her request, they may let off slightly, but never so far as to risk failing in their duties."

"Do not worry," said Balyssa. "I do not expect anything so exciting to happen today." She beckoned Julia, Entaurion, and Engar to follow her. "Come. It is time to go."

"Be safe," said Alana as they formed up to leave. "And may the Goddess watch over you."

Julia waved goodbye. Many of the women and young men in the town furtively watched as the four made their way through the courtyard, sneaking glances as their labors allowed.

"I think they're looking at us," Julia muttered under her breath, leaning toward Engar.

"Indeed!" said Engar, puffing out his chest. "They're wondering how you got so lucky as to have such fine company."

"Is that so?" Julia asked, her tone thick with sarcasm.

Engar looked back at Julia and burst out laughing. He shrugged. Entaurion rolled his eyes.

"Oh, lighten up, Entaurion," chuckled Engar. "All that time in the guardhouse has made you dull! You should come join me back at the forge—we'll bang a little metal around like true Guardian men and see if we can't beat some humor back into you!"

"My friend," said Entaurion, shaking his head, "with all the hot air you bellow, it's a wonder you even need a forge."

Engar laughed loudly again and gave Entaurion a friendly whack on the back. The guard opened the main gates as they approached, exchanging salutes with the party as they passed.

"We are not going to the monastery quite yet," said Balyssa. "There are things to do in the forest, first."

"Uh, like what?" Julia asked, surprised.

"There are many hidden things, young Vorraver, that you must learn to see."

Julia tried to wrap her mind around Balyssa's words. "Nothing too dangerous, right?"

"The forest is safe for you; you need not worry. And we have two great warriors traveling with us, besides."

Julia looked behind at Engar and Entaurion, who seemed to be embroiled in the sort of whisper-argument Julia and her brother used to have in the back of the family car. She laughed.

At the intersection with the main road, Balyssa led them south, away from the bridge, and deeper into the forest. They followed the road for the better part of an hour, reaching a particularly dense area well out of earshot of the river. Then, without clear cause or warning, Balyssa stopped. "Here we are," she declared.

Entaurion scanned the trees around them. "But—"

"Say nothing," Balyssa commanded. "This is part of her training."

Entaurion was taken aback by the hushing; he scowled but obeyed.

Balyssa came around to Julia's side. "What do you see here?" she asked.

Julia looked around at the trees. As she had noted several days before, the great majority were very old conifers with gnarled bark and patches of green moss. Thick vines climbed across trunks and limbs, and there were holes in some of the trees or jagged edges where branches had broken off. The forest floor was blanketed by low-lying plants and dead needles, amid which a few new trees had taken root. Looking through the deep green canopy, Julia could see occasional patches of streaming light and blue sky when the wind pushed the treetops apart. However, no matter where she looked, she couldn't see anything unusual.

"I see the trees," she finally replied. "And treetops with branches swaying in the wind."

"What else?" Balyssa pressed.

"And, uh, some patches of sky above?"

"Are there any animals? Any birds?"

Julia scoured the upper reaches of the canopy for another minute, then shook her head.

Balyssa nodded. "Alright then." She turned to face the two

Guardians. "Entaurion, Engar, may I ask you to wait here a moment?"

"Why?" asked Engar. "Where are you going?"

"I wish to take Julia up the road only a very short way," Balyssa replied. "I need her to focus, and I fear that being near you might break her concentration."

Entaurion looked at Julia. "Are you alright with this?"

"I guess so," said Julia. "I mean, it's why we're out here. Thank you for looking out for me, though."

"We will stay nearby, watching closely," Entaurion said. "Call if you need us."

"We'll be ready," Engar said in Balyssa's direction.

Balyssa ignored him. She turned and began walking farther down the road. "Come, Julia," she called. "This way."

Julia followed. She was relieved when Balyssa came to a stop only a hundred feet or so from where they had been.

"Look back, and you will see Engar and Entaurion," Balyssa said, her voice hushed. "And they can still see us. I only wished to get far enough away that we could speak privately."

"Why can't they hear us?" Julia asked.

"Because it is best that they not know—not yet, anyway—about what I am going to teach you."

Julia raised her eyebrows.

"You doubt yourself, but you are very special," Balyssa said. "Your necklace is a powerful artifact to which only the Vorravers are attuned. As I told you before, it is a key. But it's also more than that. It is enchanted with the energies of both the Goddess and the Shaper, and so it gives you power in both of their spheres."

Julia looked down at her necklace. "Power in their spheres? What does that mean?"

"It means that once you learn to focus, to draw on the energies of the artifact, stone and earth, wood and plants, and all of the many creatures that fill the domains of the Goddess and the Shaper will be open to you. You will not be able to control them as if you were a god, but you will be able to hear them, understand them, and learn from them."

Julia felt a strange conflict within her. These words seemed absurd; yet as she listened, she sensed that she already knew what she was hearing. The same intuition had come over her many times since arriving in Aevilen.

Hear them. Understand them. Learn from them.

"That is how I came to understand the letters my grandmother wrote," Julia said, her tone reflecting her budding epiphany. "And the language … "

"That's right," said Balyssa. "The paper shared its memory of what was placed on it many years ago, and your necklace enabled you to hear and understand those words. You should also be able to understand creatures that the Goddess created, like the Sylvan. The same holds true for the Shaper and his Rokkin. But your powers do not end with understanding these creatures; as I said before, all of the Goddess's and the Shaper's domains are open to you."

"What does that mean?" Julia asked.

Balyssa pointed to a particularly large tree just off the road. "Go place your hand against that tree. Open yourself to it."

Julia walked over to the big tree. She let her gaze fall loosely on its trunk. As her mind relaxed, she began to see the tree in ways she had not before: agedness and wisdom in the bark; vitality and life in the artery-like roots reaching into the earth; playfulness in the needles dancing in the wind above. Feeling centered, she reached out and placed her hand gently against the side of the tree and closed her eyes. Her necklace came to life, its warmth spreading across her chest. Suddenly a great tsunami of sensations overcame her. She felt like she was being pushed and pulled in a million different directions, and a great cacophony of sound and a blur of shapes overwhelmed her ability to make sense of any one in particular. Countless eyes flashed scenes from all around her, producing an overlapping mosaic of sky, branches, needles, and the forest floor.

She gasped and pulled away from the tree, her heart beating rapidly in her chest. "What was that?" she exclaimed.

"You were sensing what that tree senses," said Balyssa.

Julia put a hand on her chest, still trying to catch her breath. "Trees don't have eyes, and I was seeing a million things all at once."

"That tree may not have eyes like yours, but it is very sensitive to light. Every one of those needles above can sense very small changes in the composition and intensity of the light hitting it. When you attune to the tree, you experience that as sight."

"Amazing," said Julia, looking up at the vast blanket of green needles in the canopy above.

"You need to learn to focus your experiences. Much as you have learned to focus your own sight, smell, and hearing, you need to limit your attunement to the tree so that you gather only as much as you can understand."

Julia nodded. "I-I think I get it."

"Good. Touch the tree again. This time, try to look down at us from the needles on a nearby branch."

Julia spotted a suitable lower branch and tried to keep a picture of it in her head as she closed her eyes. She placed her hand against the tree again, and soon her mind was flooded with physical sensations, sights, and sounds. This time, however, she didn't detach; she wrestled with the overwhelming amount of sensory information, trying desperately to control it. She found the branch and tried to hone in on its outputs. It was like trying to hear whispers in a noisy hallway, but she refused to give up. Each time she felt herself losing control, she forced herself to refocus. Slowly, over what was probably seconds but felt like hours, the tide began to turn. She was able to block the branches on the other side, then the canopy above, then the trunk of the tree, until finally all that remained was the target branch and its many needles. Julia then relaxed her mental grip on the needles and let their individual outputs combine into an expansive view of the forest on that side. It was like seeing through an undistorted fish-eye lens. She looked down at herself from sixty feet above, awestruck by the experience.

"That was incredible," Julia said breathlessly as she pulled away from the tree. "I could see so much."

"Well done," said Balyssa. "Now I have another test for you. Let us return to Engar and Entaurion. I want you to try again to tell me what is in the trees around them."

Julia nodded firmly. "Let's do it."

Julia and Balyssa walked back to the two Guardians, who seemed grateful for their prompt return.

"You know, if you had told us that all you were going to do was have a quick chat and rub a few trees, I think I would have felt a bit less concerned about letting you go," said Engar.

"Well, I'm glad you let me go," Julia said. "It was—"

Balyssa held up a hand. "Guardians, can you turn around for just one moment?"

The Guardians looked at each other, confused.

"Is this what you would like, Julia?" Entaurion asked.

"Yes, Entaurion," Julia replied, sensing that it was a part of her upcoming test. "It's okay."

"As you wish," said Entaurion.

"What happened to telling us what's going on?" asked Engar, frowning.

"I'm sorry guys, just a bit longer," said Julia. "Please?"

The two Guardians turned around, giving their backs to Julia and Balyssa.

Balyssa drew very close and whispered into Julia's ear, "Use what you've learned to look into the forest around us. Tell me what you see."

Julia moved over to a nearby tree. She placed her hand against the trunk as she had before, and almost immediately felt the rush of sensory experiences. She focused on the needle clusters to get a view from above, but even going branch-by-branch around the tree she couldn't see anything unusual. She decided to listen for sounds. The needles were too sensitive to allow her to distinguish sound from wind, so she switched to the trunk. For a few moments, she let the sounds of the forest fill her: swaying branches, a scurrying, squirrel-like critter on a nearby tree, a bird calling from overhead. Then she heard something else: the birdsong-like sounds of Sylvan. They were too faint for her to resolve, but even muffled whispers were enough to rekindle the fear she had felt her first day in the forest. She disengaged from the tree and looked back at Balyssa.

"Do not worry," whispered Balyssa, her voice calm. "They will not harm you."

After taking a moment to collect herself, Julia placed her hand on the tree again. She used the trunk to isolate the sounds, then she switched to the needles in order to see the hiding creatures. Sure enough, camouflaged nearly perfectly against a nearby tree were two small Sylvan. They were very still, and they seemed to be watching Julia and her companions with great interest.

Julia opened her eyes and looked at Balyssa.

"There are two Sylvan over there," Julia whispered as she pointed over to where she had seen them.

"Entaurion," called Balyssa with a full voice. "Can you turn around, please?"

Entaurion complied, though his scrunched face betrayed a growing frustration.

"What did you see in the trees?" asked Balyssa.

"Now you wish to know?" he grumbled.

"Yes," said Balyssa.

Entaurion shook his head and gestured toward a tree nearby. "There was a Sylvan in a tree over there."

"Are you sure?"

"Yes, quite sure."

Balyssa turned toward Julia. "So, Julia, what did you see?"

"Um, I saw two Sylvan in that area. One clinging to the trunk about three-quarters of the way up, and another lying against an adjacent branch."

Entaurion's expression changed in an instant, from annoyed to surprised. He looked up at the tree and squinted, then he took a few steps to his right and looked again. "Well scouted," he said quietly. He tipped his hood at Julia. "I would not have thought it possible that you might see something in this forest that I could not."

Engar spun around and cheered. "Hoorah! Well done! Perhaps now Entaurion will stop mocking my eyesight!"

"You can barely see the trees," Entaurion muttered.

"Indeed, well done," said Balyssa. "A god's favor is no small thing. Now that you are aware of your power, I believe that the secrets of the monastery will reveal themselves to you. We will go there now, but we must hurry. I believe the Administrator expects us back before nightfall."

As Balyssa began walking down the road, Julia looked up one last time at the tree she had touched. She marveled at the thought that she had been able to connect with it and share its experiences. And yet, this power had not come free of cost. It was connected to the necklace, which Balyssa had used to summon her here against her will. Now, Balyssa had introduced her to an incredible ability, but what did it mean? Why was Balyssa helping her? The wheels of fate were turning, and Julia was beginning to understand that she had been assigned a role in what was coming. The road ahead would lead to the monastery, yes, and hopefully to the hidden "Champion's Gate" Balyssa sought. But would that be the end? She could only hope.

The trees cast their shadows over the forest floor, the ever-shifting light offering a steady stream of illusions coming into and out of existence. Julia turned to follow Balyssa, breathing in deeply.

I am in control of my destiny, she tried to convince herself. *This road is going to lead me home.*

20

The sun was high overhead in central Aevilen when Lothic and Thezdan approached Domin's stone house. Set into a hillside south of Riverstride, the home stood out in the landscape as the only intact structure amid a sea of derelict buildings. In all directions were the remnants of homes and businesses abandoned in the last Purge, some having been burned by the People's Army but most having been left to rot, their thatched roofs long since caved in from years of inattention. In times past, this had been a famously beautiful part of Aevilen, known for its stone terraces built into the hills. Whereas once those terraces had teemed with flowering plants and fruits, now Lothic and Thezdan could barely see the stones beneath the thick vines and brush that spilled over them.

"We are almost there, Eodan," Lothic announced in a forlorn monotone.

"Is everything alright?" Thezdan asked, sitting up and wiping the grog from his eyes.

" ... Yes," said Lothic. "We're close now, and we need to be alert."

Thezdan realized that Lothic probably hadn't been through here since before they fled the Trebain. "It is not only the South, you know. Much of the North and West have suffered the same fate."

"I've heard that report from Sinox, too," Lothic replied. "Still, I was not prepared to see it like this."

Thezdan caught sight of a charred ruin just off the road, a simple hearth and stone floor all that remained of the home. The iron pot hanging in the hearth brought him back to his boyhood in the Trebain, when his mother would cook fragrant stews as he played with his carved wooden *faeron* on the floor.

His expression hardened. "This is why I train, Lothic," he said. "This is why I left. I will fight the evil that has done this, whether it is a death cult or not."

"I know, Eodan. I know ... " Lothic brought the cart to a halt and looked north toward the twin spires of Riverstride. "I do not think you were wrong to leave."

"What? Why do you say that?" Thezdan replied incredulously. "What do you know about my choices?"

"We all take the path we think best," said Lothic. "Some, like you, choose to fight; I could not. But we all hope for the same thing: to serve our people as best we can. Hopefully a day will come when you understand what happened at the Trebain."

Thezdan bristled at the mention of their former home and the allusion to the battle that claimed it—the battle that Lothic had fled. He closed his eyes, counting his breaths to suppress his rising anger.

"We came to find Domin, not to discuss the past," he said finally.

Lothic offered a shallow nod and whipped the borum back into motion.

As the cart neared the house, Thezdan and Lothic kept careful watch of the building and surrounding area, keen to find signs of life. Lothic drew a sword from under his tunic. He placed it on the driver's bench between them.

"Let us both be ready," he said.

"Is that sword going to be of any use against Domin, if he is as you described him?" Thezdan asked.

"It is not Domin I'm preparing for; I'm worried about Party loyalists. We cannot be sure that this is still Domin's house. The Party may have evicted him but kept this place for the distillery out back. His liquor was always quite popular in Riverstride."

As a precaution, Lothic drove the cart past the house along the road. When their passing caused no obvious disturbance, he turned around and pulled the cart onto the grass near the front door.

Thezdan jumped down from the driver's bench.

"Wait," called Lothic in a loud whisper. He gingerly lowered himself from the cart and limped over toward Thezdan. "Go look through the window. If it's clear, gesture with two fingers up. If you see any activity inside, wave your hand over the ground. Alright?"

"Alright," Thezdan agreed. He crept over to a position beside one of the windows. With his shoulder against the wall, he craned his neck and peered into the house.

He was shocked by what he saw.

The interior was covered in polished stone, with magnificently ornate, metal buttresses rising from the floor to support the arched ceiling. From the ceiling's center hung a mirrored glass apparatus that cast light throughout the room, creating a beautiful, shimmering effect inside. There was very little furniture. The only pieces he could make out were a circular, stone table carved from a single piece of white stone that resided under the chandelier; a set of metal stools tucked under the table; and a legless stone and metal seat resembling a winged armchair set against the wall.

Thezdan pulled back from the window for a moment and looked up. Above him were the wooden eaves and thatched roof that had been the house's most identifiable feature from the road. He realized now that these features were but a disguise, masking the extraordinary metalwork and stonework that lay within.

Thezdan turned back toward the cart and made the two-fingers-up gesture he had been shown before. Lothic repeated the gesture back, and began hobbling over toward the house.

"What is this place?" Thezdan asked.

"It is Domin's house, as I've told you," said Lothic.

"Yes, I know, but it is not a normal house. What is that device that hangs from the ceiling?"

Lothic looked in the window and smiled. "Oh yes. I had forgotten that you have not seen Ymreddan. Imagine a place nearly the size of Riverstride, but buried within a mountain and filled with light like this. Here the light is probably coming from a hole in the ceiling. In Ymreddan ... well, perhaps you'll one day see it for yourself. It is no surprise that Domin has tried to create something here that reminds him of his home, though I would imagine that it does little to relieve the anguish of his exile."

"If this is all by his hand, then his skill is formidable."

"Indeed, it is. This is what's possible with three hundred years of steady practice."

Thezdan nodded. "In any case, the master is not home. What should we do now?"

"I don't see anything inside that might help us," said Lothic. He stepped back and pointed to the other side of the house, in the direction of the still. "We should work our way around the house, starting over there. If we're lucky, we'll find something that will point us in his direction."

Suddenly a voice called to them from nearby. "Hello? Who are you? What are you doing here?"

Thezdan turned to see a young man holding a long fire poke in his hands. He was well-fed, unusual for someone living outside the cities, with a broad, cherubic face. He affected toughness, but his soft body and the uncoordinated way he ambled with the fire poke made him more comical than threatening.

"We're looking for Domin," Thezdan said. "We've brought grains for his stills."

"No, you haven't. I hand-cut the grains myself, and our supplies are sufficient for the next month." The man stopped right in front of them and leaned forward into Thezdan's face, his breath reeking of dark spirits. "You wouldn't be the first peasants who thought they could sneak up here and steal from us. I think you should go before you feel the pain of Rokkin pole technique."

Lothic let out a deep belly laugh.

The man scowled. "Don't think I won't—"

Thezdan quickly slapped the man with his right hand, then he snatched the pole from him with his left. The man was too shocked to yell; he just rubbed his face, eying Thezdan.

"As I said, we're looking for Domin," Thezdan said. "Is he here?"

The man looked over at the cart and saw Lothic's sword; no peasant would have carried such a weapon. He took off running. "Help! Thieves!"

Thezdan hurled the fire poke like a spear at him, catching the man flush in the back with the blunt side. The man fell to the ground, shrieking. Thezdan leapt on top of him and covered his mouth with his hand.

"Look at me," he said to the wriggling man. "LOOK AT ME."

The man finally lay still, the color draining from his face.

"Good," said Thezdan. "Now, do you know where Domin is?"

The man shook his head.

"Are you lying to me?"

The man winced and shook his head again.

"How could you not know where you master is?"

The man's eyes welled with tears.

"You don't need to cry," said Thezdan, letting up a bit. "I just want to talk. So long as you don't scream, nothing bad will happen. Do you understand?"

The man nodded rapidly.

Thezdan removed his hand from the man's mouth and rolled off of him. The man sat up and held his head in his hands, sobbing.

Thezdan turned to face Lothic, who had come up beside him. "What do you think we should do?" he whispered. "He could give us away."

"Nothing," said Lothic. "He is innocent, Eodan. We cannot fault him for trying to protect his master's property."

"But if we leave him, he will alert a Party guard or patrol. Are we choosing his life over ours?"

Lothic nodded. "Perhaps, but maybe I can tilt things in our favor." He walked over to the man and knelt by his side. "What's your name?"

"S-s-suni," the man choked out. "Are you going to kill me?"

"No, Suni," said Lothic. "Did Domin ever mention a person named Lothic to you? Or perhaps Sithic?"

The man shook his head. "Domin doesn't talk to me much. I'm only here because my uncle on the Provisions Subcommittee of the Party got me this job. Domin gives me orders, and I do what he says."

"But he taught you Rokkin pole technique?"

The man looked up and wiped his eyes. He nodded and offered a shallow smile. "Yeah. Well, sort of. We were robbed once, so he taught me a few things."

Lothic reached for the fire poke and stood up. "Did he show you this?" Lothic raised the weapon above his head and spun it like a helicopter blade, then he pivoted on his good leg and swung the weapon with tremendous force. It whizzed right in front of the man's nose, making an intimidating *woosh* as it passed by.

The man lurched backward and covered his face, toppling over in the grass. A moment later, he sat up again and looked at Lothic. "You swing almost as hard as he does. How do you know how to do that?"

Lothic smiled. "That's a long story that I'm afraid we don't have time for. I need to find Domin. It's urgent."

"I don't know where he is," said the man. "He went north this morning, but there are lots of places he could have gone."

"Could anything here give us a clue?" Thezdan asked.

The man almost said something, then he hesitated. "Y-you promise you're not thieves, right?"

"We're not," said Thezdan.

The man sized them up again, shaking his head at his own predicament. "He'd be so mad if he knew I told you." He pointed toward what looked like a grassy hill nearby. "You should probably check his aging cave, over there. I'm not allowed in there, but if you tell me which barrels he took, maybe I can help you figure out where he went."

"That sounds like an excellent suggestion," said Lothic. "Eodan, let's go."

"Suni, why don't you come with us?" said Thezdan. "To show us the way."

The man got up and reluctantly led them in the direction of the nearby hill. As they got closer, Thezdan noticed a set of thin wheel tracks in the grass leading straight up to the slope, but they seemingly ended there. He was intrigued. The group followed the tracks all the way to a grayish, vine-covered object set into the hillside. The camouflage had worked from a distance, but now, close as they were, it was clear that this was something that didn't belong. Thezdan went over and cast the vines aside, revealing a simple, metal door.

"Lothic, you stay here with our friend," said Thezdan. "I'll have a look inside."

"Very well," said Lothic. "Let me know if you need help with that door."

Thezdan raised his eyebrows. He grabbed hold of the iron ring handle and pulled. The door proved much heavier than he expected; his initial tug barely cracked it open. Heavy it was though, he was determined to open it without Lothic's help.

He rubbed his hands together and grit his teeth. Grabbing hold of the ring, he pulled again with all his strength. The door lurched forward, opening just enough to let a man pass through. Thezdan turned around and raised an arm in victory. Lothic smiled and mimicked the gesture.

Thezdan squeezed through the crack he'd opened, finding himself in a short antechamber leading to a large, nearly pitch-black room beyond. It took a while for his eyes to adjust, but soon Thezdan was able to resolve a row of barrels arranged horizontally along racks. The room seemed to be shaped like a "P," its walls and ceiling supported by less ornate versions of the buttresses he had seen in the house. The left wall of the cellar featured a row of barrels resting sideways on fitted supports, along with a number of jugs on the floor. A center rack held a similar row of barrels trailing off into the darkness.

Thezdan pushed forward, using his hand to feel his way through the obstacles as he moved farther in. Around the corner, he noticed a change in the arrangement of the barrels. They stood on their ends here, with at least two or three arranged like this nearby. Suddenly, his shin collided with a hard, metal object. The object tipped over and hit the ground with a shrill clang.

"Shaper smite you!" he cussed, grabbing his leg.

"Are you alright?" called Lothic from the antechamber.

"I'm fine. I just banged myself on some sort of metal rod."

"Can you see anything back there?"

"Not really," said Thezdan. "I can't tell how far back it goes. There are a few barrels standing on their ends here, and I think I can see the outlines of some sort of contraption behind them."

"You might be right. It would make sense for there to be a filter-transfer device in there somewhere."

"Could it tell us anything?" Thezdan asked.

"Maybe, but can you find that thing you tripped over?"

Thezdan groped around in the dark for the offending object. He soon found it, a long, metal shaft connected to a flat plate at the bottom. It was warm to the touch. He took it back to the doorway and passed it to Lothic.

"It's warm … that's good," Lothic said. He turned around to

examine it in the light. "Eodan, can you tell me if the standing barrels are full?"

Thezdan walked back into the aging cave and tried to rock one of the large barrels from side to side. It was impossibly heavy. He returned to Lothic. "Yes, they are."

"Alright, then," said Lothic. "I'm pretty sure I know where our distiller has gone."

Thezdan followed Lothic out of the cellar and saw that the metal object was a stamp of some kind. "What is that?" he asked.

"It's a barrel brand. That's why it feels warm: the bottom was heated up until it was very hot, and then it was stamped against a barrel. The heat sears a name into the wood; in this case, the People's Rest. That's where Domin has probably gone."

"What makes you think we'll find Domin there? What if Suni is just lying to us and the Party has taken over the distillery, as you said?"

Lothic pointed at the brand's handle. "There's no wood here. A Rokkin's hand could tolerate the heat; a man's hand, not a chance. If the Party had taken over, these brands would have been sheathed with wooden grips by now."

Thezdan grinned. He could not deny Lothic's intelligence. "Hey, Suni," he called to the man seated nearby, "where's the People's Rest?"

The man pointed toward Riverstride. "I think that's the one just south of the southern drawbridge."

"He's right," said Lothic.

"You know it?" Eodan said, surprised.

"Quite well," said Lothic, showing a sad half-smile.

"Alright, Suni," said Thezdan. "We have to go, but I don't trust you to not make a bad decision."

The man covered his mouth, his face contorted with dread.

"Don't worry, we're not going to kill you," Thezdan continued. He ducked into the aging cave and returned a moment later with a stoppered jug. "But you have to choose. Would you like us to lock you in the hill, or would you like to drink this until I say stop?"

"Please just let me go," the man whined.

"I'm sorry, but I can't," said Thezdan.

The man slouched and reached for the jug. "I guess I'd rather drink."

Thezdan sat beside him and removed the stopper. The alcoholic vapors wafting out made his nose burn.

"Here you go," Thezdan said, passing the jug to the man. "Three good swigs, please."

"Ugh," the man groaned, smelling the liquor himself. "*Ashen Rain*. This one's so strong."

"I'm sorry," said Thezdan. "I hope you'll excuse our caution."

The man nodded meekly. He took a swig, holding the liquid in his mouth for a second before choking it down. He coughed wildly then wiped his face on his sleeve.

"One," said Thezdan.

The man took another swig and swallowed. "Ughhhhh," he groaned.

"Two," said Thezdan.

The man took a final swig. He shook his head from side to side, his eyes bugged out. "There, I did it! Now let me go!"

"Very well," said Thezdan. "Please come see us off, then you're free to go."

"Really?" said the man, smiling. "Okay, I can do that."

The group got up and headed back to the cart. About halfway there, Thezdan heard a thump behind him. He turned to see the man lying unconscious on the grass.

"He's going to feel that later," said Lothic. "*Ashen Rain* is indeed very, very strong. I'm surprised he even made it to a third hit on the bottle back there."

"Me, too," said Thezdan. "Come, Lothic, it's time to head out. The People's Rest awaits."

Lothic shook his head. "Eodan, that's too far into the heart of Party territory. Not only that, we would have very little chance of making it home by nightfall. We would have to hide somewhere or risk exposing ourselves to the Night Reapers. Why not wait a few days? We'll be able to meet up with Domin here eventually."

Thezdan peered into the eyes of his companion. His mind harkened back to his father's warnings to him when he was just a young boy. *Adhere to the curfew, and beware the Night Reapers, Nodan. They are much stronger than normal soldiers, and they kill anyone they find breaking curfew.* Even Eobax, strong as he was, had seemed afraid. Thezdan had never gone against his father's admonition, but today was different. He felt an urgency inside him that wouldn't allow for caution.

"I'm sorry, Lothic," he said. "I need to go today. You may wait here if you wish, and I will go alone, but I will not wait."

"What is going on, Eodan? I've never known you to be reckless."

Thezdan turned away. "It's the Vorraver girl. I feel a duty to her. Finding Domin may help us uncover some of the mystery around her arrival and purpose here." He rubbed his neck, trying to come to terms with the powerful feelings running through him. "I need to get back to her. I need to protect her myself. Aevilen is a dangerous place. I need to be there with her, Lothic. I don't trust anyone else."

Lothic paused to consider what Thezdan had said, a faint, almost imperceptible smile appearing on his face. "These feelings are your heritage, Eodan. But you must realize that you cannot serve her by getting killed or captured by the Party."

Thezdan was about to respond when Lothic raised his hand. "Of course," he continued, "your father would have said that the path of the Eo does not allow for the exchange of duty for safety. Very well. We will go find Domin, but we will have to be very careful."

Thezdan looked back at Lothic, seeing the resolve of a Guardian Prime. It was a side of him he hadn't seen since the Trebain. For once, Thezdan did not bristle at the mention of his father; instead, he felt a quiet pride that the man before him, the one Eobax had trusted over all others, could see the Guardian legacy in him.

Thezdan reached out and clutched Lothic's shoulder. "Thank you, Lothic."

Lothic saluted. "Of course, Eo."

Thezdan banged gently against the side of the cart. "Scylld, we've had a change in plans. We're going north. Our trip has gotten more dangerous. Be still on the roads, but also be ready to fight."

A rumble came from the back of the cart, causing some of the grain on top to bounce around. It was all Thezdan needed to hear.

"We are ready, Lothic," he said. "Goddess protect us."

Thezdan and Lothic climbed up onto the cart and took their seats on the driver's bench. A familiar crack of the reins put the cart back in motion.

"Let us hope that she can," whispered Lothic as he pointed the borum in the direction of Riverstride's distant, looming spires.

21

"Stop! Stop!" Julia shouted as she sank to her knees by the monastery gates. She panted, exhausted from the difficult climb up the mountain road.

Engar rushed to her side and helped her to sit. He offered her a drink from his pouch.

Julia took a swig and lay back against a gateway pillar. "Thanks," she said between breaths. "Just give me a second. I'll be fine."

Balyssa stopped and watched Julia and the two Guardians as they rested. "It would be best if we kept going."

"Do not push the girl too hard," Entaurion replied. "This is a tough trek for nearly anyone, and we have kept a very demanding pace."

"Tell me about it," said Engar as he took a big drink from his pouch and leaned against the wall.

Entaurion smirked. "It would be easier if you switched those two heavy hammers out for a bow."

"And then, instead of being tired for a moment, I would be weak all the time!" Engar replied.

"How strange to see the two of you show so little respect for the sacrifice of a Guardian Eo," Balyssa interjected. "Do you not know what happened here? Do you not know that this is the place where Eovaz returned to the Spirit Winds?"

Engar and Entaurion fell silent.

After a moment, Entaurion came forward and stood next to Balyssa. "I'm sorry. I was told as a child about Eovaz, but I didn't know that this was where he fell."

Balyssa pointed toward the library tower. "I watched from that window as Eovaz fought alongside the Order of the Key monks to keep the invading forces at bay. He was very skilled, but in the end, he could not resist so many."

"This is a remarkable place," said Entaurion, his eyes catching sight of the two great statues of the Goddess and Shaper. "To think that men could once carve stone like that … " He turned toward one of the old, dried trees emerging from a nearby building. "And tend trees for centuries until they were like living sculptures." He looked down at his own hands, rough beyond their years from hunting and foraging among the forest thickets. "What happened? What has become of us?"

"Do not despair, young Guardian," said Balyssa. "I have walked this world in service of the high and most beautiful Dancer for centuries. There are ebbs and flows to all things: to seasons, to lives, to eras. In periods of plenty or scarcity, happiness or sorrow, good or evil, the seeds of the other are inevitably sown. You are right to say that much has been lost, but it is not irretrievably lost; we are not yet beyond hope."

Julia made her way over to Entaurion and Balyssa. For her, the sight of the monastery library elicited anxious memories of her arrival. "Why are we here, again?" she asked.

"Because there are important things hidden here that you can help uncover," said Balyssa. "You need not be frightened."

Julia scanned the compound, taking in the jagged landscape and abandoned buildings. "I can't help it," she replied. "This place frightens me."

"You will be alright," said Engar, gently clutching her shoulder. "Entaurion and I will see to that."

"Thanks, Engar," Julia said. She was grateful to the Guardians; their presence certainly made her feel safer.

Balyssa began walking up the path toward the library. "Come. We have much to do."

Julia looked through the collapsed walls and open doorways of the buildings they passed. She saw into charred interior spaces that revealed small hints of the pre-Revolutionary past. There was a broad, metal basin, perhaps used for washing; a wood and metal chest, partly burned, standing in a corner; and, in one particularly long house that had been nearly completely destroyed, two rows of rectangular, stone slabs set against the walls at regular intervals, the bunks that the inhabitants had once used.

"Why did the Party attack this place?" she asked, imagining what it might have been like when hundreds of monks inhabited it.

"They destroyed as many of the religious sites in Aevilen as they could," Balyssa replied. "I grieved to see the shrines to my beloved Dancer defiled, along with countless others celebrating the Goddess and Shaper. This monastery, in particular, was special enough for them to risk significant losses to their army at the hands of the Sylvan. I once thought it was because they were chasing princess Elleina. I now believe that they destroyed this place because this is where Aevilen's Champion rests."

Balyssa's pace slowed as she approached the threshold mosaic set in the road. "Engar, Entaurion, may I ask you to give us some privacy again?"

Engar and Entaurion looked at Julia for direction.

Julia nodded reassuringly.

Entaurion patted Engar on the back and led him to one of the scorched buildings below. They sat down against a wall to wait.

Balyssa knelt down and placed a hand against the mosaic. "Stone has great memory. It cannot see like the leaves, but it will hold its message for eons if it has been carved or arranged."

Julia knew where Balyssa was leading her. "I remember reading a carved stone wall when I first came here. So that was like what happened with the trees, right?"

"Yes. Your necklace gives you power in both the Goddess's and the Shaper's domains, as I said earlier. These stones fall in the latter."

"Can you read what they say?"

"Only partly," said Balyssa. "The ornamental script is an early one, long out of use, and many of the words are archaic, their meanings forgotten or changed. This is why you are so important. You are not just reading the words when you touch them; you are experiencing them. In doing so, you are able to understand them in the same way they were understood by their original authors centuries ago."

Julia looked to the mosaic below their feet. Her eyes were drawn to its center, to the symbol that matched the centerpiece of her necklace and the thick, blue letters that had inspired a feeling of dread that first day.

"There's something about this mosaic," she said, thinking out loud. "Something very serious. It bothered me the first time I saw it."

"That's not surprising," Balyssa replied. "The text follows later forms of the Code that I've seen. When you look at the mosaic, you are probably seeing sacred law."

Julia dropped to her haunches and placed a finger against a block of text at the left side of the mosaic. As she began to trace the words, she could feel her necklace grow warm against her chest. A moment later, she heard a voice, though this one was far deeper than she had expected.

"The Fifth Principle: Seek Excellence. The Goddess and the Shaper exalt achievements that are the fruits of great effort, patience, focus, and skill. Pursue excellence in all your labors."

"This one is the 'Fifth Principle,'" Julia relayed. "There was something strange about it, though … The voice I heard was very deep, and it spoke without any inflections. It didn't sound like a man."

"Then it was Rokkin," said Balyssa. "That means that the mosaic was laid by Rokkin hands. It is strange now to think of man and Rokkin working so closely together, but I believe that there are many other works in this monastery of Rokkin origin."

Julia looked back at the mosaic and placed her finger against the blue tiles at the center. She traced the words slowly, still feeling an unsettling intuition as she looked at them.

"We Shall Protect Aevilen and its Champion, and We Bind Ourselves to this Purpose with the Forces that Bind Us."

"Bind ourselves with the forces that bind us?" Julia repeated in a whisper. "What does that mean?"

She began retracing the words:

"We shall protect."

Suddenly her ears detected something new. An anomaly.

"Aevi[pitter]len [pat]and [pitter] its,"

The sound was faint, but growing louder by the moment.

"Cham[pat]pion [pitter],"

Julia popped her head up in alarm. "I think something's coming!"

Balyssa turned toward the front gate. "Are you sure?" she asked. "I do not hear anything."

Julia placed her hand against a roadway brick behind her, and sure enough, the pitter-patter sound of an approaching animal came through again. "Yes. It sounds like a horse. Maybe a dog."

For the first time, Julia saw a look of concern come over Balyssa. Balyssa tilted her head forward, trying to hear the sounds Julia described. Suddenly, the electric energy in her eyes pulsed violently, and she ran down the valley toward where Entaurion and Engar were sitting.

"Rise! Rise, and be ready!" she shouted toward the two Guardians.

Engar rose first, his hand instinctively reaching for one of his hammers. "What is it?" he shouted back.

"Something approaches!" She suddenly stopped in her tracks and pointed. "There!"

Engar spun around. Just coming through the front gates, not more than 200 yards away, was an enormous, black wolf with a thick, white mane. It was easily taller than a man at its shoulder, and it ran with its mouth agape, showing the sinister white and red of its teeth. Churning toward them at tremendous speed, it inspired the terror of a nightmare made real.

Engar shuffled backward, transfixed, fumbling to draw his hammers. Entaurion ran up the path toward Balyssa as he worked to unsling his bow.

"Engar! Focus!" cried Balyssa.

Engar regained his wits and hopped over a nearby collapsed wall. He grabbed a large rock from the ground and waited. He could hear the beating footsteps of the wolf getting closer and closer. Then, as it came into range, he leaned out of the doorway and shouted, trying to draw its attention.

The creature didn't seem to notice. Its gaze was fixed on Julia.

Julia's necklace burst to life, flashing brilliant, blue light. She screamed and turned to run.

Entaurion notched an arrow and dropped to one knee. "Please, Goddess," he whispered under his breath. He faced the wolf and let his arrow fly.

A moment later, the arrow found its mark in the creature's front leg, splintering the bone above its paw. The creature let out a pained howl and fell. Engar saw an opening and rushed forward from the doorway, heaving his rock at the wolf's head. It struck but missed its target, glancing off the creature's shoulder.

The wolf rose to its feet; now Engar had its attention. Reaching down, the wolf grabbed the lodged arrow with its mouth and snapped it off at the wound. It locked stares with Engar and unleashed a hellish roar that pushed Engar backward.

It was then that Engar saw the otherworldly, red light emanating from within the creature's eyes. "Goddess save us … " he whispered.

"Engar! Up here!" Entaurion shouted, snapping Engar from his trance.

Engar turned and saw Entaurion standing amid the columns of one of the sacred buildings. He pushed off and ran as fast as his legs could take him up the valley toward where Entaurion waited. He could hear the wolf running behind him, getting closer with each step.

Entaurion notched another arrow and drew back his bowstring. "Down!" he shouted.

Engar leapt into a forward roll. He heard the hiss of the arrow as it whizzed by overhead and an angry growl from the wolf as the arrow lodged somewhere in its body. As he came out of his roll, the wolf roared again. Engar fought to keep his balance, waving Entaurion inside as he sprinted toward the building. Reaching down, he drew one of the hammers from his belt; this would be his only chance.

With all his energy, Engar burst forward and swung his hammer at one of the thin columns of the building. It met the stone with a tremendous thud, fracturing the rock. He pivoted and swung in the other direction, a huge chunk dislodging from the column's center. The wolf lunged forward as debris began to cascade around them; Engar raised his hammer in defense. The wolf's mouth collided with the shaft, its teeth stopping only inches short of Engar's throat. The weight and momentum of the massive creature hurled Engar through the air, his body crashing into the front wall of the building. The world seemed to spin around him as he gasped for breath. The last thing Engar saw before passing out was the building's façade collapsing, the great wolf howling as the stones fell around it.

"ENGAR!" screamed Entaurion. "ENGAR!"

Engar groaned. There was not a part of his body that didn't hurt, and Entaurion's voice sounded like an out of tune horn blaring in his ear.

"You're alive! You borum-brained fool, you're alive!"

Engar opened his eyes and saw Entaurion standing over him. The room was dark. Only a narrow stream of light beamed in from nearby.

"Get up!" Entaurion commanded, heaving against Engar's arm. "We have to go!"

Engar sat up and clutched his head with his free hand. "Where … "

"Now, Engar, now!" repeated Entaurion. "It's still outside! We don't have time!"

Engar rolled to his knees and tried to stand. Entaurion saw him begin to topple, and he slipped under Engar's arm to support him.

"What … what's … " Engar mumbled.

"That fen wolf is still outside. That noise is the sound of it digging through the rubble. I was barely able to pull you inside the temple before the columns came down!"

Engar cracked a smile. "You're stronger than I would have guessed," he slurred.

"And you're heavier than I would have guessed," Entaurion grumbled as he strained to hoist Engar up the first few stairs of a grand staircase leading to the second floor. "I sent Balyssa and Julia ahead. Hopefully, they've found a way out."

They were halfway to the top when they heard Julia's cry out, "There must be a way out of here! Come on!"

"That doesn't sound good," said Entaurion. "Come, Engar, we have to catch up."

Engar grunted, trying to propel himself along.

At the top of the staircase, they faced a long corridor with a brightly lit room at the end. Engar and Entaurion followed Julia's voice, arriving at a conservatory with a glass ceiling that offered a view up to the afternoon sun and sky. The whole room was bright green from the thick ivy that covered the walls and the moss that blanketed much of the floor. There was a persistent trickling sound from a circular fountain at the room's center that sent water out across a network of channels carved into the floor. On a dozen pedestals arranged around the fountain were the remains of potted trees that had been planted and carefully sculpted, but they were now withered and dead from neglect. Watching over it all, at the very head of the room, was a human-sized statue of the Goddess seated on a flower petal throne.

Julia and Balyssa were pacing around, looking for a doorway or stairway hidden under the ivy.

"You have spent time in the monastery; don't you know the way out of here?" Entaurion asked Balyssa.

"I have spent time here, yes, but I have never been inside this temple. It would have been inappropriate," Balyssa replied.

"What do you mean?" asked Entaurion, frustrated.

"This is not the time!" said Balyssa. "Julia, come read this!"

Julia looked over at Balyssa and saw that she had found a carved block of text behind a patch of ivy on the wall. She rushed over, adrenaline coursing through her body. She ran her finger along the words, and a man's voice came to her:

"May these trees reflect our Meditations and our Prayers to the Goddess, she of ever-true and ever-changing beauty."

"There's nothing here!" Julia exclaimed, pulling away from the wall. "Just religious words!" She looked around the room again, hoping to feel an intuition of the sort she had felt in the past. Nothing.

Entaurion lowered Engar down against the front wall and hurried to join Julia and Balyssa. "What do we do?" he asked, his eyes scanning the room.

"Keep looking," said Balyssa. "There must be something here."

Julia went down the wall looking for hidden switches or passages. "Should we go back to the entryway?" she asked frantically. "Maybe there's another way out over there! Or a connection to the library!"

Just then, Entaurion looked up and saw a possible way out. He ran back to Engar and took a hammer from his side.

"I knew this day would come," Engar teased weakly.

"Save your energy, Engar," said Entaurion as he smiled at his friend. "And besides, it's not what you think."

Engar shot his hand forward and grabbed the dagger concealed in Entaurion's belt. "It's a trade, then," he whispered as he drew the dagger out, revealing its long, curved blade.

"Don't get too comfortable with that," said Entaurion. "I'll be back for it in a moment." He moved into position midway down the wall. "Move over toward the statue, quickly!" he called to Balyssa and Julia.

"What is it?" Balyssa asked.

"Just do as I say!" Entaurion barked.

Once they were clear, he gripped the hammer with two hands and let it swing down between his legs. He looked up through the glass ceiling to the mountainside and sky overhead.

"Goddess, guide my hand or receive my body."

Calling on every ounce of strength he could muster, he hurled the hammer upward toward the skylight. No sooner had it left his hand than he dove away, covering his face and neck, and bracing for the inevitable impact.

There was a deafening crash as the hammer tore through the glass. Entaurion lay still as the shards fell around him, some smaller pieces tearing at his exposed skin. Once the shrill rain of glass had come to an end, he uncovered himself and looked up. Above their heads was a small hole in the ceiling, four or five feet in diameter. He could see the open sky beyond.

Entaurion stood and wiped the blood oozing from his hand, then he brushed the clinging shards off his body. He grabbed hold of a thick vine on the nearby wall and began to climb.

Suddenly, a terrible roar came rumbling through the corridor.

"We're out of time! The beast is nearly through the debris!" said Balyssa as she rushed to the center of the room. She looked over at Entaurion and pointed in Julia's direction. "Quickly, go anchor yourself and Julia to the wall. Grab onto the vines and hold tight!" She glanced at the hole in the ceiling. "We may yet be saved."

Entaurion knew that they no longer had time to climb to safety. He would have to trust Balyssa to deliver them from the beast, though he didn't know how. He ran back to Julia, holding her tightly in one arm as he gripped the nearby ivy with his free hand.

Julia's necklace glowed, helping keep her panic at bay. She grabbed hold of a vine herself, strengthening their anchor.

"Be strong," Entaurion whispered.

Another roar came, followed by the sound of bricks crashing down onto the stone floor. The last of the blockage had given way.

Amid the harrowing sound of the wolf's footsteps, Balyssa raised her arms at her side and began speaking in a language none of the others had ever heard. Her eyes crackled, arcs of electricity leaping across her face and arms as a strong wind gathered around her, drawn through the hole in the ceiling. Her chant crescendoed, the air in the room swirling faster and faster until it became a furious maelstrom that made the ivy convulse against the walls. Julia held on with all her might, barely maintaining her grip.

Just then, Entaurion caught sight of the red-eyed beast in the corridor. "It's near!" he yelled.

Balyssa raised her arms over her head and began floating above the floor. The winds grew stronger, pushing the potted trees off their pedestals and sending them crashing to the ground. The wolf fought to hold its ground, using the force of its roar as a counterbalance. Pane after pane of the glass roof shattered as Balyssa maintained her assault, pushing the creature back farther and farther into the corridor. Julia screamed, her strength failing. Entaurion wrapped his leg around her and hooked his foot in the ivy.

Then Balyssa began to falter. Her arms dropped to shoulder height, and the winds slowly tapered. The wolf muscled forward again toward the light; it would soon be upon them, leaving the group nowhere to run.

Engar saw the fear on Entaurion's face and knew that he had to act. Steadied by a long vine wrapped around his arm, he struggled to his feet and pushed forward toward the corridor, fighting against the wind. Then, as the wolf came into the light, Engar leapt forward, using the vine as a tether to swing into the corridor. The great wolf lunged toward him for the kill. Seeing his chance, Engar thrust his vine-entangled arm into the creature's gaping mouth; it bit down viciously, its teeth rending his flesh, muscle, and bone. Engar felt no pain as he jerked the wolf's head upward and buried Entaurion's dagger deep into its chest. He could see the primal agony in the creature's eyes as it bit through the last of his arm.

"Ouch," Engar deadpanned as he pushed the blade in further.

The beast stepped back and dropped Engar's arm from its mouth, gasping for air. Then it gave way to the winds, falling backward and disappearing into the darkness of the corridor.

Balyssa dropped her hands and fell into a crumpled heap. No longer supported by the winds, Engar was pulled backward by the vine and fell, writhing, to the floor.

Entaurion squeezed Julia. "I think we are safe now," he whispered, struggling to contain his emotion. "I have to go check on Engar!"

He ran through the room and knelt down next to his friend, a growing pool of blood gathering around his sandals. Engar flailed about, trying to prop himself up against the wall, his face contorted with pain.

"What did you do?" gasped Entaurion as he tried to make sense of what had just happened. "Engar, what—"

"Like the old stories, my friend!" gurgled Engar. "My arm is gone … but the beast … is slain!"

Entaurion looked down at the shorn limb and the life leaking from the open wound. "You saved us, Engar." He felt a tear run down his face, the first in a long time.

Engar forced a smile. "It was all for the … girl … of course."

Entaurion chuckled between tears, placing a hand against his friend's neck. Even as he lay dying, Engar's spirit was still very much alive.

"The Council will hear about this," Entaurion said. "They will give you the hero's title. I will tell my children that I fought beside Jagar, and they will be proud."

"Jagar … " Engar muttered, offering an almost imperceptible nod. "I like it."

But then, suddenly, a new hope: Entaurion caught sight of the remaining tangle of vine around Engar's arm. He knew that there might be a chance.

"Engar, forgive me!" he said, quickly shifting his body to pin Engar's arm against the wall. Engar groaned, but did not resist. Grabbing the vine with both hands—one above and one below—Entaurion pulled his hands apart and twisted. Engar offered only a muffled grunt as the tourniquet bit into his arm, staunching the flow of blood. Entaurion removed several arrows from his quiver and inserted them into the space between the vines. He twisted further to tighten the tourniquet, winding it tighter and tighter until the bleeding had stopped.

Engar let out a deep, guttural yell, no longer able to tolerate the pain.

Entaurion was grateful to see such a response; it meant that his friend might live. He removed his belt and used it to secure the tourniquet then knelt down beside Engar again.

"Engar, can you hear me?" he asked. "Are you aware?"

Engar beckoned for Entaurion to come close. "That … " he muttered, "that … HURT!" He brought his free hand over and pushed Entaurion sideways.

Nearby, Julia let out a sobbing laugh, born more of relief than humor. She came forward, wanting very much to give Engar a hug but thinking the better of it once she saw his condition. "Oh, Engar …"

"You're safe, Princess," he responded between winces. "The creature's dead."

Julia didn't dare look at his arm, which was mostly concealed by the vine tourniquet. She could see the blood though. She was glad to see Engar sitting up and responsive despite the trauma.

"Engar, I don't know what would have happened without you," said Julia. "Outside, when I saw that thing running at us—"

"Yes, I saw it too," said Engar. "In its eyes. The red fire in its eyes …"

"A red fire? In its eyes?" Entaurion repeated. "Are you sure?"

Engar nodded. "It was not natural. That beast was here to kill us.

I am certain of it. We can't stay."

"Let's get Balyssa and go," said Julia. Looking over her shoulder, she spotted Balyssa lying in a heap on the ground. "Balyssa?" she called.

There was no response.

Julia rushed to her side. "Balyssa?" she repeated.

Pulling back the cloth of her hood, Julia saw Balyssa breathing shallowly, the skin on her face and neck an almost transparent yellow-white. She had an iridescent glow like the one that she had displayed at the fort, but this time it lacked vitality, hanging like an ethereal fog around her. She seemed to be fading from this world.

"Balyssa!" Julia cried. "Are you okay? Balyssa!"

"Help me sit," Balyssa whispered in a weak monotone.

Julia reached down and grabbed a hold of Balyssa's arm, slipping her hand around her back to prop her upright.

"Thank you," Balyssa said. "It is too soon for me to return to my beloved Dancer." She pulled her hood back up and over her head. "I can sense that Engar's spirit has not left him. Is he alright?"

Julia looked back at the Guardians. Engar seemed to be in great pain, but he was talking.

"I think so," Julia replied. "He was very badly hurt, but I think Entaurion has stabilized him for now. How about you?"

"I will need to meditate to recover. I have very little energy remaining, and it will be difficult for me to travel with you." She paused to breathe a few times before continuing. "We must find the Champion's gate. We must know if it's here."

Balyssa strained to rise to her feet. When it seemed as though she was going to lose her balance and fall, Julia reached out and grabbed her arms.

"Are you sure you can stand?" Julia asked.

Balyssa nodded. "Yes. I just need to adjust to my present weakness."

Julia backed off as Balyssa rose to her full height and slowly walked over to where Engar and Entaurion were waiting.

Engar looked up at her. "Are you alright, Balyssa?"

"Yes. Weak, but alright. And you, Guardian?"

"I still breathe."

"My most high and beautiful Dancer's gift to man," said Balyssa, smiling. "Can you also walk?"

"I think so," Engar said, beckoning for Entaurion to help him up.

Entaurion came up beside him, wrapping an arm around his torso and helping him to his feet. "Are you sure you're ready to walk?"

Engar motioned his head forward.

"Very well," said Entaurion as he took a small step.

Engar grit his teeth and took a step of his own, and soon the Guardians were shuffling slowly but steadily down the corridor toward the entry hall. Julia and Balyssa followed behind. The light changed as they neared the end of the corridor, the entry hall gradually coming into view. They were almost to the stairs when Julia spotted an obstacle between them and the exit: a giant, black mass lying still on the ground. The carcass of the wolf.

"Oh, god," she murmured.

Entaurion heard her, and tried to offer reassurance. "It cannot hurt you anymore. Just ignore it, and focus on the daylight. We will be out of here soon."

Julia could feel a slight breeze coming through the corridor, evidencing Entaurion's words.

Focus, Julia, she told herself. *You're almost out of here.*

Julia closed her eyes, putting one foot in front of the other. For a moment, she thought she heard the sound of the wind growing stronger, and then something strange happened. She felt her necklace warming against her chest.

Her eyes sprang open.

Little had changed over the course of the few steps she had taken. Engar and Entaurion were a bit farther ahead now, but nothing about their body language suggested trouble. Behind, Balyssa was still following, her glow so dim that it barely reflected off the nearby walls.

Julia tried to close her eyes again. Another breezy sound whisked through the corridor, and this time she heard it: the faint translation of a new voice.

"Forgive me, Goddess."

Julia stood still, trying to understand what was going on. Balyssa came up beside her and stopped.

"Is something wrong, Julia?" she asked.

"I don't know, I think … I think I'm hearing things on the wind."

It came again: *"Forgive me, Goddess."*

Julia's eyes grew wide. "Did you hear that?"

"Yes," said Balyssa. "Those are the dying breaths of the fen wolf.

Its spirit is nearly ready to leave its body. Do not worry, it is much too weak to be a threat to you.

Julia shuddered at the thought that the wolf still lived. But looking over at the black mass again, she felt an unexpected feeling come over her: compassion. She heard the creature's words echoing through her mind, and she felt an intuition that this was not the same creature that had attacked her. She felt drawn to it. Despite her fear, she cautiously made her way to its side.

"Julia, what are you doing?" Balyssa asked.

Julia knelt down next to the wolf. She reached out and placed a hand against its shoulder.

The creature stirred slightly. "*I feel ... the Goddess ... in you. I beg ... forgiveness ... for what I have done.*"

Julia stroked its magnificent, white mane, the lower part of which was now wet and heavy with blood.

"*I am ... Shahelea. You must tell Nain. My will was ... taken ... I was ... so angry ... hungry ... It was ... a lifestone ... Tell ... Nain.*"

The creature exhaled for the last time.

"I forgive you," Julia said under her breath, letting her hand fall still on its side.

"It is gone," said Balyssa.

"I heard her speaking, Balyssa," said Julia, looking up. "She was pleading for forgiveness."

"Did it tell you anything?"

Julia nodded. "Yes. That she was being controlled by something called a 'lifestone.'"

Balyssa's expression changed. "Lifestones? Are you sure that's what you heard?"

Julia nodded again.

"Lifestones … " Balyssa repeated, her voice trailing off.

"Julia?" Entaurion's voice came reverberating up the corridor. "Are you coming?"

"We'll be right there!" she called back. She looked at Balyssa, seeing the lingering concern on her face. "What's the matter?"

Balyssa shook her head. "I would not have thought it possible, but lifestones in any form would imply Rokkin involvement."

"What does that mean for us?"

"I do not know. But I assume that we will soon find out. We should keep going. Entaurion and Engar are waiting."

"Okay," Julia said. "I will follow you."

Julia and Balyssa clambered over the rubble at the building's entryway. Entaurion and Engar were waiting just outside.

"What was the delay?" Entaurion asked.

"The wolf wasn't dead," said Julia. "I spoke with her."

Entaurion's expression hardened. For the first time, Julia saw anger in his eyes. "What do you mean? After Engar was nearly killed trying to protect you from that creature, you risked your life to talk to it?"

"You should trust her, Entaurion," said Balyssa. "What she senses can be very powerful."

"Don't worry, it was too weak to hurt me," said Julia. "Before it died, it told me something that might explain why it attacked us."

"What was that?" Entaurion asked skeptically.

"That someone was controlling it using lifestones. It said that we had to tell Nain."

The mention of lifestones meant nothing to Entaurion. But Nain … Nain was a name he knew. He shook his head, confused but no longer angry. "I do not understand what you've described, but Nain is the leader of the Sylvan. If you need to speak with him, then Sinox might be able to arrange it."

"Okay, then I will talk to Sinox," said Julia, relieved to see Entaurion's disposition soften. "Engar, how are you doing?"

Engar forced a smile. "Don't worry about me."

"He needs further treatment back at the fort," said Entaurion, "but he'll live. He's as tough as the iron he forges. You and Balyssa should quickly take care of whatever business you still have left to attend to here. I will see to Engar and wait for you."

"Is there anything I can do?" asked Julia.

"No," said Entaurion. "You go. We'll be fine."

"Try to hurry," Engar added. "This place is not safe."

"The Guardian is right," said Balyssa. "We should work as quickly as we can."

Julia nodded. "Okay. We'll be back soon. Be strong, Engar. We need you."

22

As Julia and Balyssa crossed the open threshold of the library, Julia's eyes darted around the interior's many shadowy spaces. The recent attack was still very much on her mind. Here, in this huge, cavernous space, she felt as though hidden monsters could lurk anywhere. She knelt down to touch one of the stones underfoot, waiting a few moments to hear its report.

Nothing.

"Are you alright?" Balyssa asked.

"Yes. I don't sense anything moving inside the library."

"You need not worry. It would be very difficult for something to hide from me in an enclosed, stone structure such as this; the air would bring me its sounds almost immediately. If we are going to be attacked again, our attacker will come up the valley as before."

Julia placed her hand against her necklace and took a deep breath to regain her composure. "Okay. Let's keep going."

At the top of the stairs, Julia glanced over toward the room where she had woken up her first morning in Aevilen.

"We're lucky that the Revolutionaries didn't find that room," said Balyssa from behind.

Julia stood in silence, thinking about her arrival. Not much time had passed, but so much had happened that that morning seemed more distant in her memory.

"Come," said Balyssa. "We're close now."

Julia followed Balyssa through the maze of standing and toppled bookcases, stepping over the dust-covered books that lay scattered across the floor. Along the way, they passed the last of the great columns, this one rising through the center of the floor. It was ringed by ornate, metal cabinets, each with a glass window offering a view inside. The cabinets were empty.

"What was in these?" Julia asked.

"Religious artifacts, artworks, legal manuscripts," Balyssa replied. "There were even some old weapons and personal items that belonged to Aevilen's heroes."

Julia looked at the empty cases and imagined them with their contents, like a display at a museum but illuminated by the multi-colored light of the library. "Sad that all that history is now lost."

"That was their aim: to strip Aevilen of its past. A people disconnected from their past are less likely to honor the gods of their ancestors, less likely to fight to preserve their culture and way of life. By destroying religious shrines and old monuments, by forcibly moving people away from old family homes and farms, the Party made subjugating the people of Aevilen easier."

Julia shuddered. "Frightening."

As they came around to the far side of the column, Balyssa pointed to a large, metal panel at the head of the library. "That's it," she said. "I believe that that mural hides a doorway to a secret archive."

"Really?" said Julia, walking up to it to get a better view.

At the mural's center were seated versions of the Goddess and Shaper, she with her ivy covering and floral, wreath crown, and he with his massive beard and shin-high boots. Their hands were extended, palms up, in the same sort of formal greeting Julia had seen Alana perform, though their heads and eyes looked straight ahead at the viewer. To the right and left of the figures were panels engraved with ornamental text, and across the top of the mural, in the same script, ran a line of words inlaid with silver.

It was a beautiful work of art, but nothing about it suggested that it might conceal a door.

Julia stretched her arm up to read the words running across the top. As she traced the letters, her necklace grew warm, and a Rokkin voice came to her:

"Aevilen's Future Is In Our Hands."

She shifted her attention to the panel at left, reaching out a hand to trace its words. She heard the same Rokkin voice:

"Passion United With Reason."

Julia shook her head, confused. *Why does Balyssa think that this is a doorway?*

She moved to the right and ran her hand over the final panel's text: *"Informed Always By Truth."*

She shook her head again then turned and shrugged. "It looks like artwork to me. I don't see any keyholes, latches, or knobs. Just religious iconography and some text."

"Did you read the words?" Balyssa asked.

"Yes, I did. Nothing special, just things like 'The Future Is In Our Hands' and stuff like that."

"Interesting."

"Interesting?"

Balyssa nodded. "Yes. The Rokkin have been known to use hidden mechanisms to lock doors. 'In our hands' may reference the statues themselves. Perhaps they conceal a hidden switch or lever."

"Do you really think that's possible?" Julia asked.

"I do."

Julia raised an eyebrow. "Uh, I guess I'll check again."

She stepped forward and looked more closely at the mural, probing the surface of the artwork for signs of hidden latches or unusual protrusions. When she got to the arms of the Goddess, she felt them give way ever so slightly to her touch. She pushed again, and, sure enough, the arms moved again. After a few tries, realizing that she wasn't getting anywhere, Julia also tried pushing on the Shaper's arms; those, too, moved slightly. But no matter how she manipulated the statues, nothing changed. The mural remained a solid, metal surface in front of her.

What are you hiding …

As she stepped back, her eyes were drawn to the text blocks on either side. She moved in front of the left panel and ran her hands over the words again.

"Passion United With Reason."

"What are you hiding," she repeated aloud as her eyes ran up and down the panel.

She placed a single finger in the first word, and slowly traced it out.

"PASSION."

And then the next: *"UNI—"*

Suddenly, as she was tracing and hearing the final part of the word, the metal moved slightly under her finger, shifting backward into the mural. Intrigued, Julia pushed hard against the word with both thumbs, to no effect. She explored the metal with a single finger again, and in a few spots on the right side, the pressure from her finger caused the metal to shift backward. She grabbed hold of two ornamental protrusions on either side of the word and pulled. The word, with an inch of metal plate on all sides, slid forward. She pulled again, and the metal plate came free, slipping from her fingers and falling to the floor with a loud clang.

"What was that?" Balyssa asked.

Julia reached down and picked up the plate from the floor, holding it up for Balyssa to see. "The words detach."

"What is that word you're holding?"

"It says 'United.'"

Balyssa pored over the mural, trying to make sense of this new clue. "Try changing the order of the words. What are the other words on the panels?"

"The panels say 'passion united with reason' and 'informed always by truth.' I'm not sure how those phrases could be rearranged … "

"'Passion united with reason' speaks to the combined influence of the Goddess and Shaper on Aevilen. Passion is in her sphere; reason in his. 'Informed always by truth' may refer to this library, or to the commitments made by the Rokkin and Humans when they made this place. But you're right; the words do not seem misarranged. There must be something here, though." She paused, then she stepped back and smiled. "I trust in your blessings, Julia. I will let you focus. Focus and believe, and surely all will be revealed."

Julia reached up and ran her hand over the banner text again. *"Aevilen's Future Is In Our Hands."* She looked down at the heavy, iron plate in her hand. This strange puzzle-door, if it was a door at all, seemed like a dubious test of her patience more than anything else. But as she looked down at the strange script, she was reminded of the intuition that had drawn her attention to the panels earlier.

Focus and believe.

Putting the metal piece on the floor for a moment, Julia placed her hands over the central figures of the Goddess and the Shaper. She closed her eyes and very deliberately ran her fingers over the contours of the statues, aware of every twist, turn, and bulge in the metal. A few times, she thought she heard whispers in the back of her mind, but they remained unintelligible. Slowly, though, her experience began to change, her mind becoming more attuned to the will and intentions of the artist long ago. She felt momentary impressions of his devotion to the Shaper and of his respect for the Goddess. And then, deeper down, she felt something so brief and fleeting that she wondered if it were real. For a moment, Julia became aware of the connections between the parts on the mural, her mind flashing the panels, the banner bar, and, finally, the hands of the deities themselves.

"The future of Aevilen is in our hands!" she exclaimed.

Her heart racing with excitement, Julia reached down and picked up the metal piece from the ground and carefully placed it into the outstretched hands of the Goddess. A moment later, she heard a soft 'click' sound from inside the mural. She then looked over at the Shaper.

Now what do I put in yours?

Julia ran her hand along the right panel again, trying to remind herself of its words.

"Informed Always By Truth."

It did not take long for her to find the pair; it was the only word that could make the phrase fit the spirit of this shared land and monastery. She plucked it from the right panel and delicately dropped it into the Shaper's hands.

United Always.

For a second, nothing happened. Then, the Goddess's and Shaper's arms began to drop, followed by the sound of moving cogs and gears. There was a loud pop, and then, starting from just below the banner text and running down the center of the mural, Julia heard bolts being violently pushed out of place, one by one.

Clang.

Clang.

Clang.

Clang.

Clang.

When the sound reached the bottom, Julia knew that she had solved the puzzle. "I-I think we're in," she said, staring at the mural.

"Excellent," said Balyssa, coming forward again. "Open it."

Julia pushed gently with a single hand. The center of the mural split in two, swinging open to reveal a short corridor in front of them. It was very dark and seemed to lead to a small room lit only by a single, narrow column of bright, white light from above. As Julia entered, the floor at the room's center began to shift, a mechanical contraption rising into the light.

"What the … ?" Julia said, shuffling back into the library.

"Do not worry, it will not harm you," said Balyssa.

Julia watched as the section of floor rose up further and split into four pieces, each piece using a reflective surface to redirect the light from above. The pieces tilted, and no sooner had they fallen into place than a complete network of prisms and mirrors revealed itself throughout the room, replacing the earlier darkness with a shimmering light. Julia stared back at Balyssa in disbelief.

Balyssa gestured forward. "The Rokkin are quite good at making dim spaces bright, aren't they?"

"Yeah," said Julia, awestruck as she took in the illuminated room. It had an oval shape perhaps twenty-five feet long by forty feet wide, with a high-domed ceiling supported by two smaller versions of the pillars in the main library. Eight elaborately carved bookcases holding large books ran along the perimeter on either side. But it was what lay beyond the light-directing apparatus that most caught her attention: a huge, iron door inlaid with gold and silver.

"Could that be it?" Balyssa wondered aloud, hurriedly making her way to the door. "Is this the Champion's Gate? I think we've found it!"

Unlike the mural from before, this was unmistakably a door. It featured a triptych of figures and scenes: the first panel, on the left side, showed a human woman with a golden crown standing in front of a walled town; the second, in the center, showed a Rokkin with massively thick limbs and a golden beard standing before a high-backed throne; and the final panel showed a Sylvan, a gold and silver headdress-like object atop his head, sitting against a tree. Running horizontally through the door's middle, bisecting each of the figures, was an iron braid with a giant, circular lock in the middle. The lock was inscribed with a ring of silver words.

Julia ran her finger over the words, soon hearing a Rokkin voice: *"Our Unity Will See Us Through."*

"What does it say?" Balyssa asked.

"It says 'our unity will see us through.'"

Balyssa smiled. "It makes sense! Julia, you've done it! This has to be the Champion's Gate! Aevilen's salvation lies just beyond this door! As I told you before, the Rokkin and Humans each received a piece of the key to open it. Those pieces will have to be unified to function. But ... " Her smile faded as she surveyed the triptych again.

"But what?"

"The door shows a Sylvan, too. I was not aware of a Sylvan piece."

"If I'm going to speak with Nain I could ask about it," Julia said.

"Yes, he would know. This gives you even more reason to speak with him. You must go as soon as possible."

"And what exactly would I ask him? Do you think he'll know about this doorway?"

"Blessed Sylvan like Nain can live longer than a thousand years. He will know."

Julia pursed her lips. "Alright … but what about the last piece, the Rokkin one? What happens if they won't give it to us?"

Balyssa shook her head. "I do not know much about it. Judging by the size of the hole in this lock, it's larger than I had thought. And if the Senior Elder will not give it to us, then we will have to find a way to take it from him. Domin used to be an Elder; he can unlock the door."

"Wait, what?" said Julia, startled by the suggestion.

"Hopefully it will not come to that, but we cannot let anything stop us." Balyssa came around and stood in front of Julia, staring deeply into her eyes. "You must always remember the stakes. This gate is the only path to victory. If we fail, the Still Lord will consume all that the Creator gods, in their beneficence, brought into being here in Aevilen. Afterward, when the Still Lord's army has grown even stronger from the slain left in its wake, the lower continent will be invaded. Many, many more will die a permanent death, outside the cycles of the Spirit Winds. Eventually the whole world will fall, and there will be only stillness. Oblivion. This is what we face. You must be willing to take any action or make any sacrifice in order to prevent that from happening. Life, even with just a handful of survivors, can begin anew. But should the Still Lord prevail, there is only the final end: nothingness."

Balyssa's words hung in Julia's mind like the ring of a dissonant bell. She looked into the bottomless, black pupils of Balyssa's eyes, the surrounding purple irises crackling with energy, and felt like she was falling.

"Go," said Balyssa, breaking her stare. "Retrieve the key pieces and bring them back to the monastery. I will remain here and research the key and the Champion. I expect some of these volumes to be recent enough for me to read and understand; even if not, I should be able to piece some information together. Once we have opened the Champion's Gate, if my strength permits it, I will send you home. Work quickly; we do not have much time."

Julia remained frozen from their encounter, watching Balyssa slowly make her way over toward the bookcases.

"Go, Julia," said Balyssa calmly, without actually looking at her.

Julia turned toward the doorway. After a few steps, she picked up her pace to a jog, never pausing to look back. Then, as she neared the grand staircase and caught sight of daylight coming in through the main doorway below, she ran. Her legs carried her down the stairs at a breakneck pace.

She was stuck in a divine contest of incomprehensible scale and consequence. And it was becoming clear that she had to follow the arduous, dangerous, and potentially cruel path down which Balyssa was leading her. She had no choice, not really; choice had always been an illusion.

Julia burst across the threshold and out of the library. Entaurion stood to greet her. He quickly realized that something was wrong. He rushed toward her, and she fell into his arms.

"Did she harm you?" Entaurion asked, keeping his eyes on the library and waiting for Balyssa to emerge.

Julia shook her head against his chest. "No," she said as she fought for breath. "No … "

Entaurion took a half step back and gripped her gently by the shoulders. "What's the matter? What happened?"

"I can't … " She shook her head again.

"Can't what?" Entaurion pressed.

Julia felt her necklace warming. For the first time, she resisted its influence, her trust shaken. But the longer she resisted, the more broadly the warmth spread until finally she gave in, allowing it refocus her. "I had hoped that this was it," she said quietly. "That I was going to come here, find the gate, and get sent home. But it's just the beginning! Now so much is riding on me, and I-I still feel so confused, like I don't even know what's going on! I don't know if I can do it, Entaurion. I just—"

Entaurion reached up and pulled his hood back, letting it fall to his shoulders. He looked at Julia and brought his arm up in a Guardian salute. "Whatever destiny has in store for you, you will not have to do it alone. We Guardians will be with you as long as you are here, no matter the stakes."

"He's right," called Engar from the ground. "I have a few more limbs left to give in your service. I am ready."

Julia smiled, some of her spirit and confidence returning. In these Guardians—and in Thezdan—she had found courageous and loyal companions. It comforted her to know that no matter how long the road ahead might be, she could count on the Guardians to be with her to the end.

"Thank you, Engar, Entaurion," she said. "It's hard for me, but I'm lucky to have you guys." She looked off into the distance, spotting the sun still several hours above the horizon. "Maybe we should go so that we can make it back by night. Besides, I'll feel better after someone's looked at Engar's arm."

"I'll be alright," said Engar, standing up under his own power.

Entaurion chuckled. "As I said, tough as the iron he forges."

Balyssa watched from the window of Julia's arrival room as Julia, Engar, and Entaurion made their way out of the monastery.

"Oh, my most beautiful and beloved Dancer," she whispered to the sky in the Eternal Tongue, *"Hear me, marvel of all the gods, the ancients, and the creatures of creation: I near the day of my redemption!"*

She spun around and headed back toward the hidden archives. The day had gone better than she had hoped. But there was still much to do, and she had precious little time.

23

Thezdan's eyes burst open. He lurched forward in the cart, reaching for his sword. "Julia!" he shouted, panting.

"Quiet, Eodan!" Lothic scolded in a whisper-shout. "Waellin is just ahead!"

Thezdan's body was covered in sweat, the nightmare shaking him even now that he was awake. The beast had seemed so real ... those eyes, with the unnatural, evil, red fire burning inside them ...

"Are you alright?" asked Lothic, sensing something was wrong.

Thezdan swallowed hard, still struggling to regain his breath. "A too-real dream. I fear something has happened to Julia."

"Do you sense that she's alive?" asked Lothic, suddenly concerned.

Thezdan closed his eyes for a moment, and somehow knew that

she was. He nodded. "Yes, I think so."

"Those may be the Whispers, Eodan. You may be bound to her in the way the old Guardians were to the Vorraver queens and kings they served. What you are feeling is likely what she herself felt. She must have been in danger. If she is alive, she is likely safe for the moment, but we'd best hurry."

Thezdan let his head fall into his hands. "I should not have come here. I should have stayed with her!"

"Do not forget, you are serving her now. Persuading Domin to help us will surely get Julia closer to her return home. Keep your head about you. The sooner we do what we came to do, the sooner we can return to her."

Thezdan breathed in deeply and exhaled. Reaching back, he pulled the hood of his tunic over his head and tried to steel his mind. *Keep her safe, Goddess,* he prayed silently.

Waellin was a small fringe town that extended out from the southern gate of Riverstride. It had never been rich, though it had once possessed a certain mercantilist dignity, bustling with the activity of tradesman and traders hawking wares to travelers and local shoppers. In recent years, it had been reduced to a collection of drab, ill-maintained row houses. All that remained of the town's past vibrancy were a few colorful patches of paint clinging stubbornly to the walls. There was little activity visible from the road.

"Does that look like it is still in use?" Thezdan asked, pointing to the stone tower standing ominously at the town's entrance.

"I do not know," said Lothic. "But we should assume it is."

"It's not going to be easy to talk our way through if we're stopped by guards. They're skittish these days, Lothic, much worse than you probably remember. It might be better to look for a different route, or even prepare to fight."

"Fighting is not an option, and there are no other routes. If you want to see Domin, you're going to have to trust me, Eodan."

A moment later, they saw the tower door open slowly, the blade of a Revolutionary Army polearm peeking out from behind the wood.

"You're a farmer," said Lothic.

"As you wish," Thezdan muttered.

The guard who emerged was slight in stature, his leather tunic hanging loosely on his frame. He fumbled around awkwardly with the polearm he carried, too weak to bear its weight. Unlike Domin's distillery aide, the guard showed the hardness of a man who had lived the difficult life of a low-level Party soldier.

Moving to the head of the road, the guard thrust his hand in the air. "Halt!"

Lothic dutifully brought the cart to a halt and waited for the guard to come forward.

"What business do you have in Waellin?" he asked gruffly. His cheeks were hollow, and he had a large, open sore on his temple.

"Hail Defender," said Lothic. "We're bringing grains for the troughs at the People's Rest, and then we will continue to Riverstride."

"Where are you coming from?"

"The Western Territories, near Breslin."

"Breslin?" the guard repeated, his curiosity piqued. "Did you witness yesterday's crimes?"

"Witness? No," said Lothic. "But we certainly heard about them. Hopefully the Revolutionary Guard will find the ones responsible."

"Indeed … " said the guard. He gestured at the sickly animal pulling their cart. "Do you have a permit for the borum?"

"I do," said Lothic. He reached into his tunic, pulled a piece of paper from an inner pocket, and casually held it up at his side.

"Give that to me," the guard ordered.

Lothic reluctantly handed over the paper.

The guard examined it for a moment then looked back at Lothic. "This is old, citizen," he said, his tone betraying his growing suspicion.

"Yes, it is," said Lothic. "But it's still valid."

"Is it?" the guard spat. "I don't recognize the signature. Strange, since Revolutionary Grimmel has been personally signing all borum permits for years."

Thezdan shifted in his seat, preparing to draw his sword. Without turning, Lothic reached back to stay his motion.

"Listen to me," Lothic said, his voice suddenly gratingly serious. "Do you know why my permit is old? It's old because I have been providing feed for the personal borum stock of senior Revolutionaries since the earliest days. Why don't you tell me your name so I can know who will go to the Pit in my place when Committee members are walking around with starving borum?"

The guard stepped back and tightened the grip on his weapon. He stared icily at Lothic as he grappled with what to do next.

Lothic turned and grabbed a small sack out of the wagon and

held it to his side. "You have done your duty. Let me do mine."

The guard examined the sack in Lothic's hand, imagining what it might be like to feel full again. If this man was who he said he was, stopping him could mean a year working the Pit, or worse. He offered a shallow nod as he handed back the permit and reached forward to receive his bribe.

No sooner had Lothic passed the sack over than he whipped the borum back into motion. "Be well, Defender of the Revolution!" he called as they drove off.

Thezdan held his position—and his tongue—as the cart moved past the guard tower and onto the narrow road that snaked through the village. The cart wheels clacked loudly against the cobblestones underneath, the sound amplified as it bounced back and forth between the houses walling them in on either side. All of the windows at ground level were shuttered closed even though it was well before dark.

"That was awfully close back there, Lothic," Thezdan said finally, tilting his head forward.

"Yes, it was. You were right about the guards being skittish. It makes me concerned about what awaits us ahead."

"Why? What is it?"

"The People's Rest used to be a preferred tavern for merchants and the occasional Rokkin. After the Revolution, it became a tavern for People's Army soldiers and mid-level Party leaders."

"I see," said Thezdan. "We're going straight into the *faeron's* mouth, then?"

"Yes, we are."

"If we're discovered, we'll be trapped. Your injury means that you cannot run, and this town looks to be sealed more tightly than a dungeon."

"Indeed. We must be careful."

"Yes, careful," Thezdan agreed. "And lucky."

Continuing down the road, they passed a slow, steady stream of tunic-clad townspeople, each carrying a small, wooden bowl in his or her hand. In the town's central square, several soldiers were serving stew out of a giant cauldron at the square's far end. The townspeople lined up to have their bowls filled. Even from a distance, Thezdan could smell the fetid odor of rotten meat, and he grimaced at the thought of anyone eating anything so foul. The townspeople, however, appeared to be less picky; those already served sat at long communal tables hungrily choking down the contents of their bowls. They rarely looked around at their tablemates, and they seemed to avoid conversation entirely.

Thezdan shook his head. Despite his occasional trips to Breslin, he didn't know that living conditions in the towns had deteriorated so greatly in recent years. He spotted the remains of a destroyed temple on the other side of the square, an old statue of the Goddess effaced beyond recognition.

"Better to look ahead, Eodan," said Lothic under his breath.

Thezdan snapped back to attention. He clenched a fist, aching for the opportunity to exact his long-sought revenge. But Lothic was right. With all the potential eyes around them now, he couldn't afford to look out of place.

Lothic guided the cart through the square and up the road at the far end. As they came around a bend, they saw the southern drawbridge leading to one of the four Great Gates of Riverstride in the distance. It was a different town ahead of them. Gone were the townspeople and ill-kept, row houses, replaced by empty streets and larger structures stretching nearly to the river.

"Let me guess," said Thezdan.

"As with the tavern," said Lothic, anticipating the question, "once merchant, now probably mid-level Party and army."

"Think they eat the sludge being served back there?"

"Probably not. But just so you know, the tavern we're going to is owned by a couple, Cobran and Elda, and Cobran has occasionally made things that smell so bad you'd have wished he were serving that stew."

"That doesn't seem possible," said Thezdan. "What would you do when he served it?"

"Eat it, of course," chuckled Lothic. "It almost always tasted better than it smelled."

"Almost always?"

"Almost always. You'll see soon enough; the tavern is just up ahead."

Thezdan looked up to where Lothic pointed. It was a two-story stone building not unlike the merchant houses surrounding it, distinguished by the size of its door and the large, open lot beside it. There were two black borum attached to Party chariots feeding from the lot's troughs. Beside them, farther in from the road, sat a large, metal wagon. It had an exotic, highly ornamented skeleton frame holding a complement of barrels, and four oversized wheels. There was no animal attached to the wagon but rather a long pole extending from the front axle, hinged near the frame, that had been tilted upward so as to allow it to fit in the lot.

"Thankfully, it appears that Domin is here after all," said Lothic.

"Even the Rokkin are not allowed to have borum?" Thezdan asked.

"The Rokkin don't use borum. Animals like borum are not suited to life underground, so the Rokkin have never kept them. They pull their carts themselves."

Thezdan smirked. "I know what that's like."

Lothic carefully pulled into the lot and parked behind Domin's wagon, hoping to partially conceal their cart from the road. He cinched the reins to the catch mounted in front of his seat then turned toward Thezdan.

"Eodan, I think I should go in alone. It could attract attention if we were to go in together, and you can keep our cover by transferring some of our grain to those troughs."

Thezdan shook his head. "No. If you get in trouble in there, you're going to need my help."

"If I get in trouble in there, there will be no helping me," Lothic said firmly. "Stay here with Scylld; if you hear anything that sounds wrong coming from that tavern, I want you to get in the cart and go."

"No," Thezdan repeated, looking back at Lothic with equal resolve. "I will not abandon you. I am coming in."

Lothic was silent for a moment, then nodded in resignation. "Alright. But be careful to not bring attention to yourself."

"Of course," said Thezdan. He checked the road behind them to make sure it was clear then spoke quietly into the cart bed. "Scylld, wait for us here. If something should happen, cry out, and we will come quickly."

The grain bales shook ever so slightly.

Thezdan climbed down from the cart. He heard a loud snort and glanced over to find the nearest of the Black borum looking back at him. There was something strangely captivating about the animal's large, black eye, filled with bestial menace. It brought him back to his dream, to the evil, red fire he had seen in the eyes of the wolf. And then, inside, he began to hear a rising voice, a dissonant, otherworldly growl.

You are late, Guardian! Aevilen will be mine!

"Are you ready, Eodan?" Lothic whispered, gently grabbing his arm.

Thezdan gasped as Lothic's voice brought him back to reality. His heart beat rapidly, the vision still anchored in his subconscious.

"Eodan?" Lothic repeated, sensing his unease. "Are you alright?"

Thezdan breathed in and out several times to calm himself. "Yes … still feeling the effects from my dream."

"I see. Gather yourself; we will not be here long. When we go into the tavern, wait near the front wall, over toward the bar. There should be a dark place for you to stand and observe."

"Alright. I will wait there and watch. If I see trouble, I will rap against the wall to alert you."

Lothic led Thezdan to the front door of the tavern. "I will listen and hope to hear nothing." He raised the latch and pushed it open.

It took a few moments for their eyes to adjust to the dim light of the room. Even with the tavern lit from the late afternoon sunlight and the steady candlelight from the table lanterns, Thezdan and Lothic couldn't make out anything more than general outlines of the patrons. Several large chandeliers overhead remained unlit, as did the many wall sconces; darkness here was by design. Even those who wore the fine tunics of Party bureaucrats hid in the shadows with their hoods up, leaning over their food or drink. In the back, two horn players rotely played some up-tempo tune. The music did little to relieve the heavy atmosphere of the tavern. The patrons were not here to converse and cavort; they were here to drink, eat, and forget.

Thezdan knew that every eye in the room was probably looking toward the door to see who had come in, and so he made a great effort to seem unremarkable. He followed Lothic down a few steps and over toward a long, wooden bar behind which an older woman stood, busy wiping down glassware as she furtively sized up her new guests.

Thezdan stopped short, ducking into an alcove. Lothic approached the bar and tapped gently against the wood to get the barmaid's attention.

"What can I get you, hunter?" she asked tentatively.

Lothic leaned over the bar, his hood hiding his face. "A braen of river white and the haerrit pie, warm."

The woman froze. Shocked, she nearly dropped the glass from her hand. "I'm sorry. We haven't served those things for a long time."

"A shame," said Lothic. "I never much cared for the rest of Cobran's cooking."

The woman swallowed hard. "W-Who are you?"

Lothic reached up and pulled back his hood just enough to expose the features of his face. "It's nice to see you, Elda."

The barmaid nervously checked left and right then slowly leaned forward. "Sithic?" she said. "How can it be? How do you still live?"

"I fled before the Trebain fell. I survived, living in hiding."

"Sithic, it is not safe for you here," Elda said under her breath. Her eyes darted around the room again. "It is not safe for anyone here!"

Lothic pulled his hood forward again. "I will not stay long. I've come looking for Domin. Have you seen him?"

Elda paused for a second then nodded. "I gave him a table and stool in the storeroom so he could take a drink after his deliveries. He usually likes to be left alone ... but if you need to see him, you can go knock twice on the storeroom door. He should still be there."

"Thank you, Elda. I'll be on my way. I don't want to cause you and Cobran any trouble."

Elda shook her head, her eyes showing a suppressed sadness that told Lothic all he needed to know.

"I'm sorry," he said quietly.

"These are bad times, Sithic," said Elda, choking back her emotions. "Don't come back here—for your own sake."

Lothic tipped his hood goodbye, then he turned and headed toward the doorway. Thezdan watched the room carefully as Lothic opened the door and went outside, wanting to be sure that no one in the bar would follow. After a few moments of no activity, Thezdan made his way out himself.

He found Lothic waiting for him back by their cart. He had a forlorn look about him, but wasted no time in beckoning for Thezdan to come.

"The storeroom door is over here," Lothic said gruffly.

"Wait," called Thezdan. "What is it, Lothic? What troubles you?"

Lothic halted in his tracks. "It doesn't matter," he said, his fist tightly clenched at his side. He took a deep breath. "It's too late now, anyway. We need to focus. Be ready." He walked over to the storeroom door and pounded out two strong, deliberate knocks.

Bang ... Bang ...

Several moments passed without a response. He knocked again.

Bang ... Bang ...

This time, there was movement inside. Thezdan could hear the muted thuds of heavy footsteps just beyond the door. He grabbed hold of Lothic's tunic and pulled him back a step, just far enough that he might have time to react if the Rokkin attacked. There was a scratching sound from a sliding lock, followed by the clanging of a chain being unwound. Suddenly the large door sprang open, revealing an enormous figure looming in the doorway. He was nearly Scylld's size, and he wore a simple pair of leather pants with a sleeveless, wool tunic on top. Though his features were exaggerated, he looked in many ways like a human man except for his ashen-gray complexion and short, wiry, metallic-gold facial hair.

Lothic quickly raised his hand in a fist to his side and bowed his head. "Borrenon ommag Domin," he said, his voice quivering faintly.

There was silence as the giant figure stared down at them expressionlessly. When finally he spoke, the air shook with the contra-bass rumble of his voice.

"Sithic," he said. "I thought you had been reclaimed."

"No, Domin," said Lothic, looking up. "I still live." He paused a moment, trying to gauge Domin's intentions. "Do you wish it otherwise?"

"You believe I wish the unmaking upon you?" Domin asked. He let out a rumbling chortle. "No, I do not."

Lothic bowed his head again. "I have missed seeing you all these years, bren Simarron."

A faint smile appeared on Domin's face. "You remember our tongue, yor Domin barrog Simarron. Come in, let us speak inside. I know the risk you took in seeking me here, so I am sure you have something important to discuss."

Thezdan and Lothic entered the storeroom and Domin closed the door behind them, resetting the sliding lock and chain.

The interior was darker than the bar, illuminated by a single candle on a large, round table. Thezdan could only barely see that they were standing in a two-story space, the nearby tall, mostly-empty shelves extending almost all the way to the ceiling. On the floor were several barrels standing on their ends. He tried to resolve their stamps, wanting to compare them to the one he had seen in Domin's cellar earlier, but it was too dark to do so.

"Sithic, is your companion of you?" came Domin's voice in the darkness.

"No, Domin," said Lothic. "He is not my son. He is Eodan, son of Eobax, the leader of the Guardian Clan reclaimed when the Trebain was sacked."

"Yes, I met Eobax," said Domin, his footsteps receding. "He was well-made. Enbor ymad nal Brod Simarron."

"What did he say?" Thezdan asked in a whisper.

Lothic leaned in close. "It was a blessing. It translates as 'May the Great Shaper grant that he be recast.'"

Domin came back toward them, his golden beard reflecting some of the candlelight.

"Thank you for your words," said Thezdan. "My father was a good man, a good leader."

Domin placed a clutch of candles on the table and set about lighting them. "And you, young Guardian," he said, looking up at Thezdan, "you bear the Eo title. Tell me: where do you lead your Clan in this difficult age?"

"I am not an Eo, nor is Sithic, as you knew him, still Prime," Thezdan said, shaking his head. "I am Thezdan, a Searcher; and he is now Lothic, Prior-warrior."

Domin let out a deep laugh that reverberated off the wooden floor and walls of the building. "I have never understood your titles. Has he who was once Prime really ceased to know the things that made him a great warrior? Is he to be trusted less in matters of war than the youngest En?"

"Domin, much has changed," Lothic interjected.

"Indeed it has," said Domin. "But has time really extinguished the warrior's fire within you? And you, young Thez, who once led men well enough to be called Eo, are you not what you once were? Will others no longer follow you if you lead?"

"Bren Simarron, we have important things to discuss," said Lothic. "Let's—"

"I would hear his answer, first," said Domin, cutting Lothic off. "Tell me, Searcher, will others no longer follow you?"

Thezdan was lost in the candlelight, his mind replaying the flight from the Trebain to the forest. He tried to pull those memories forward, imagining what it might be like to be to lead his Clan again. "I do not know," he answered finally.

"I see," said Domin. "Then you should keep searching." He turned toward Lothic. "Tell me, Sithic, what has made you come to see me after all this time? What is so urgent that you would follow me to the gates of Riverstride?"

"It is urgent, yes, though much of it remains outside my understanding. Eodan brought a lost woman to our settlement yesterday. He had found her alone wandering in the western forest. She claimed to be Princess Elleina's granddaughter."

"Was she?"

"I believe so, yes. She wears an artifact, a magestone artifact."

"Magestone?" Domin repeated skeptically. "Are you sure?"

"Yes, Domin."

"This artifact, what did it look like?"

"Like the symbol on the royal crest."

Domin rumbled pensively. "Does she show any powers?"

"Actually, she does," said Thezdan. "Her necklace shines brightly when she's in danger, and she seems to have remarkable facility with language. She was able to understand the Sylvan despite not being a Guardian."

"I believe she also shares the ancient Guardian-Vorraver connection with Eodan," Lothic added.

"I see," said Domin, pausing to think. His breath hummed like wind passing through a cave. "Then there can be no question that the girl is who she claims to be. Her artifact sounds like one of the fren sin alburred, the three key pieces, that contain the blessings of Gahaella and Brod Simarron. It would not offer its powers to someone unless they descended from the Vorraver bloodline."

"There is more, Domin," said Lothic. "Another woman appeared shortly after the Vorraver did. She announced herself as Balyssa, and she claimed to be the one who had summoned the girl."

Domin's expression changed at the mention of Balyssa. "So the spirits stir? I met Balyssa during the early days of the human Revolution. She is Keffig yor Kalon, one of the Spirit Dancer's Handmaidens, and she was indeed involved in Princess Elleina's flight. I have never known to where Balyssa sent Princess Elleina. I am not surprised she returned with one 'of Ellenia' and not the Princess herself because humans live such short lives."

"But why now? Is there a reason she is here now?" Lothic asked.

"Surely," said Domin. "The Keffig do not typically insert themselves into the affairs of the living. Their task is to ensure that the cycle of spirit release and return to the Spirit Winds continues, and that is a process with which very few things can interfere. For a Keffig to have appeared suddenly, with a bearer of a key piece, is an ominous portent."

"Perhaps then it is as we were told," said Lothic. "Balyssa claims that a cult of the Still Lord has established itself here in Aevilen, and that it is working to summon a Champion."

"Kron Diggur … " said Domin gravely under his breath. "For the Rokkin, even discussion of him, he you call the 'Still Lord,' is a grave offense. You say that a Keffig has warned you that one of his Champions is to be summoned? I dare not believe it."

"Yes, I also thought it impossible at first," said Lothic. "But perhaps it makes sense. How else does one explain the Party's depredations? Perhaps the Party is, as Balyssa claims, a front for the Still Lord's cult."

"The Party?" Domin echoed, his tone growing tense. He turned to the side, leaning against the warehouse racks. "The Party is a cult? The Party … Kron Diggur … NO!"

Suddenly the giant Rokkin dropped to his knees, the floorboards cracking under the force of the collision. With a massive blow from his fist, he shattered an empty barrel beside him.

"REDYAR!" Domin boomed. "My mind burns, Sithic! My mind BURNS!"

"Watch out, Lothic!" Thezdan exclaimed, grabbing Lothic's shoulder and pulling him away.

"Falbor nal Brod Simarron!" Domin groaned, gripping his head in his hands. "I am weak-minded, Sithic! I knew, years ago in Ymreddan, that the Party was supporting Redyar from outside. Now he still lives, which, as even back then he was showing the grod yor balog, the death glow, should not have been possible! But you have brought me the explanation!"

"The Cult," Lothic murmured.

Domin let his hands fall. He slouched, his heavy breathing making the candle flames tremble. "We are forbidden to speak of Kron Diggur because this has happened before. Generations ago, the Elder Fargius discovered a way to extend his life. He took blessed fildreman arrod, the high lifestones mined from the caverns of Ymreddan, and corrupted them with the dark magic of Kron Diggur. Those energies bound his flesh together again, but they also came to control him. Eventually he was not a Rokkin at all, but a soulless golem bound to an evil god. Through the promise of extended life, other Elders were persuaded to give themselves over to Kron Diggur. It was only Uleric, Senior Elder of the Council, who stopped it."

"Wait," said Lothic. "Uleric, whose statue fills the entry hall?"

"Yes," Domin replied. "Our most honored ancestor. As Fargius and other Elders were turning from the Brod Simarron, seeking eternal life through the desecration of His gifts, Uleric chose to be an example of the old ways. Already gripped by the grod yor balog himself, he sat in the main hall and meditated. For weeks on end, he barely moved, and all in Ymreddan—from the young to the Elders—could watch as day by day his deathlight grew stronger. And then, finally, he crumbled, his cloak found resting upon the shards of his former being. He reminded us that *this* was the way of the Rokkin; *this* was what the Brod Simarron had intended when he shaped us!"

"But what became of the cultists?" asked Lothic.

"A great and harrowing battle inside the halls of Ymreddan itself. It is why we treat the blessed lifestones so seriously, and why you and I were exiled over the one found in your quarters."

"I had not put it there!" Lothic protested. "I would never have betrayed you!"

"I know," said Domin. "It is clear that it was Redyar. He follows the path of Fargius, I am sure of it now. He is not conducting the corrupting rituals in Ymreddan; he could not keep such a thing secret. But once you told me the Party masked a cult of Kron Diggur, the evidence all fell into place. They are his conspirators. It was there in front of me all along. Ymreddan may be in the grip of the darkest of the Dark Lords."

"Then we may be in terrible trouble," said Lothic. "Balyssa told us of another Champion, Aevilen's Champion, that may be able to save us. But to get to it, we would need to reassemble a divided key, one piece of which is in Rokkin hands."

Domin rose from his knees and stood at his full height. "She is right! We must rouse the draeggor, the beast that slumbers deep in the great mountain! With it at our side, we will wipe the stain of Kron Diggur from Ymreddan and Aevilen both!"

"But if Redyar is indeed aligned against us, I cannot see how we could possibly get the Rokkin piece," said Lothic. "We cannot ask for it, and we do not have the strength to take it."

"There may be another way," said Domin. "Even if Redyar has turned, I am sure that some of the other Elders remain true-cast Rokkin. We will go to the Elder Council."

"What?" said Lothic, startled by the suggestion. "Even if we could, what good would that do?"

"Every Elder is told the secrets of the alburred keys and the draeggor when they ascend to their seat; such has been the case since the last time the Champion's Gate was sealed over a millennium ago. There is also an oath that is taken that requires the Council to give audience to any Sylvan or human bearing one of the key pieces. This is how we will proceed. We will have the Vorraver girl request an audience, and she will stand before the Council and tell them what you have told me. The Elders will award her the key piece ... and perhaps Redyar's treachery will be revealed!"

"Wait," Thezdan interjected sharply. "You would send the girl before the Council when we believe that the Council's head allies himself with the Party? The moment she steps foot in Ymreddan, she will be killed!"

"You do not understand our oaths," said Domin. "She will be safe. Elder Ormold and the entire warrior caste will ensure it."

"And what if Ormold has turned? What if he too is corrupted?"

"He is not. I have known Ormold for seven times longer than you have been alive. He is the one Elder I would never doubt."

Thezdan shook his head. "I cannot … !"

"If we were to try to gain an audience with the Council," Lothic interrupted, "how would we go about it? Are you sure it's even possible?"

"We would have to take the girl to meet with the Ambassador in Riverstride," said Domin. "He would bring word back to Ymreddan that she has requested an audience."

"Do you think we can we trust the Ambassador?" asked Lothic. "Would he tell us if an audience were safe for the Vorraver girl?"

"Ullor? He was once as you were to me, Sithic: yor Domin barrog Simarron. He was the first apprentice I shaped. He continues to visit me even though the consequences would be severe were he discovered."

Lothic nodded. "That is certainly reassuring." He looked over toward Thezdan. "Eodan, will you at least agree to a meeting with the Ambassador?"

"Perhaps, but would it be possible to meet outside the city? At your house, Domin?"

"No, Eodan," said Domin. "I cannot be a part of the initial meetings; I am jobbur, unwelcome. Ullor would risk his position by accepting a formal invitation from me. The only way for this to happen is for you to arrive at the embassy with the girl and to request the meeting directly. Do not worry; I can provide you cover to get there."

"That's it?" Thezdan said, his frustration rising. "We just walk up to a Rokkin warrior in Riverstride and demand a meeting? And trust them not to alert a Party patrol?"

"As I said before, it would be against Rokkin tradition to do so," said Domin. "We handle our own affairs. Turning you over to Party patrolmen would be bidroddam."

"Dishonorable," Lothic clarified.

Thezdan sighed. He put his elbows on the table and leaned over in a slouch. "You're convinced, aren't you Lothic? You think that this is the only way?"

"Yes, Eodan," Lothic replied. "For now, yes."

"I don't like it," said Thezdan. "It comes with great risk for Julia, and the result is too uncertain. But I know that she cannot sit idly by, as that will bring her no closer to her return home … We should go back to the fort with Domin. We'll talk to Julia and Balyssa and see what they say. If they approve, then we can go to Riverstride tomorrow."

"What do you think, Bren Simarron?" Lothic asked.

"I think he suggests a wise and measured approach," said Domin.

"Very well," said Lothic. "I will go with Domin and show him the way. It is getting late, though; perhaps we should wait out the morning at Domin's house."

"No," Thezdan replied. "It is still several hours until dusk. We should be far enough west by then to be clear of the Night Reapers."

"But the three of us cannot leave together," said Lothic. "It would arouse too much suspicion. Even with a meager, thirty-minute delay, the later cart would be at great risk."

"Given your leg, I think Scylld and I might fare better than you and Domin should trouble arise," Thezdan replied. "But I'm not worried. It should be easy for me to make it through the western plains by nightfall, even with the delay."

"Perhaps you should go ahead, Eodan?" asked Lothic. "Even with a night in Domin's house, he and I will be back at the Fort before midday tomorrow."

Thezdan recalled his unsettling intuition that something had happened to Julia, that she'd been in mortal peril. Then he heard the voice in his head again. *You are late, Guardian! Aevilen will be mine!*

"Something is happening," said Thezdan. "With each moment the danger for Julia, for everyone, is growing. We cannot spare any time at all; we must all go tonight."

"That is the resolve of an Eo," said Domin, smiling. He turned and made his way over toward the barred door of the storeroom. "Come, Lothic; his mind is made. Let us go."

"As you wish, Eodan," said Lothic, resigned. "But do not risk being seen by the by the Night Reapers. Remember, you can do no good if you are dead."

"I will follow in half an hour," said Thezdan. "We'll meet back at the Fort this evening."

Domin unwrapped the chain and pushed the bolt aside. He opened the door slowly this time, scanning the alleyway and road beyond.

"Mor boddir nal Brod Simarron," he said, turning toward Thezdan and raising his massive hand in a clenched fist at his side. He then stepped out into the afternoon sun.

Lothic followed and pushed the door closed behind them, leaving Thezdan alone in the storeroom. Thezdan let out a long exhale and turned back toward the glowing candle at the center of the table.

"Don't fail me, light."

24

The sounds of heavy footsteps and clanking chain mail filled the cathedralesque throne room, punctuated by a sudden thud as the chest hit the floor. Late afternoon sunlight streamed through the windows of the second-floor gallery, casting long shadows from the statues of Aevilen's heroes above. Two young Rokkin, their chest-length beards hanging over colorful dress tunics, stood at attention on either side of the chest.

"We present these blessed fildreman arrod to you as a gift of friendship between our peoples," said Redyar from behind, lifting a raised fist in salute. Over the woven gold of his Senior Elder's shawl flowed his giant, silver beard, a trophy grown over a centuries-long lifetime. Its strands matched the two long, silver streaks that ran from his eyes down his cheeks.

Grimmel leaned forward in his throne and admired the box. Even half full, it would be an excellent harvest indeed.

"Thank you, Elder Redyar," he said with unctuous gratitude. "Your gift will heal many of Aevilen's sick and wounded. Surely there could be no greater token of your great and enduring friendship."

"Of course, Revolutionary Grimmel. May our friendship last as long as the mountain stone."

Grimmel stood and waved his hand, dismissing the human and Rokkin soldiers gathered in the room. "Leave us, all of you. I wish to have private audience and counsel with Elder Redyar."

Redyar nodded at the assembled Rokkin, who then turned and filed out. When the heavy door closed behind the last departing guard, Grimmel rose from his throne and descended several stairs to where Redyar stood.

"It appears you have done very well," Grimmel said, his tone pleased but no longer obsequious.

"I am working the miners hard, as you instructed," said Redyar. "It is not without risk. Already some of the Elders question the impact of our pace on the structural integrity of the shafts below Ymreddan. I may not be able to keep them in line for long."

"It does not matter," said Grimmel. "We are very close to our aims; we will not need their assistance much longer." He gestured toward the chest. "Now, show me what you've brought."

Redyar reached down and pulled open the top. The red crystals inside radiated a soft light, and they were large—larger than usual.

The Master would be pleased.

"Outstanding!" Grimmel hissed, his gaze fixed on the gleaming treasure. "Are there any great lifestones?"

"Not in there, Lord, though we have finally found another."

Grimmel looked up, his nostrils flaring. "Where is it?"

Redyar reached into a pouch under his tunic and brought forth a very large, radiant stone. Unlike the others, this one shone with a brilliant, prismatic light. "No finer fildreman arrod has been found in a century," he said without emotion. "This one would have grown to be an Elder, surely."

Grimmel reached out and received the crystal. He turned it around several times, examining it from all sides. It was flawless, a thing that in the hands of the Master would yield such pure, magnificent power that Grimmel's mind swirled even to consider it.

"Grimmel," Redyar interrupted. "My deathlight is getting brighter. I will not survive much longer without assistance."

Grimmel looked back at Redyar with a malevolent grin. He tucked the crystal into his pocket and withdrew a different, smaller crystal that emitted a deep, red-black glow.

"The Master knows that you have been a good and faithful servant, Redyar," he said. "You should live to see the hour of our triumph."

"Terrenon sim boddir nal Kron Diggur," said Redyar as he received the crystal. "I will be ready."

Redyar turned away from Grimmel and popped the crystal into his mouth, swallowing it whole. He closed his eyes, groaning as he felt it work inside him. He reached down and pulled his golden shawl and tunic nearly up to his chin, looking for visual confirmation of what his body felt. A deep wound glowed a bright reddish-brown color at the center of his chest. A web of shallow fissures fanned out from the injury all the way to his sides. As he watched, some of the fissures began to close, and then others. Bit-by-bit, the stony-gray flesh of his body sealed his death glow away. Within a minute's time, virtually his entire chest had healed; the only remnant of his former condition was a smaller version of the central wound.

Satisfied, Redyar let his clothes back down. "I will take my leave and await your summon."

"It is time to begin your final preparations, Redyar. We will call for you shortly."

Redyar's body burned with the essence of the corrupted lifestone. Combined with his strength—that of the most ancient of all living Rokkin—his new energy would ensure that none would be able to resist him in these final days. Such was the power of Kron Diggur.

25

Thezdan walked over to the storeroom door and cracked it open, scanning the open lot outside. Only his cart remained; beyond, the street looked empty. A half hour had passed since Lothic and Domin had left. It was time to go.

He slipped out into the lot and moved quickly across the open ground, unhooking the borum from its hitching post before climbing onto the driver's bench. He reached behind into the grains and pulled out his sword just far enough to expose the top of the hilt, giving him easy access should he need it.

"O-na," he called, sending the borum ambling toward the street with a flick of the reins. He discreetly elbowed the storage bed behind him, producing a muted thud that ran through the old, wooden boards of the cart. "You back there, Scylld? We might have a busy evening."

Scylld let out a rumble from beneath the grain.

"Alright," said Thezdan. "Be ready."

Thezdan whipped the borum to a trot, guiding it around the bend leading to the town square. The sun was still a couple hours or so above the horizon, but the streets had already cleared. The residents knew all too well that the curfew was not to be taken lightly; it was better to be inside well before sundown than to be outside and under increased scrutiny from the guards. As he passed one of the houses, a pair of arms shot out of an upper window, grabbed hold of the open shutters, and quickly swung them closed. There was an almost palpable dread that hung in the air. Thezdan thought he could sense eyes watching him through cracks and slits as he moved up the road.

Suddenly, he heard a shout. Up where the road intersected with the square, a wiry man wearing a tattered, Party tunic tumbled onto his side. The man scrambled to right himself. Though Thezdan was still some distance away, he could hear the man pleading with someone.

"Please, please! I haven't done anything!"

A guard captain appeared, strutting over toward the man with his polearm held out menacingly in front of him.

"I stole nothing!" whimpered the man as he cowered before the guard.

The guard spun around and delivered a brutal blow to the man's arm with the shaft of his weapon. The man fell over sideways again, writhing in pain.

Thezdan continued on, doing his best to ignore the cruelty.

The guard looked up at the cart for a moment, then he turned back toward the man. "You thought we wouldn't see you scraping the bottom of the cauldron? Do you think you deserve to eat more than the other citizens?"

"I didn't! I–I'm sorry!" the man wailed. He closed his eyes and braced for another blow.

"Make way, please, Revolutionary," Thezdan called ahead. He was loath to bring attention to himself, but he needed to pass. He also hoped the distraction might spare the man further punishment.

The guard captain looked up at the cart again. "Who are you, and why are you out so late?"

Thezdan stopped the cart and waited for the guard to approach. "It is still more than two hours before curfew, Revolutionary, and I need to get this grain down south. I just finished a run to the People's Rest, and a Rokkin distiller I found there told me that he was very low on grain stock. It is less than an hour from here, and he has offered me a roof for the night. I figured that if he's supplying the People's Rest, then his work is important to the Revolution."

"Are you aware that we don't make exceptions for curfew?" the guard asked.

"I am."

"It is your life to lose, then. Move on."

The guard stepped aside, and Thezdan whipped the borum back into motion. He was quietly pleased to discover that the battered man was gone, having scampered off to hide somewhere. He could only hope that the guard had lost interest in hunting the man down.

As the cart passed through the square, Thezdan looked toward the spot where the townspeople had been eating earlier. He saw a small group of citizens wearing the tattered tunics of lowest-level peasants busily scrubbing the tables, cobblestones, and the large, black cauldron. Guards loomed over the peasants carrying heavy, leather flogs on their shoulders. As Thezdan watched, one of the guards swept an unlucky peasant from his feet. No sooner had the peasant fallen than the flog came down against his side with a loud "snap." The man yelped, but none of the other citizens looked up from their work.

Thezdan needed an outlet for the anger and malice he felt swelling within him. He bit his lip until it began to bleed. The pain and the taste of his own blood was clarifying: intervention would mean death, and survival was his only aim tonight.

He heard another crack of leather hitting some other poor soul. This time, he didn't turn to look.

As Thezdan neared the guard tower at the edge of town, the door swung open and out stepped the guard with the sore on his temple that he and Lothic had dealt with earlier. The guard moved to the middle of the road and held up his hand, commanding Thezdan to stop.

"Why are you here again?" he asked suspiciously. "Weren't you going to go north after your stop in town? Where is your friend?"

It dawned on Thezdan that Lothic had probably been smuggled through the checkpoint. "The plan changed," he said, his voice quivering slightly. "Now I need to get this grain to the Rokkin distillery down south."

"What about your friend?"

"He is staying at the People's Rest for the night. I am going to come back tomorrow so that we can continue our deliveries up north."

"Really?" said the guard. "I don't recall seeing a permit for either of you to stay here." He grinned spitefully. He had trapped Thezdan in a lie. The guard knew that this interloper and his companion, who had so irritated him a few hours ago, would almost surely be condemned to the Pit; more importantly, he would be rewarded with extra rations for his diligence. "People smuggling is a very serious crime. You're going to have to speak with the Captain."

The guard turned to shout for assistance, clearly unaware of the danger he faced. Thezdan's blade struck just below the base of his helmet, deep enough to kill instantly but not so deep as to risk the mess of decapitation. The guard flopped to the ground, his polearm clanging loudly as it met the stone.

Thezdan returned the sword to its spot hidden in the grain and hopped down to collect the guard's body and weapon. Even wrapped in armor, the guard's body was surprisingly light; Thezdan had little trouble hoisting it onto his shoulder and then up and onto the cart.

He grabbed the polearm and tossed it in the back, then he returned to his seat on the driver's bench.

The ground where the guard had fallen was stained red, but not obviously so; Thezdan's careful strike had left little evidence of the guard's violent end.

"Sorry about the new passenger, Scylld," Thezdan said into the cart bed. "He'll be getting off soon."

Thezdan drove the cart out into the countryside. He waited anxiously to hear the alarm horn sound. Thankfully, it never came. He stopped the cart at the intersection with the road that would take him west toward the forest. He retrieved the guard's body from the grain bed and dumped it among some bushes nearby. He thought about asking Scylld for help concealing it but decided it was unnecessary; it was more important to keep the Ogar hidden. He scavenged around for nearby rocks and twigs until he had covered the body. No one would find it for several days, until the smell became strong.

"Goddess, forgive this desperate fool," he said as he looked at the partially obscured and lifeless body.

Thezdan returned to the cart and grabbed the polearm. He thought about discarding it with the body but quickly changed his mind. He may have been clear of the town now, but he still had a long trip ahead of him. It was later than he had hoped it would be at this point in his journey, and there was a real chance that he might not make it to the far western plains by nightfall. He checked the blade of the polearm; while it was not to Guardian standards, it was sharp enough to kill. It might be useful.

Thezdan put the polearm back atop the grain and returned to his seat. The sun hung ominously in the western sky, a great luminescent timer ticking down all too quickly. Thezdan tried to whip the borum up to a faster pace, but received only snorts in response. He was on a collision course with the night, and he could only hope that his Guardian instinct had not led him to make a fatal blunder.

26

"Look guys, we made it!" said Julia as she caught sight of the path leading to the fort.

It was getting late, the increasingly dim light making the trees on either side of the road start to blend together. Her legs were heavy from the day's journey. Thankfully, Entaurion and Engar had been good company, and Engar's irrepressible spirit had continued to shine despite his injury. Julia still worried about him, but she was growing ever more confident about his prognosis.

As they turned up the path, Julia began to hear a few birdsong-like chirps overhead—brief, not even translatable, but unmistakably Sylvan.

"Are they following us?" she asked.

"I doubt it," said Entaurion. "They watch over the whole forest, so it's not that unusual to hear them around here."

Just then, Julia caught sight of a hooded figure up ahead.

"It's Sinox!" said Entaurion.

"It is a good day when the Prime welcomes you home!" said Engar proudly.

Sinox rushed toward them with long, silent strides. He had an almost feline grace that now, at dusk, made him seem like a moving shadow.

"Engar!" he called. "Are you alright?"

Engar held up his wounded arm. "I lost something. Don't worry though, I'm sure Lothic can help replace it!"

Sinox came up to him and held out his hand. "Let me see. The Sylvan sent word that you had been injured."

Engar gingerly placed his arm in Sinox's hand.

"By the Goddess, Engar, I am grateful you are alive," said Sinox. "You will have to have Alana treat this immediately."

"I will, Sinox," Engar replied.

"Entaurion, escort him back and see that he's treated right away," Sinox commanded. "Leave me with the girl; I need to speak with her privately."

The two younger Guardians looked at each other, confused by his order. They were not quite prepared to leave Julia's side, as they had not yet delivered her home.

Sinox sensed their hesitation. "I will escort her back to the fort personally. But please, leave us now and seek treatment. Engar, that wound poses a danger to your life."

Julia's necklace turned cold. She felt an impulse to say something but suppressed it, not wanting to put Engar and Entaurion in a difficult position. "Uh, Sinox, why don't we speak back at the fort. It's late. I'd be happy to meet with you in Alana's quarters if you'd like, maybe after I've had a quick bite to eat!"

"Alright, that should be fine," Sinox said. "Why don't we head back together?"

Engar beamed. "See? The Prime is escorting us!"

Sinox bowed his head at the two Guardian En. "You brought honor to our Clan today. Lead us home to the hero's welcome that awaits you!"

Engar and Entaurion looked at each other. Entaurion nodded, at which point Engar turned and began walking up tbe path to the fort, Entaurion beside him.

"Do you still promise to say all those nice things about me, Entaurion?" Engar asked.

"Of course," Entaurion said, chuckling. "You earned it, my friend."

"You're going to tell your sister first, though, right?"

"You cheeky … !"

Julia laughed. She and Sinox followed right behind. Her necklace was still a bit chilly, but she was excited to get back, have a proper meal, and catch up with Thezdan. It had been quite a day.

"Julia?" Sinox whispered quietly.

"Yes?"

" … I am sorry."

Before Julia could say anything, Sinox thrust out a hand and covered her mouth. He moved his body behind hers in a single deft motion. Julia felt a prick in her mid-back, followed by a powerful tingling sensation spreading through the region.

"I had no choice. You would be the death of us all," Sinox whispered in her ear.

Julia tried to scream, but her energy had already drained out of her. She watched Engar and Entaurion walking farther up the path, still jostling and joking back and forth, oblivious. Sinox reached around and grabbed her necklace with his free hand. When it burst to life a moment later, only faint traces of its brilliant light escaped through his fingers. He pulled her into the forest.

A few moments later, Julia heard Entaurion calling out to her and running footsteps nearby, but it was too late. Slowly, inexorably, she slipped into blackness.

27

Thezdan heard the Whisper like a scream calling out inside him:
Help me!

His pulse accelerated. He closed his eyes and sensed that Julia
lived, but he knew that something had happened to her. She was in
danger again.

He flailed at the borum, shouting at the highest volume he could
without his voice carrying across the landscape. "GO!"

It was for naught; the creature had no more to give. It would soon
be better to proceed on foot. A few minutes later, the very last sliver
of the sun slipped behind the horizon. Thezdan perked his ears and
caught the faint wails of faraway horns calling to the towns and villages
within range: curfew had begun, and with it, the Night Reaper patrols.

Thezdan pulled the cart off onto an adjacent field and parked next to a thicket. This was the end of the line.

He grabbed his sword and the polearm and hopped down.

"Scylld, we have to go!"

The grain in the cart began to shift, Scylld's massive, gray figure rising from the middle. With one giant step, he dismounted, the cart creaking loudly as its undercarriage sprang back into place.

Thezdan walked to the front and cut the borum free, patting it on its thick, sweat-soaked hide. "Thank you for your efforts," he said, delivering a swift smack to its rear quarter that sent it walking off into the grass. He turned back toward the Ogar. "Scylld, can you hide our cart?"

Scylld rumbled affirmatively. He reached out, grabbed the back of the cart, and pushed it part-way into the thicket. He then took a step back and dropped to his knees, placing his two giant, claw-like hands against the ground. As he began humming a prayerful song, the thicket began to change, new branches and leaves growing out and slowly enveloping the still-visible portion of the cart. Little by little, the bush grew until the cart was completely concealed, devoured by a thick mass of branches and leaves.

Scylld stopped his chant and stood up.

"Surely the Goddess still favors you," said Thezdan admiringly. He surveyed the landscape around them. "We need to hurry. Something has happened to Julia. It is only two or three rests to the river, and if we move quickly, we should be able to keep our lead on the patrols."

Scylld gestured with a single claw toward his own eye, then he took his other hand and pointed backward from the base of his neck. Thezdan watched and puzzled over the display for a moment, but soon realized what the Ogar was suggesting.

"Eyes in both directions?" he asked.

Scylld nodded. He turned to present his back to Thezdan, one of his mammoth hands turned upward behind him as a seat.

Thezdan bristled at the sight of the Ogar offering him a ride. But he put his pride aside, recognizing that it was a good idea. They had no margin for error, and having eyes in both directions would make it easier for them to spot an approaching patrol. He pressed himself up into Scylld's awaiting palm; so great was the Ogar's strength that the hand did not budge as Thezdan added his weight to it.

"Ready!" Thezdan said.

Scylld rumbled and began walking westward, doing his best to stride evenly across the terrain as Thezdan kept a lookout behind them for Night Reaper patrols.

They had barely covered half the distance to the river when Thezdan caught the dreaded sight he had been watching for: a white light, still a full rest behind them, that seemed to be shifting left and right and back again across the countryside. Even from this distance, he could tell that it was closing on them quickly.

He rapped his knuckles against Scylld's side.

"Scylld!" he called in a pressing whisper. "Reapers! Behind!"

Scylld stopped and turned around, bringing his hand out from behind his back so that both he and Thezdan were facing the light.

"Do you see it?" asked Thezdan, pointing to the flashing dot. "It's moving fast. We won't make the bridge in time. We're going to have to hide."

Scylld offered a brief, low rumble in acknowledgement. Thezdan hopped down from Scylld's hand and looked around for cover, but saw none.

"Do you see anything? Any cover? Shelter?" he asked with rising urgency.

Scylld rumbled again and began walking toward a shadowy space nearby, a bit closer to the road than their course had been taking them. Thezdan followed behind, placing a hand against Scylld to guide him as he kept his eyes on the rapidly approaching patrol. When Scylld stopped, Thezdan turned around. Before him was an old, collapsed house, its thatched roof having long ago rotted away and its interior space overgrown with vegetation. He kicked in the old door, the force of the strike separating the wood from the hinges.

"Only fight if we're found," Thezdan said, standing in the open doorway. "But if you hear me yell, then we fight for our lives." He moved inside and tossed the polearm to the ground, then he crouched against the near wall to wait out the Reapers. Scylld remained outside, rolled into a ball against a collapsed region of the wall; from afar, he would be nearly indistinguishable from the stones.

Thezdan craned his neck to watch as the light came closer. Before long, he could see it in detail, a cone of brilliant white tinged with occasional streams of reds and blues shining across the landscape, fully illuminating whatever it fell on. As the light crossed back and forth, it occasionally revealed the patrol itself. From these brief moments, Thezdan was able to make out that it had at least three members: two men riding large, galloping, black borum, and a third riding behind in a chariot who controlled the searchlight. They were all well-armed, bearing large swords, heavy, bladed armor, and wide-brimmed helmets that spread nearly to their shoulders.

Thezdan continued watching as they drew nearer. Their faces were invisible, hidden behind dark masks. For a moment, he thought he saw something when the lead rider looked over in his direction. Then it flashed again, this time clear as day in the low dusk light: the red glow from his dream, emanating from the Reaper's eyes. Thezdan whipped himself away from the doorway, breathing hard where he sat.

He clenched his teeth and reached down to grip his sword, the sound of borum hoofbeats growing louder around him. The patrol was dangerously close now. He sat motionless as the ambient light around him increased, a sure sign that the Reapers were searching the nearby terrain. Then the light shot through the open doorway, shining brightly against the back wall. Thezdan closed his eyes and held his breath. The light seemed to be lingering, the hoofbeats of the borum slowing …

Goddess, receive me!

Just as his eyes sprang open, the light disappeared from the room. Thezdan's head spun, his heart pounding as he held his breath a second longer. When it became clear that the Reapers were continuing down the road, he let the air slowly drain out of him, his head falling back against the old, stone wall.

Once he could no longer hear the borum, Thezdan peered out of the doorway again and watched the patrol on its westward path. A minute later, all that he could see of them was the beam of the spotlight crisscrossing the landscape. He grabbed the polearm from the floor and made his way out of the house. Scylld heard him exit and rose from the ground nearby.

"They're heading toward the river," Thezdan said. "They'll probably turn north at the bridge. We should be safe if we follow, so long as we keep our distance."

Scylld turned around and presented his upturned palm for Thezdan to sit in again.

Thezdan paused, his mind grappling with the danger they faced. It was surely significant, much more so than he had realized when he had committed to the journey just hours before. Then he thought about Julia and the Whispers that had told him that she was in trouble. Any tentativeness he felt disappeared.

"Let's go, Scylld," he said, climbing up into the Ogar's hand.

As the Ogar began walking again, Thezdan looked up briefly at the twin moons tracing their joint path across the night sky, the larger, gray moon, Aras, trailing the smaller, brighter, delicately blue Fremma. It was something he had glimpsed thousands of times in his life, but tonight was different; tonight, the moons reminded him of his destiny as a Guardian. The constancy of the heavens—he as Aras, Julia as Fremma—a connection he felt at his core.

"Rem sikk einheryan, vom err Eo," Thezdan whispered in the tongue of his ancestors. He asked them to guide him, to help him come into his heritage so that he could hear the Whispers fully. They would lead him to her.

When Thezdan caught the faint sounds of the river in the distance, he knew the forest—and with it, safety—was only minutes away.

He turned around and pulled himself up to look over Scylld's shoulder, spotting the dark backdrop of the trees ahead. They had made it.

Call to me, Julia … tell me where you are.

He spotted a faraway flash, which he tried to rationalize as moonlight reflecting off of water droplets from the river. Then he saw the telltale cone of light spreading out along the north road.

"Down!" he cried.

Scylld stooped down amid the deep grasses. Their bodies poked out slightly, but it was unlikely that the Reapers would be able to see them from this distance.

"They must be by the bridge!" said Thezdan. He looked around and saw that there was no available cover nearby. "Stay low. Let's see where they go."

Scylld and Thezdan remained in the grass, watching the Night Reaper spotlight cross the terrain. Then it switched off.

"Can you see them, Scylld?" Thezdan asked, confused.

Two grunts: no.

Nervous seconds faded into minutes as Thezdan waited for some sign of the Night Reapers. Then the light returned and scanned the landscape in front of the bridge again. To his horror, Thezdan realized that the Night Reapers would not be moving along after all.

They're guarding the bridge!

"Scylld, they're not moving!" Thezdan said. He glanced east and felt a surge of adrenaline run through his breast; there was another light in the distance approaching them through the fields.

He jumped down from Scylld's palm. "Another patrol, behind!"

He looked around for anything in the nearby terrain that he could use to his advantage, but he saw nothing. He was growing frantic now. Discovery by one patrol would mean discovery by both, and he knew that his chances of survival in such an encounter would be slim. Breathing hard, he looked back at the bridge and realized that they only had one option.

"Scylld, we're going to have to fight at the bridge," he said. "At next pass, run west!"

Thezdan remained low until the moment the faraway light crossed them again, then he rose and sprinted toward the bridge. He bounded over the uneven ground, holding the polearm at his side as his eyes carefully tracked the path of the Reaper beam. Thezdan could hear the loud crashing steps of Scylld keeping pace with him behind, which he could only hope would not draw the Reaper's attention. As the light neared their position again, Thezdan slid forward, his momentum carrying him several yards farther into the grass. Scylld rolled into a ball next to him, and they lay still as the light passed overhead.

Only a few hundred yards now separated them from the Reapers by the bridge. Thezdan rose to a squat and crept forward. When it appeared as though the spotlight was clear and moving away from him, he stood and ran again, closing to within fifty yards before sliding down once more. Scylld had not kept pace this time, instead moving forward slowly, quietly. Thezdan lay on his side until he heard the sounds of Scylld's footsteps nearby. He peeked up in the grass and whispered in Scylld's direction, "Scylld! Here!"

The Ogar heard his call and came over to where he waited.

"Are you ready?" Thezdan asked.

Scylld offered a quiet rumble.

"Place a snare here, and make sure it's dense," Thezdan instructed.

Scylld waited until the Night Reaper light switched off, then he rose to his knees, placed his hands against the ground, and began to hum. A vine in front of him began to grow, covering the ground in a thick, low-lying tangle; soon it was large enough to suit its purpose, and Thezdan tapped Scylld on his side.

"Good enough, Scylld."

Scylld stopped humming and sat up.

Thezdan pointed at a spot close by. "Get set over there. I'll try to lure the Reapers this way. The lead rider is mine. You surprise the second when he gets here. The chariot will probably lag; we'll deal with it last."

Scylld acknowledged the plan and quickly moved over to the spot Thezdan had identified. He rolled into a ball and waited.

Thezdan sat behind the tangle watching the shadowy figures ahead. He checked over his shoulder. The other patrol was now less than a full rest away. The moment of truth had arrived. He had to act now.

He placed the polearm he had been carrying on the ground a few feet behind the tangle, its blade facing toward the bridge. He then took one last deep breath.

"Goddess, guide my blade or receive my body," he whispered into the night.

Ready, Thezdan faced the bridge and rose to his full height. He drew his sword and held it high over his head. "I am Eodan of the Guardian Clan!" he shouted defiantly. "I do not fear the night!"

The spotlight switched on immediately, filling his eyes with blinding, white light. The air erupted with the tumult of approaching battle, the mix of thundering borum hoofs and horn blasts signaling that a new victim had been found.

Thezdan dropped his sword but held his position, challenging the Reapers to come get him. Closer and closer the borum came, the outlines of their riders coming into view as they passed between the light source and where Thezdan stood. They held their massive swords aloft, ready to mete out a swift execution.

Thezdan counted down until the critical moment arrived, the Reapers only seconds from striking.

"Now, Scylld!" he shouted as he dropped to one knee and tilted the polearm up from the ground.

The lead Reaper's borum crashed into the tangle, its front legs buckling under the force of its body's momentum. The borum let out a whinnying groan as it fell forward, hurdling the Reaper toward Thezdan. Thezdan braced the polearm with all his strength; a moment later, the Reaper let out an otherworldly screech as the polearm's blade sank into its breast. Thezdan quickly pivoted and sent the impaled soldier tumbling to the ground. Reaching behind him, he grasped the hilt of his sword and lunged away from the second Reaper, tumbling into a backward roll. He sprang back to his feet in time to watch Scylld grab hold of the rear legs of the second Reaper's borum and toss it like a child's doll toward the road. The Reaper came unseated and fell to the earth nearby.

Thezdan looked over at the bright, white light of the rapidly approaching chariot. "Scylld, get the chariot!" he bellowed. "I'll finish the other one!"

Scylld grunted loudly and turned toward the chariot-borne Reaper.

Thezdan ran to where he had seen the second Reaper fall, hoping that he could find it dazed in the grass. He heard a loud sound as the chariot overturned, its light veering away. Thezdan shot a glance over his shoulder and saw Scylld rushing to engage the dismounted charioteer. Looking forward again, he could see by the spotlight's penumbras the black figure of the second Reaper rising. It turned to face him, the sinister, red glow of its eyes inspiring a second surge of adrenaline that ran through his body like lightning.

"By my blade you fall!" Thezdan shouted as he raised his sword and charged.

The Night Reaper answered Thezdan's aggression with a soulless shriek from behind its mask, the sound so brutally piercing that Thezdan felt like glass was shattering inside his mind. Unbowed, Thezdan focused and swung his blade toward the narrow opening between the long, sloping sides of the Reaper's helmet and the body armor beneath. The Reaper deftly avoided the blow, ducking underneath the sword's path and whipping a leg into Thezdan's shins. Thezdan was caught off-guard but instinctively allowed his legs to fly free under him as he rolled forward and out of the fall. He rose quickly and turned, seeing the Reaper reach down into the grass to recover its sword.

Thezdan dropped into a defensive stance. The Reaper lunged with a strong, thrusting attack that Thezdan parried, then it raised its sword and feinted a follow-up strike. Thezdan quickly switched stances to avoid the blow, realizing too late that he'd been fooled. The Reaper sliced upward toward his wrist with a cut designed for sudden, brutal dismemberment; it was only a reflexive, last-moment bend away that saved his hand. Thezdan let out a pained growl as the Reaper's sword cut into his forearm. He looked across his sword at the Reaper. It seemed to be anticipating his techniques, his movements, and his defenses.

It's fighting … like a Guardian.

"What are you?" Thezdan yelled as he stared down the ghoul.

The Reaper hissed beneath its mask, slowly pacing around him. Thezdan sprang forward and sliced at the Reaper with a swift cross-cut, carefully watching its movements in response. The Reaper redirected the strike and switched its stance, countering with a series of thrusts and swings of his own. The strikes were strong and precise, though, for Thezdan, predictable. When a brief opening presented itself, Thezdan delivered a strong kick to the Reaper's side, pushing it away from him. He no longer doubted what he was seeing: the Reaper was undoubtedly using Guardian techniques.

How do you beat a Guardian? Thezdan asked himself, racking his mind for the answer.

The Reaper screamed and charged toward Thezdan. They collided in a dance of blades, trading slashing strikes and parries, lunges and ripostes. Then it suddenly appeared, in the blink of an eye, as Thezdan narrowly sidestepped one of the Reaper's thrusting attacks: the opportunity he had been waiting for. Thezdan's intuitive brain played out the sequence of strikes and counters his father had taught him in the training grounds of the Trebain years ago. He grabbed the Reaper's wrist with his free hand, extending the Reaper forward as he spun to its rear. The Reaper responded with Guardian tactic, countering the motion by ducking lower and slicing toward Thezdan's legs. Thezdan had seen it coming. Using his grip on the Reaper's arm as a pivot point, he leapt upward into a side-flip, driving the point of his sword down into the ghoul's exposed lower back.

The force of the strike was so great that the blade drove through the Reaper's lower abdomen and out the other side. The Reaper let out a deathly yell and fell to the ground, where it fought desperately to push out the protruding blade. A brilliant, red light flashed from its eyes, then a moment later it lay still on the road.

Thezdan picked up the Reaper's sword and turned to join Scylld in his fight. He could see that the charioteer's weapon had found its mark several times in Scylld's arm, breaking off chunks of rock from the previously intact surface. The Reaper was even worse for wear, its helmet gone and a large piece missing from the front of its armor. Scylld stepped forward and swung a fist, which the Reaper dodged. The Reaper spotted Thezdan, but it was too late for it to avoid the true-flying sword from Thezdan's hand. The weapon buried itself in the ghoul's chest, and another otherworldly scream pierced the night air. Scylld silenced the Reaper with a crushing blow to its head.

"Scylld!" Thezdan shouted as he ran to the Ogar's side. "Are you injured?"

Scylld shook his head and buzzed twice: no.

Thezdan checked over his shoulder. The other Reapers were no more than a minute away.

"Get over the bridge! I will meet you on the other side!"

Scylld waved for Thezdan to join him.

"I'll come soon—I need to see something. Go!"

Thezdan ran back to the Reaper he had fought and yanked his sword free from its abdomen. He reached down and turned the ghoul over, pulling back the helmet and facemask to expose its face. Even in the very faint light, he could make out the ghostly, drawn features of his attacker, and it shocked him to his core.

Ennik!

It was his father's brother, a beloved uncle from his childhood and as true a Guardian as he had ever known. Ennik had stood at Eobax's side as the People's Army had approached the Trebain, and Thezdan had always assumed that he had died in the fighting.

How could this be? Thezdan wondered. He felt an aching pit in his stomach amid the thousand conflicting thoughts and emotions that filled his mind. He looked up. The second Reaper patrol was much too close for him to waste even a single second more. His curiosity would have to wait.

Thezdan mustered what was left of his strength and picked up Ennik's corpse, slinging it over his back. He ran toward the bridge. As he sprinted past the overturned chariot light, he struggled to make out the shapes of the terrain beyond. He did not have to struggle for long. The brilliant beam of the onrushing patrol's spotlight suddenly illuminated him from behind, bringing the bridge into view. He lowered his head and ran faster, hearing the sound of thundering borum hooves closing on him quickly.

As his feet met the stones of the bridge, he closed his eyes, summoned the last of his strength, and tried to run faster. He was barely a quarter of the way across when he first heard hooves hit stone, and he knew he was in trouble.

"AAAHHHHHH!!!!" Thezdan screamed, urging his legs to carry him forward, just these last few steps, to deliver him from the Reapers.

Suddenly he heard whizzing sounds overhead, followed by a loud borum snort. He opened his eyes and saw Scylld standing at the end of the bridge, hurling large stones toward the Reapers. He kept running, but he could hear the Reapers starting to slow behind him. Near the end of the bridge, Thezdan heard the whistling sounds of at least a dozen Sylvan high up in the nearby trees. The borum hoofbeats stopped, then they began to move away, taking the light with them. Though surrounded by darkness, Thezdan knew exactly where he was. Several strides later, his feet met dirt and he collapsed, the corpse rolling forward off his shoulders and onto the ground. He let out one final scream, trying to expel all his fear, malice, and confusion. Then he closed his eyes and breathed.

Thezdan opened his eyes again and looked up to find Scylld standing over him with a hand extended. Thezdan took it and rose to his feet, his eyes spotting Ennik's limp body tucked under Scylld's other arm.

"I would not have survived without you," Thezdan said quietly.

In the moonlight, he could see Scylld stand at his full height and raise a clenched hand across his body in salute.

"No, my friend, no," said Thezdan, shaking his head as he put a hand against Scylld's arm. "You owe me no further service."

Scylld continued to hold his salute.

Thezdan shook his head again and smiled. "At the very least you must rest for a while. I saw the wounds in your hide; you need time to heal. Give me Ennik. I will carry him home."

Scylld rumbled in acknowledgement and passed the dead body to Thezdan, who carefully slung it over his shoulder.

"Rest well, Scylld," said Thezdan, raising his own free arm in salute.

Scylld rumbled once more and turned to head west into the forest. Once the Ogar had passed from sight into the trees, Thezdan trudged down the road in the direction of the fort. Heading up the footpath, he could see the ambient light of the courtyard was brighter tonight than usual.

"Announce yourself!" a guard called as he approached.

Thezdan looked up toward the tower. "Eodan," he called back. "Tell Alana and Lothic to meet me right away!"

"Of course, Eo!" shouted the guard.

Thezdan passed through the gates and immediately caught sight of his mother and Lothic rushing toward him, a crowd of No and En holding torches in the background.

"Oh, Eodan," Alana said emotionally, reaching past the body to clutch the back of his neck. "Are you alright?"

"Yes, Mother," he said. He lay the corpse on the ground. "Where is Julia?"

Alana looked at the body, then she reached down and turned the head to face them. She gasped loudly, recoiling in shock.

"Goddess … " Lothic mumbled loudly. "It's Ennik."

"He was afflicted by some kind of evil magic," said Thezdan. "We should try to understand what it was. But first, I need to find Julia. Do you know where she is?"

Lothic didn't respond, appearing distracted. Alana stared back blankly.

"Mother, where is Julia!" Thezdan asked pointedly. "Is she safe?"

Alana reached out a hand. "Eodan, we—"

Her hesitation communicated all that Thezdan needed to know.

"Is that a search party?" he asked, pointing toward the torch-bearers. "What happened to her?" Just then, he spotted Entaurion standing among the young warriors. "How is it that Entaurion is here? Where is Julia?"

"With Sinox, Eodan," Lothic interjected. "They are both missing."

Thezdan's eyes flashed with fury. "WHY?" he roared. Then, amid his anger, clarity.

"We don't know yet, Eodan," said Lothic. "We are forming up search groups to go looking for them."

Thezdan ignored Lothic; he already knew where they were. He grabbed one of the torches mounted against the front wall and ran back through the gate.

"Eodan, stop!" yelled Lothic from behind, to no avail.

Thezdan sprinted down the path, his legs rejuvenated by his Guardian's fire.

Call to me, Julia! I am coming!

Acknowledgements

First and foremost, I'd like to thank my wife, Julia, whose life provided much of the inspiration for this book. She was also generous with her support and expert eye as an editrix—and without those things, I doubt I ever would have finished *The Lost Princess of Aevilen*. I'd also like to thank and acknowledge Mike Varley, my friend and freelance editor, who helped me to shape the story in its earliest days.

D. C. Payson

DC Payson is a biotech entrepreneur who chases down exciting new therapeutics for Parkinson's disease by day, and builds expansive fantasy universes by night. Inspired to write by the birth of his son, Henry, DC began working on the *Lost* series in 2012, basing it loosely on real-life events in his wife's life.

When not working or writing, DC enjoys spending time with his family in New York, playing video games or badminton with his kids, and relishing the affection of his furry companion/sidekick, Freya the Mini-Schnauzer.

CONNECT WITH US

Find more books like this at http://www.Month9Books.com

Facebook: www.Facebook.com/Month9Books
Instagram: https://instagram.com/month9books
Twitter: https://twitter.com/Month9Books
Tumblr: http://month9books.tumblr.com/
YouTube: www.youtube.com/user/Month9Books
Georgia McBride Media Group: www.georgiamcbride.com

OTHER MONTH9BOOKS TITLES YOU MIGHT
LIKE

MYKONOS BLUE

GARDEN OF THORNS AND LIGHT

THE MATRIARCAS